WHAT
GOES
ON
TOUR

SAM
DERBYSHIRE

Matador
9 Priory Business Park,
Wistow Road, Kibworth Beauchamp,
Leicestershire. LE8 0RX
Tel: (+44) 116 279 2299
Fax: (+44) 116 279 2277
Email: books@troubador.co.uk
Web: www.troubador.co.uk/matador

ISBN 978 1780884 844

British Library Cataloguing in Publication Data.
A catalogue record for this book is available from the British Library.

Typeset by Troubador Publishing Ltd, Leicester, UK

Matador is an imprint of Troubador Publishing Ltd

Printed and bound in the UK by TJ International, Padstow, Cornwall

Chapter 1

Steve Sinclair looked at his watch, four-thirty pm and the office was already preparing itself for the early Friday exodus into the wine bars of Glasgow's city centre. The day had been mild and intermittently sunny and as a consequence the office was warm, the staff languid and already mentally ordering their first drink of the weekend. Steve didn't mind his staff leaving early on a Friday; he pushed them hard during the week. He appreciated that all of them could be relied upon to put in the extra hours when deadlines loomed; an early exit on a Friday was easy payback and his staff were more than happy to oblige. Despite the recession, Steve, through sheer hard work and a great deal of charm, had managed to keep his graphic design business on track and business and morale for the moment was good.

At four thirty-five pm, Paula, his good humoured and surprisingly efficient PA, popped her head around the door.

"Anything else you need doing before we head off?" she asked cheerily.

Steve could tell that she wasn't expecting to be given anything else to do on a Friday afternoon, as already fully made up for a night on the town, her body language signalled that her mind was already on her first vodka.

"No thanks Paula. Have a good one. I don't think there's anything that we didn't discuss this afternoon. Remember, Donnie is quite capable of dealing with any issues while I'm away and tell him only to contact me if its life or death. I'm sure you can all manage for a few days without having to call me."

Paula laughed her mischievous, throaty laugh, her recently

whitened teeth clashing with her glossed lips and expensively applied bottled tan. She was attractive, but smoking from the age of fourteen was already taking its toll.

"I'm sure we can Steve, enjoy yourself and don't do anything I wouldn't do," and with a wink she was gone.

That leaves me a pretty blank canvas then, Steve thought to himself as he watched her wiggle her way along the corridor in her ridiculously high heels and tight black skirt. Not his type, but as he eyed her buttocks straining at the fabric, he had to admit she had a great arse.

Four forty-five pm and the office was empty; silent, apart from the intermittent buzz from the water cooler and the background hum from the rush hour traffic outside. His mobile rang; it was Mike MacDonald, keen for his usual Friday night pint.

"Bloody hell Mike, are you out already?"

"Stevie boy," Mike shouted down the phone trying to talk above the din of the already busy wine bar, "are you coming down to Dawson's? Thought we might get revved up before we head off tomorrow, shit, I'm so excited. Callum's coming, not sure about El Divo."

Mike MacDonald, forty-eight, property developer and an all round great bloke was, as usual, firing on all cylinders. Despite being on the small side, Mike was a magnet for women, his outrageous sense of humour and Tom Cruise smile appealing to all types and all ages. Mike, however, was devoted to his lovely wife Christie.

"Not sure yet Mate, got a few things to finish up here. I'll do my best. I'll text you if I can make it." Steve stared at the computer screen trying to assess how long it would take him to tie things up.

"Come on Stevie Boy, it can wait till you get back, that's what your staff are for. Come on, it's party time!"

Putting down his mobile, Steve scanned the e-mails,

searching for any that may need his attention before he left. Most of them were from the rest of the boys about to embark on the annual Scotland England golf trip, the usual juvenile banter along with confirmation of hotel bookings, flights, costumes purchased. song lyrics to learn and team sheets. Shit, he hadn't even looked at the song sheet, which was bad news. Punishment this year for being crap on any part of the tour was likely to be severe, this being the twentieth anniversary and a big one. Myles Cavendish was in charge, and he was dangerous. He never missed a trick. Forfeits were his speciality. His phone rang again. It was Lucy, his wife.

"Hi darling, what's up?"

"I was just wondering what time you would be home this evening as the kids would like to see you before you head off tomorrow. Jamie wants you to help him with his talk."

From the tone of her voice, Steve realised that a pint was probably a bad idea. He hated the way she used the kids to make him feel guilty.

"Tell him I've got a few things to finish up here, and I will try and get on the six-thirty, if not it will definitely be the seven, I promise."

"Please Steve, it's really not that much to ask."

"I said I would be back as soon as I can, I will definitely be on the seven, I promise. Tell him to have his bath, and I'll help him when I get back."

Steve returned to his e-mails and draining the last of his coffee, printed off the song sheet. Bloody hell, how many songs were there? Cavendish was a complete bastard. It was alright for him, he didn't have a wife and kids to deal with every evening, having been divorced or dumped by every woman who had ever been daft enough to get mixed up with him. Steve knew that Lucy couldn't stand Cavendish, having described him recently as an arrogant shit, and her unhappiness with this trip stemmed from the fact that Cavendish was in charge. Cavendish was also not one of the original founders of the trip, having been drafted in a few years ago when one of the London boys had had to call off at the last minute. If he was honest, Steve didn't trust him either, considered him a bit of a pompous twat, full of his own importance, and as far as Steve was concerned, he had no right to be organising. But as usual he had muscled his way in, and as no one else had complained, he had had to let it go. For a fleeting moment he began to wonder whether he was getting too old for all this. He forwarded a few more e-mails to Donnie and Paula and looked at his watch, five-thirty, just time for a pint. Picking up his mobile, he sent a text to Mike.

Lucy slammed down the phone in exasperation. Men are such complete shits, she thought to herself, selfish bloody shits. Taking a tube of tomato puree from the fridge she squeezed it angrily into the Bolognese sauce. She knew he would go for a pint, he wouldn't be able to help himself, wouldn't want to let the boys down. It was alright to let her down, that was part of the game for them, seeing how much they could get away with, how far they could push without the walls crashing down. Lucy realised, however, that the more barriers the wives put up, the more they tried to circumnavigate, not being able to resist any form of challenge. She had learnt early on that ignoring their games made it a lot less fun for them. Boys' trip was the right word for it, certainly none of them had grown up yet, and how the hell they managed to run successful businesses was anyone's guess. She poured herself a glass of white wine and left the sauce to simmer. In reality she didn't really mind Steve going away, quite enjoyed having one less person to cater for in the house and the bed to herself for a few nights, but there was always something nagging at the back of her mind. It annoyed her that he enjoyed his time away from her so much, that he obviously found a trip away with the boys a lot more fun than a holiday with her, but she could cope with that. If she was honest, she often preferred the company of her friends to him. The difficult thing to cope with though, was her lack of trust. Steve had never in their fourteen years of marriage given her any reason to doubt that he had been anything other than faithful, but the golf trip always made her nervous. A combination of boys, booze and too many egos was, in her mind, a recipe for disaster. She was in no doubt that he would flirt, would enjoy any attention at his age, but would he actually have sex with another woman, had he had sex with another woman or worse still, in her mind, actually enjoy the company of another woman? She didn't know. If he had, would she want to know? This year, the fact that Cavendish was in charge and the trip was abroad, made her more uneasy, for as far as she was concerned, Cavendish was without any moral substance, having cornered her at a recent party. She had dealt with it, possibly she had been slightly flattered and hadn't told Steve. She didn't know why she hadn't told him, it was probably because she hadn't wanted to rock his world, to shatter his illusion of the solidarity of the brotherhood, the brotherhood of which she was undoubtedly jealous. If it wasn't for the kids, she wondered whether she would still be with him. Pouring herself another glass of wine, she realised that she probably would.

Standing out on the fag end strewn steps of Dawson's, Mike combined his nicotine fix with a call to Christie. Hopefully he would catch her before she left work.

"Christie babe, are you still at work?"

Christie stepped outside the studio and took the call in the corridor.

"Are you in the pub already? Christ Mike, you'll be wrecked before you leave and you haven't even packed yet. Where are you?"

"Dawson's, I'm just having a quick one with Steve. Do you want to come down here and then grab something to eat before we head home? I've spoken to the kids, they're fine, going out anyway, said they would do their own thing."

"Yes, I bet they will." Christie said anxiously. She looked at her watch. "I think we'll be finished in about twenty minutes," then lowering her voice added, "this shoots been a bit of a disaster, bloody woman's a bitch of a client, I could do with a drink. I'll text you when I'm leaving, mine's a gin and tonic."

Christie leant against the wall of the corridor. She was exhausted, the shoot had been a nightmare and the prospect of a few days alone with three teenage boys, without the support of Mike, filled her with dread. She had been beginning to wonder whether full time working really was such a good option. She didn't need to work and loved her job, but over the last few months she had begun to think that the boys needed taking in hand, and at the very least needed one of them in the house at the end of the school day to keep things under control. Taking a deep breath, she walked back into the studio, promising to give it some serious thought over the weekend.

As Mike handed Steve his pint, Steve felt himself start to relax. The last few months had been difficult, and long hours had taken its toll on both his health and his marriage. Lucy had been understanding, but by taking on most of the responsibility for the kids and taking little time for her own needs, it had given their relationship an edge, an edge he understood was born of resentment for what she saw as his freedom. As far as he was concerned, he would be quite happy for her to take a break or get herself a part time job, anything to get her out of the house, but she always found some excuse and usually it was his fault. The golf trip was not great timing, but he needed some time off, needed a few days without responsibility. He would make it up to her when he got back. Snapping himself out of it he raised his glass to Mike.

"Here's to a good one, just hope Cavendish hasn't overdone

it." Mike raised his eyebrows. "So do I, pretty bloody expensive this time, I haven't actually told Christie the full price. The hotel sounds top drawer though, it's got a casino."

"Aye but Cavendish worries me, I'm not sure he knows where to draw the line. It's one thing going overboard in this country, but getting us arrested abroad is a different matter. Just as well we're taking a lawyer or two. Talking of lawyers, I thought Callum was coming for a pint."

"Nope, Maggie put her foot down and he thought better of it. Thought he might find his passport in two pieces if he didn't go straight home. She's so bloody scary Maggie, I love her but I wouldn't want to argue with her. One of the kids has got a recital or something." Mike drained his glass.

"Only a child of Maggie would be doing a recital, poor little bugger. Do you want another one? Christie's on her way, but she'll be half an hour."

Steve looked at his watch, six- thirty, he'd be risking it, but as Lucy was already in a bad mood it wouldn't make much difference now.

"Yeh ok then, it's my turn, what you having?"

At seven-thirty, Lucy dialled Steve's mobile, but before it had a chance to connect, she hung up. What was the point?

"Jamie," she called up the stairs, "sorry darling, Daddy's going to be late again, go and get your talk and we'll practice." Settling herself at the kitchen table, she poured another glass of wine.

Letting himself in at ten-thirty, Steve found an empty bottle of wine and an empty bed. He knew Lucy would be in the spare room again, and as the door was pointedly shut, he left well alone. At least that gave him chance to pack, and he could avoid any confrontation. Whatever he said or did was wrong these days. He didn't have the time or the inclination for any melodrama. He could deal with it when he got back.

Chapter 2

As Callum Dunbar sat in the usual Friday night traffic jam on the M8, he tried desperately to put his workload to the back of his mind. With a major case looming, he could ill afford the time away, but the threat of being eliminated from the tour for the next three years for not showing, had ensured his participation. If he was clever, he might be able to manage to sneak some time while they were away, but in reality, he knew he was kidding himself. If Maggie knew, she would go ballistic, and in all honesty, she would be justified. Business was cut-throat these days and this case was major, lose this one and things would be tight, tighter than they already were. With his wife's stables, three sets of school fees and an ageing country house to finance, he was feeling the pressure. He had to admit, he'd been relieved when Maggie had banned him from going to the pub tonight; he'd made up the bit about the kids recital, it had sounded better than admitting that he had given in to his wife. The boys, knowing that Maggie was a force not to be reckoned with, had not pushed him, and for that he was grateful. He could stay up late tonight and hopefully sleep on the plane tomorrow. The golf trip was the highlight of his year, a chance to let go, have a laugh. And by God, how he needed to laugh.

Picking up her gin and tonic, Maggie carried the beautifully ironed golf shirts into the bedroom and hung them on the back of the wardrobe door alongside the kilt. Callum's case lay open on the bed, methodically and efficiently packed by herself, with everything he could need for his trip away. His passport and currency lay beside it, along with his wash bag and adaptor. Maggie Dunbar was formidable, running her family and their respective lives as she would run a business, her ultimate goal to produce and support a successful husband and offspring and in her determination she was tireless. As a result, the Dunbar family life was time managed to perfection, with any attempt at deviation being efficiently deflected before the instigator even realised what had happened. Everyone knew their place and what was expected of them and as far as Maggie was aware, everyone was happy. Taking her gin and tonic with her, Maggie went back down to the kitchen and checked the oven and then herself in the mirror. She had always made a point of looking good when Callum came home, after all, why he would he want to come home at all if she let herself go. Mentally she made a note to phone Lucy this weekend, as there was a woman who was definitely on the slippery slope. With a good looking husband like Steve to hang on to, it was a dangerous slope to be on. She would need to have a word.

In the unused kitchen of his London city apartment, Myles Cavendish spooned the last of the take away onto his plate and took it through to the TV. Picking up the remote control, he flicked through the channels, the usual Friday night dross offering little inspiration. Settling on football, he shovelled the remainder of the curry into his mouth. Usually he would be drinking himself into oblivion on a Friday night or trawling the wine bars and night clubs in search of an attractive filly to warm his bed for the night. Attractive fillies seemed to be in abundance these days, especially if you had a bit of cash. They were easy, confident and basically devoid of shame. Good looking, intelligent women, however, were not or at least he hadn't found any. With two marriages behind him, cynicism was beginning to set in but the easy lays, he realised, were no longer offering any comfort. His thoughts strayed to the wives of the boys on the golf trip, all great girls in their own way, even Maggie. If he was honest, he would settle for any one of them, had even tried it on with one or two under the influence, and quite rightly, and to his relief, they had turned him down. Obviously they had never divulged. Planning this trip had consumed his life over the last six months, he was aware that he wasn't the most popular of team leaders, but hopefully, after this trip, they would see him in a new light. The hotel was immense, expensive yes, but great facilities and the entertainment had been sourced carefully. Simon had warned him about organising entertainment as it hadn't been done before and a few of the boys were uncomfortable with it, but Myles had selfishly decided that the twentieth anniversary would be one to remember. Belching loudly, Cavendish got up from the sofa and leaving the take away on the coffee table and a mess on the carpet, walked through to the bedroom to start his packing. His Polish cleaner would be in on Monday, she could deal with the mess.

Packing his case in his bedroom, gynaecologist Simon Lewis felt a sense of foreboding. He had known Cavendish since they were at University together and had been the one responsible for inviting him onto the tour. He was now beginning to regret it, for as usual, Cavendish had pushed his way to the front, nominating himself as Team leader at the end of the last tour when the rest of the boys were too hung-over or tired to object. What worried him most, was the prospect of the entertainment that Cavendish had planned; entertainment that if Cavendish was responsible, would definitely involve women. There was no denying that women featured in their trips but only as part of the banter in bars; the trips usual focus being on savage competition, games, fines and beer. Sex had never been a feature, all of the other guys being married or steadily occupied. If any of the boys had opted to play away, it had been discreet and was not something that was encouraged. Tracey would go mental if she knew what was being planned and quite rightly, as she didn't deserve the deceit having allowed him free rein on his boys' trips, never complaining. She appreciated that he worked hard and allowed her the freedom to pursue her own interests, and for that she was grateful. Their relationship was solid, the children were giving them no cause for concern and life was good. Simon did not want anything to rock the boat. Maybe he should tell her, promise to stay out of it, but he knew then that she would worry and maybe even tell the other wives, who would undoubtedly not be quite so understanding. Ignorance was bliss, and staying out of it, he decided, was probably the best option.

Walking out of the Italian takeaway, Tracey phoned Simon.

"I'm just leaving the takeaway, can you lay the table please and there's a really nice Chilean white in the fridge if you want to crack it open. Either that or I'll crack it over the kids heads, you can tell it's a full moon they're a bloody nightmare this evening."

"They're boys, that's what boys do. Tell them to pack it in or it's straight to their rooms when they get home. Did you manage to pick up my dry cleaning?"

"Yes and that's another story. Have you packed yet?"

As Tracey got into the car, the boys were still bickering in the back, that constant, tiresome and unnecessary bickering that always ended in everyone shouting at each other to be quiet, each of them vying for the last word. Now in their teens, and with testosterone in abundance, leaving them in confined spaces for any length of time was always traumatic and was to be avoided at all costs. Luckily for her, they were both away on a three day school rugby tour this weekend and she felt as though a weight had been lifted from her shoulders. With Simon also away, a weekend of selfish indulgence stretched out before her like a blank canvas, and she was keen to make the most of it. Saturday morning was taken care of with a visit to the spa, and Sunday she would dedicate to her writing. But Saturday afternoon and evening was still to be filled. She would phone Sophie quickly and try to organise a night out. She turned to the boys.

"Will you two please just stop it and grow up, please I've had enough, and I need to make a phone call, be quiet."

"His leg is over my side and he keeps giving me the finger."

"He called me the C word."

"No I bloody well didn't, that's what you called me, you twat."

"Josh, move your leg, stop being so obnoxious. Max, if he's trying to wind you up, don't look at him, then you won't see him and both of you stop swearing, for god's sake boys, I said that's enough, one more word and I'll ground you both. Don't think I won't stop you going on the trip because I will."

Instantly regretting that remark, Tracey prayed that they would stay silent as the last thing she wanted was to have them at home and ruin her weekend. Simon was always criticising her for not following through on her threats, but sometimes it was easier said than done, and the bigger they got, the harder it got. Looking at them in the rear view mirror, she could see the next phase brewing.

"I'm warning you, one more word."

Thankfully they acquiesced. She dialled Sophie's number.

"Sophie, it's Tracey, sorry I haven't been in touch for so long, yes I know it's a busy time of year. Traffic awful tonight isn't it, where are you now? Look, I was just wondering as the boys are on the golf trip this weekend, why don't we go out tomorrow night?"

Tracey listened.

"No I'm sure Andy is on it, definitely, Simon's got his ticket." There was silence.

"Ok, call me back later, I'm just heading home now, I'll be in all evening."

Tracey hung up, her head spinning with the reality of what she had just done.

"Shit," she said aloud, forgetting about the boys in the back.

She looked in the rear view mirror, for once they were both grinning, united in their enjoyment of the moment, picturing the drama that was about to unfold.

"Oh dear, oh dear, someone's put their foot in it," Josh said gleefully. "I think you'd better phone Dad quickly Mum, he'll need to warn Andy or he's seriously dead meat."

Josh was loving every minute.

"Oh and Mum, please try not to swear!"

Tracey called Simon.

Sophie Ellerman slammed the front door of her terraced house in South Wimbledon and threw her bag onto the hall table. If he thought she was going to take it gracefully he had another think coming, there was no way in hell he would be forgiven this time, he'd pushed it too far. He was such a bloody liar, how the hell he thought he would get away with it, he must be more of an idiot than she thought. Or maybe she was the idiot believing his cock and bull story about pricing a new job. She should have put two and two together; the date should have been imprinted on her memory having banned him from ever attending that bloody golf trip again after the credit card bill from the last time. Fucking business my arse, she fumed. She pushed open the kitchen door. Gingerly, Simon offered her a glass of wine.

"Hi Soph, how are you?" he asked rather cautiously.

Sophie halted in her tracks, stood with her hands on her hips, her green eyes flaming.

"How the hell do you think I am? Has he called you in for protection, I hope so, because he's going to need it, where is he?" She turned to walk out of the door but Simon grabbed her arm.

"He's upstairs. Look Sophie, just listen for two minutes. It's our fault, all the boys; we talked him into it because we want him on the trip. He's our mate, we love him. I know we shouldn't have got him to lie. I'm really sorry."

Sophie looked at Simon and sighing, took the glass of wine.

He could see that she was about to cry. "No he shouldn't have lied and he shouldn't be going. We can't afford it Simon, it took us six months to pay off his bills from the last one and this has to be more expensive, especially with that dickhead Cavendish in charge, he only thinks about himself. Andy's too soft and doesn't know how to say no. He's crap at all your moronic games and it costs us a fortune. It's not that I don't want him to go, we just can't afford it at the moment, we really can't."

She sat down at the kitchen table and put her head in her hands.

"Shit, I'm sorry Soph," Simon said inadequately, "I really had no idea."

Up in the bedroom, Andy sat on the bed, his case half packed. How he was going to get out of this one he didn't know. All he knew was that he had stuffed up big time and for once he wasn't finding it very funny. The fact was, he felt a complete shit. Sophie was right, they had no money and if she knew the whole truth he doubted she would still be with him. Business was crap, he had no new contracts on the horizon and debts up to his eyeballs. The trip was nothing more than an escape from the reality that was starting to drown him, one last fling before he went under and the last bloody rites for a dying man.

Chapter 3

Lying in the bed in the spare room, Lucy heard Steve come in. Rigid with anger, and despite the wine, she hadn't been able to sleep, emotions tumbling around chaotically in her mind. He was never very quiet when he'd had a few pints and she lay there listening to him as he stumbled around, his complete obliviousness to the hurt he had caused tonight only adding to her fury. She heard him go into the bathroom, the toilet seat clattering as he fumbled it, his uninhibited farting adding to her annoyance. She knew he wouldn't flush it either, the revolting bastard. At this moment she hated him more than anything. She toyed with the idea of confronting him, she wanted him to know how hurt she was but he wouldn't get it, wouldn't understand how miserable she was, how lonely. His solutions were always so simple. Why didn't she get out and do something she enjoyed, get a part time job if she wanted, go away with friends, he would look after the kids he said, but he couldn't be trusted could he? He didn't realise how difficult it was to organise the kids if she wanted to go away, he only ever had himself to think about and the kids needed their routine. She would be surprised if he actually knew what year they were in at school or even their teacher's names, he didn't have a clue what went on when he was at work, he had no idea how difficult and dull her life had become. What she really wanted was for him to want to be with her, to help her with the kids, give up his friends for once, but he couldn't do that could he, they always came first. She heard him rummaging in the hall cupboard, searching for a case with which to pack, swearing as the tangled

15

mess that was the hall cupboard thwarted his attempts to retrieve the bag he wanted. Lucy felt slightly satisfied, pleased with anything that slowed his progress and made his life difficult. Finally the bedroom door closed, and with the realisation that he would not be coming into her room this evening, she began to cry.

As they jumped into the back of the taxi outside Dawson's, Mike took Christie's hand. He still found her incredibly attractive and loved her company. She was, after all, fun to be with and all his mates felt the same. His thoughts, however, strayed to Steve.

"Poor Steve," he said to Christie as he caressed her leg, "he didn't seem too happy tonight, don't think things are very good at home at the moment."

"Well going home at eleven when you've said you'll be back by seven won't have helped his case will it, although you can't blame him. Lucy is so miserable these days. He probably doesn't want to go home. I've asked her to come out with the girls so many times but she always finds an excuse. Steve has offered to have the kids, so has his mum, he told me to ask her but she seems to enjoy being the martyr. If you speak to her on the phone she just moans, and it's all Steve's fault, she doesn't realise how lucky she is. Lots of women would kill to be in her position. The thing is, Steve still loves her, but even he's starting to give up."

"Yeh, Steve thinks she's starting to hit the bottle too, keeps finding empty wine bottles when he gets home but she won't discuss it. Bad news that."

Mike moved his hand suggestively up Christie's thigh and nuzzled into her neck. Christie, catching the eye of the taxi driver in the rear view mirror, removed it, giving his hand a playful squeeze.

"Not sure how you're going to manage a shag as well as packing," she whispered in his ear.

"No problem," he grinned, "try me, I don't want to go away leaving my beautiful wife unfulfilled".

Christie laughed, "It's not you who should be worried and you're the one that's going away, not me."

Hearing his car coming up the gravel drive, Maggie opened the ice box and dropped three ice cubes into Callum's gin and tonic. Giving it a stir, she walked through to the sitting room and placed it on the table beside his chair at the fire place along with the newspaper. Running her hand over her elegantly bobbed hair and moistening her lips, she walked through to the hall to greet him, their two black Labradors, tails wagging, following obediently. Opening the front door she watched him get out of his car, he looked tired she thought. Hopefully the break would do him some good.

"Hello darling," she said routinely, offering her cheek for the obligatory kiss, "good day?"

Had it been a good day? Callum didn't think so. It hadn't been a good year.

"Not bad, traffic was awful, I need a drink."

He was tired, mentally drained, but to confess would have shattered Maggie's illusion of perfection. How could he tell her that the reason for his tiredness was that their perfect lives were hanging by a very precarious thread, a thread for which he was ultimately responsible.

"Are the girls back this weekend?" he asked, hoping for a diversion. He missed them when they were away at school, missed their laughter and the way they made him feel he was loved for who he was rather than what he could provide.

"Not this weekend. Susie's practising for the concert, Gemma has a hockey match and Grace is going to a friend's house for the weekend. It's a shame; you won't see them now for another two weeks. You look tired, go and have your G & T, I've done most of your packing so go and relax. Dinner will be another twenty minutes." She took his brief case and hung his jacket at the end of the banister ready to be taken upstairs the next time she went.

Callum walked through to the sitting room and sank down into the chair beside the fire. The dogs, sensing some unhappiness and eager to please, settled themselves at his feet. He took a large gulp of the gin and tonic and closed his eyes as the cool, comforting liquid glided down his throat. Relax, he sighed, he would love to bloody relax, if only life were that simple.

Maggie opened the aga door and checked the dinner; ten more minutes should do it she decided and she turned up the pan of water on the hob ready to cook the beans. Callum did look tired this evening and something about his demeanour was unnerving her. She glanced through the kitchen door, across the hall to the sitting room; he was sitting staring into the fire, the newspaper laying unopened on the table. If she was honest, she had to admit that he hadn't been himself lately and had been avoiding any form of intimacy, whether verbal or physical and her unease at her possible lack of control over the situation was growing. Hopefully, she reassured herself, the golf trip would unwind him a little, and then possibly they could talk. She needed to discuss the cash flow of the stables, quotes had come in for renewing the windows and Gemma was talking about trying to get into Oxford, which was definitely going to be more expensive than Edinburgh; all these things required his attention. Popping the green beans into the simmering water, Maggie walked through to the sitting room to announce dinner. Callum was fast asleep.

Myles Cavendish, alone for once in his bedroom on a Friday night, picked up his phone, and sent an e-mail to his contact at Party Go-ers. He needed to confirm the arrangements for the entertainment on Sunday night. He had booked a private room at the hotel for the meal and his Portuguese contact TJ had confirmed that the girls would arrive at midnight. The fee was for dancing and getting their kits off, anything extra the boys would have to sort out for themselves. TJ had e-mailed photos of some of the girls, mostly eastern European by the sound of their names, although he had roggered a girl recently who called herself Ivana, and she was from Hemel Hempstead. He scanned the photos. They all looked fit for purpose as far as he was concerned and were proving to be pretty good value too. "Happy Days," he said aloud to himself, and setting the alarm button on his phone, turned out the light.

As Simon walked into the sitting room, Tracey could tell that his visit to the Ellermans' hadn't gone particularly well. She had been desperate to find out what was going on, riddled with guilt for being the innocent cause of the problem. How was she supposed to know that Andy had been banned, Sophie hadn't mentioned it last time they met, but then why would she? The golf trip hadn't even been mentioned. She was annoyed at Simon though, he could have warned her.

"Well how did that go, what's happening?" she asked, accepting the cold beer that was being offered.

"Bloody nightmare, I feel like a complete arsehole," said Simon taking a swig from his bottle. "Apparently they're broke, that's why he was banned, not Sophie being spiteful. Andy hasn't had any decent work for the past few months; the idiot should have said something."

"Well that's men for you, you don't discuss these things. He's got his pride too and probably didn't want to admit that he couldn't keep up with you lot. Poor Sophie, I feel awful. So what's happening, he's obviously not going now."

"Yes he is actually. I had a phone around the boys and we have some money in a kitty, it's been accumulating for a few years from different bets we've put on here and there. The kitty is going to subsidise him."

"He won't like that will he, would you?"

"We've not given him a choice have we? Andy's been on the trip from the beginning and he makes us laugh, even if it's his last one he has to be there for this one. We're mates Tracey, that's what mates are for. I've discussed it with Sophie and she's ok with it, she's obviously just worried sick. I did feel sorry for her though, she a great girl and you can see she loves him to bits. He's just been living outside his means."

"Just like everyone else in this bloody country. God it makes you realise how fragile everything is right now."

Tracey looked at Simon; he was such a good man. It was obvious that the evening's proceedings had shocked him and she was proud of him for protecting his friend when he was in need. She put her arms around his neck and kissed him.

"Come on, let's get this packing done and get to bed. The boys are away so let's make the most of it. I do love you, you know."

"Yes I do know and I love you too."

Thanking God for his good fortune, Simon led her upstairs.

In the Ellerman household, Andy and Sophie lay together in the darkness, Andy cuddling up to Sophie's back, stroking her arm. He was glad that she had fallen asleep, he didn't want to talk, there was too much to say and he hated seeing her cry. God knows what he was going to do. Feigning sleep, Sophie didn't want to talk either, in the vain hope that a new morning would help her to see things more clearly and that by some miracle, someone, somewhere would wave a magic wand and make everything better. She was glad he was going away as it would give her time to think and a little space to come up with some sort of plan to get them both out of this ridiculous mess. She was terrified now. He didn't know about the huge credit card bills that she had run up and the juggling act that her own bank account had recently become. It would kill him if he found out.

Chapter 4

Steve stuffed the wad of Euros into his wallet and tucked it safely into the inside pocket of his team blazer alongside his passport. He had a stinking headache, probably the result of not eating and mixing his beer with a couple of whiskies at the end of the night. Rummaging in the bathroom cabinet for a couple of paracetamol, he knocked them back, then catching his reflection in the mirror he took note of a few more greying hairs, thankful that he wasn't losing any. He knew he was attractive by the number of advances he regularly deflected but just lately he realised that on one or two occasions he had been tempted. He didn't know what to do with Lucy, obviously she wasn't happy and her constant self pity was starting to wear him down. Christ, he needed some attention too. She had no idea how hard he had worked to get them through the last year, he had worked his arse off and she was still moaning. Too many nights spent alone in their bed was starting to take its toll. Throwing a few more paracetamol into his wash bag he closed the zip and packed it in the case. He glanced at his watch, six-fifteen am. He had arranged to pick up Mike at six forty-five and he realised that he'd better make a move. Carrying his case through to the landing he looked in at the kids. Jamie, in his blue striped pyjamas, his tousled blonde hair in disarray, was laid thumb in mouth, the wrong way round in his bed, his transformers standing silently on guard on the floor below. Steve leaned over and kissed him gently on the forehead, envious of his innocence of the complicated world that he would someday have to find his way through. Having unhappy parents wouldn't make it any easier. In her pastel pink palace, Lily slumbered and murmured as Steve kissed his little princess on her soft rosy cheek. She smelt of flowers. Shit, he had to make it work for the sake of the kids. On the landing he paused outside the spare room, but deciding against it, made his way downstairs.

Lucy awoke to the sound of the front door banging shut. She looked at the clock, six twenty-five am. She heard the beep as he unlocked the Range Rover and the slam of the boot. She wouldn't look out of the window; she didn't want to see him drive away. As the engine started, she covered her ears with her pillow, and carrying on where she had left off a few hours before, she began to cry.

At five forty-five am, sitting alone in his study, Callum decided to phone Myles. He had worked through the night and his tiredness was now all consuming. He would have to call off the trip. Somehow he had got through dinner with Maggie without having to answer any difficult questions. She, in true Maggie fashion, had put his demeanour down to a lack of fresh air and exercise which, she decided, the golf trip would no doubt resolve. He hadn't told her that he had to be in court on Wednesday morning and that he was still totally unprepared. He called Myles.

"Myles Cavendish." Myles answered briskly.

"Myles, it's Callum."

"Who?" Myles replied arrogantly.

"Callum Dunbar, golf trip."

"Bloody hell, sorry Callum, didn't quite hear you properly. What's the problem, not an issue with the flights I hope, not bloody ash again."

"No. Look, something pretty heavy's going on with work, I'm not going to make it, I'm really sorry Myles but.."

Myles interrupted.

"No fucking way, you can't call off at the last minute, you'll stuff up the whole trip, the pairings are all organised, we'll have an odd number and we won't get a replacement at this short notice. Come off it Dunbar, don't be such a wanker and get your act together, you can sort it out while you're away, that's what technology and staff are for. I'll see you at the hotel." And he hung up.

Putting his phone back in his pocket, Callum picked up his case files and took them out to the hall. He would need to take a shower. Hopefully the plane would fall out of the sky and solve his problem.

Christie looked at the clock, five-fifty am. She could hear Mike downstairs in the kitchen; hopefully he would bring her up a coffee before he set off. She would love a lie in, love to snuggle back down under the duvet and just sleep, but two of the boys had to be in Hamilton for a rugby tournament by nine-thirty and the other had a golf tie at ten. She hadn't yet thought through the logistics of this and the late night hadn't helped. She might have to phone one of the other mums for help. The problem was that her weekends were now as busy as her working week, ferrying the boys to their various sporting fixtures, catching up on paperwork, shopping, washing and ironing and of course endless cooking. During the week she had the help of Anna from the Czech Republic, a nice girl who kept the house tidy and who could be relied upon to feed and act as a taxi service if she or Mike were held up, but it wasn't ideal. The boys walked all over her and she had to organise Anna, as well as the boys, if the household was to run smoothly. Mike did his share, but she did more, and like most men, he was far better than her at taking time out for himself. Work had been pretty stressful over the past six months and her ability to cope was wearing thin. She was getting snappy and she didn't like it. Hopefully, Mike would come back on a high from his trip and she could discuss the possibility of cutting down her hours. She realised now, that being a full time working mother came with a price and she wasn't sure whether she was still prepared to pay it.

Mike put the coffee on the bedside table. He looked annoyingly handsome.

"Don't say I don't love you," he said grinning, "you are so lucky to be married to me."

Ignoring him, Christie sat up and rearranged the pillows. The coffee was a welcome treat and taking a sip she looked at Mike.

"Have you got everything, tickets, passport, money?"

"Yep all organised. What time do the boys have to be up? I'd like to have seen them play rugby this weekend."

"Oh I'm sure you won't give it a second thought once you're on the plane," Christie answered sarcastically. "Where are you staying anyway? Have you written it down somewhere? I'm very trusting you know, you're always going off and just assume that because you have a mobile phone you don't have to tell me where you are."

"I can't remember the exact name of it, Cavendish has all the details but I'll text you when I get there."

Mike wasn't sure whether he wanted Christie to Google the hotel, it wasn't exactly cheap and he'd already been away skiing. Sitting down on the bed, he began to rub her back.

"Will you phone Lucy this weekend?" he asked changing the subject.

"I suppose I should." Christie sighed. "I'll see how I get on with the boys. To be honest I'd just like a bit of peace. I'll see."

As Mike continued to rub her back she realised that she didn't actually want to do anything. She just wanted to have one day without any responsibility. The thought of dealing with Lucy's issues was really depressing and then, of course, there was Maggie. Maggie had threatened to phone as well and she wasn't sure if she could handle the feelings of inadequacy that

Maggie always seemed to generate. On the positive side, Maggie would produce food. Mike gave her shoulders a final squeeze and kissed her on the top of her head.

"Bye my darling. I'll call you later, if I'm allowed. I got a heavy fine for calling you last time."

"Oh for God's sake Mike, that's so pathetic, not being able to phone home is really quite ridiculous. Just bugger off and please behave yourself."

Standing alone in her dressing gown in the warm kitchen, Maggie stared aimlessly into the pan of bacon sizzling on top of the Aga. She had slept badly, aware that Callum had spent the night downstairs and for once in her brilliantly organised life, Maggie Dunbar realised that she was afraid.

In Steve's car on the way to the airport, Mike's phone rang.

"Myles Cavendish you arsehole, where are you?"

"Still at home, I'm heading off in about five minutes. Is Dunbar with you?"

"No, he's making his own way; he's not on our route."

"Well you can fine him big time when he gets to the airport, he's just tried to call off the tosser, don't know what he's playing at but he's in your team so you can sort him out. I'll see you at the hotel. Give me a ring when you get there."

Mike hung up. "Dunbar's just tried to call off," he said in disbelief, "bloody hell, something must be up, no one calls off at the last minute, it must be serious."

"And I bet Cavendish was his usual understanding self," Steve answered sarcastically, "you'd better phone Callum, find out what's going on. Shit, it's not like him, something must have happened."

Mike dialled Callum's mobile. "It's gone straight on to voicemail; he must have it switched off. Do you think I should try the house and risk waking up Maggie?"

"Don't worry, she'll be up," laughed Steve. "You know what she's like."

Mike called the house. Eventually Maggie picked up.

"Hello, Maggie Dunbar."

"Maggie, it's Mike, sorry, hope we haven't got you out of bed, we were just wondering whether Callum has left yet."

"Oh hello Mike, no I'm afraid you've just missed him, why, have you forgotten something?"

"No, no, it's just that we couldn't get through on his mobile, it's nothing important." He changed the subject. "Got anything nice planned for the weekend?"

"Oh a few things, I'll be calling Lucy and Christie in a wee while, hopefully I can get them to come over."

"Good on ya Maggs, they'll be delighted. Have a great weekend."

"You too Mike, keep out of trouble."

"You know me Maggs, virtue is my middle name and don't worry I'll look after that dopey husband of yours. See you soon."

Mike hung up. "Maggie says he's left, she didn't sound annoyed or concerned so I presume he's still coming. Something must be up though."

Maggie put the phone down and filled the kettle with water. Callum had looked awful this morning and he'd hardly spoken to her over breakfast. She'd never seen him like this before. She wished that she had been brave enough to ask, maybe she could have helped. She hadn't though had she, mainly because she knew deep down that she didn't actually want to know the answer.

Leaving instructions and cash for his cleaner, Cavendish locked up and loaded his golf clubs and bag into the boot of his Audi. Getting into the car he called Simon.

"Morning Fanny Man, are you on your way?"

"You are so bloody polite, Cavendish, yes I'm on my way, do

you think I'm not capable of getting myself to the airport?"

"I'm just checking that I've got a team seeing as one of the Scottish lot just tried to call off. Dunbar, of all people, bloody ridiculous. He'll regret it later; he's on for a big fine as soon as I get hold of him."

Simon was incredulous. Cavendish was so insensitive.

"He must have had a good reason Myles; did you actually bother to ask him?"

"Course not, not interested, especially as he said work. Death I would accept, possibly family illness, but work is not a good enough excuse. Anyway, not up for discussion. God I'm looking forward to this trip. How's your golf? I hope you've sorted out that bloody slice you acquired last time we played, you were fucking awful."

"Thanks for that mate, if that's an example of your positive team chat I don't hold out much hope. I'll see you at the airport, I'm picking up Andy."

"Oh yeh, I forgot about that debacle. Bob the useless broke builder, at least he's coming I suppose."

Simon gave up; it wasn't worth wasting his breath.

"Piss off Cavendish, I'll see you later."

In the Ellerman household tensions were running high, both of them aware that this weekend was a brief respite from the grim reality that they would have to face on Andy's return. Andy was trying hard to be his usual chirpy self but the issue weighed heavy on Sophie's shoulders. She realised reluctantly that she would have to come clean and knew she would be spending the weekend calculating and facing up to the extent of her debt.

"It'll be all right Soph," Andy said gently, "we'll get through it, we're not the only ones struggling at the moment." He put his arms around her and held her tight, wishing he felt as confident as he sounded. Sophie, burying her face into his shoulder, suppressed the urge to sob.

Chapter 5

At Glasgow airport, Mike cracked open the Champagne and filled up the plastic glasses of the Scottish team. Raising his glass he proposed a toast.

"Cheers boys – here's to a good trip and a thrashing for those bloody southern Jessie's." The rest of the team raised their glasses with a cheer and knocked back the contents. Refilling the empties, Mike continued.

"Fines are going to be big this year as Cavendish is in charge, so if we're going to win, we need to be on top form. I don't want you all so paralytic that you can't even hit the bloody ball. Rex, you useless bastard are you listening?"

Rex Haig, Estate Agent, smiled amiably, his unruly blonde hair reflecting the mayhem of his life.

"You had so many fines last year Haig I'm surprised you're still alive, try and keep up this time, I'm fed up with babysitting, and El Divo, if you don't make it to the tee on time you will be banned next year, final warning, no more chances. If you don't show up on the tee, we lose a match."

Davie Sutherland grinned cockily and looking around the group raised his glass with a wink.

"Depends what's keeping me back, eh boys?"

"I'm telling you, if I catch you shagging on tour Divo, I'll ban you too. Alex, you're responsible for getting him on the tee." Alex protested.

"Oh come off it Mike, I'm not responsible for that randy bastard, why do I have to share a room with him? Christ that's a full time job."

"I know, and you get it for being the weakest link last year, highest handicapper gets to be babysitter."

"I'll need a pair of bloody handcuffs then," replied Alex tetchily.

"Don't worry Alex," said Davie coyly, "I'll try and behave as long as you promise to bring me tea in bed in the morning."

The boys laughed.

"Right tour rules," Mike shouted above the din. "No swearing, fine five Euros, no pointing, fine five Euros – starting now- fines to me please. Cavendish will no doubt have a few more by the time we get to the hotel, so try not to give him any opportunity to get one over on us – cheers boys."

The team raised their glasses for the final time and as the group mingled, out of earshot, Steve spoke quietly to Mike.

"What about fining Dunbar? Have you spoken to him yet? He doesn't look too chirpy does he?"

They both looked over in Callum's direction, he was making the right moves but his body language told them that his mind wasn't on the conversation.

"I'll go," said Steve, "something's not right."

Steve slapped Callum affectionately on the back and squeezed his shoulder.

"Are you all right mate – something up?"

Callum turned his back on the rest of the group and took a drink. "Oh nothing much apart from the fact I probably won't have a job when I get back, things are pretty shit actually Steve."

"Is that why you tried to call off? Cavendish is raging and that's five Euros by the way."

Callum rummaged in his pocket and taking out his wallet he handed five Euros to Mike.

"Yeh, been struggling a bit lately, partners aren't happy, I know they want me out. I've got a case on Wednesday and I'm not prepared, I just can't think straight, can't seem to get myself together. To be honest, I think its curtains for me Stevie boy."

"Does Maggie know?"

"Bloody hell, course not, she just thinks I need more exercise." He handed over another five Euros. " I can't face the thought of telling her."

"Why don't you just go home Dunbar? This trip's not worth losing your job, or your wife over."

"To be honest mate, I don't think it would make any difference, my days are numbered, they're probably writing me a cheque as we speak, might as well go out with a bang."

"Shit Callum, do you not think you're taking this a bit lightly, what about Maggie and the kids?"

"Believe me, I'm not taking this lightly, best thing would be if I dropped dead, solve everyone's problem. And that's five Euros from you too."

As Steve handed over the fines to Mike, he felt uneasy.

"Forget fining him Mike, it's not good. In fact I think it's a real bloody disaster."

Andy and Simon sat with the rest of the English team at Heathrow airport waiting for Cavendish to arrive.

"How was Sophie this morning?" Simon asked cautiously, "did she calm down a bit?"

"Just about. I bloody deserved it though didn't I? Bloody stupid, I should have told her. We're gonna try and sort everything out when I get back, don't quite know what we're going to do yet but it'll be easier trying to sort things out together than me trying to blag my way through. It's a relief actually."

"I don't envy you mate, construction's not the best market to be in at the moment is it but it'll come back round it always does. It's easy for me, gynaecology is actually a thriving market."

Andy smiled. "What a life eh, looking at women's fannies all day."

"Believe me it's not all it's cracked up to be and talking of fannies, look who's just arrived."

Cavendish swaggered into the airport bar, pink striped shirt, chinos and sunglasses. As usual, he looked expensive.

"He's got banker written all over him," Andy grinned. "You'd think he'd keep his head down for a while."

"He wouldn't give it a second thought," Simon simmered, "once a banker always a banker, brace yourself, Exocet approaching."

"All right boys," Cavendish boomed across the bar, "come on liven up, can somebody get me a bloody drink. Is everybody here?"

"He really is such a complete tosser," Andy said quietly. "I almost feel sorry for him."

"Well boys," Cavendish bellowed, "has everyone got a drink? Well here we all are ready to give the northerners a good seeing to and here's to an all round bloody good trip."

He raised his glass.

"To Queen and Country, beer and birdies and remember boys, what goes on tour stays on tour..."

Chapter 6

Sitting at her kitchen table, Sophie Ellerman stared at the assortment of un-opened envelopes, each one containing a part of the whole unpleasant truth. Resolving to face up to her responsibility, she had gathered a notebook and pen and riffled in various drawers to find a calculator. She had made herself coffee and buttered toast, but her breakfast lay untouched alongside the unwelcome messengers. She felt sick. It seemed to have happened so easily, as one enthusiastic sales assistant after another, eager to fulfil sales targets, had offered discounts in return for easy credit. And as the store card balances had piled up, credit card companies offered 0% interest on balance transfers, put all your debt onto one card, it was easy they said. Each time she had done it she had resolved to pay it off and had cut up her store cards, but somehow it had never happened. Sophie opened the first envelope and stared at the balance £1750.88. Earnestly she wrote it down on the first page of the empty notebook. Her hands shaking, she opened the second envelope, £3457.49. She realised that this was the first time she had registered the totals, her usual method of dealing with the demands was to focus on the minimum payment only; it had seemed less brutal, less real. But now as the minimum payments had eased their way past her ability to pay, and hard hearted debt collectors had started to phone wanting their pound of flesh, she realised there was no escape.

She had nothing to show for it; a bulging wardrobe of clothes never worn, a fancy kitchen, knick knacks, frippery but nothing of substance. The pleasures her purchases had brought had been fleeting, a sticky plaster over the empty void that infertility had brought to her life. If her mountain of debt had produced a child it would have been worth it. In her mind it would have been worth every single penny.

Methodically, she opened each envelope until the pile was gone, then picking up the calculator with shaking fingers, she began to add up the figures. As she reached her final total, her stomach lurched and she vomited into the kitchen sink.

As she knew it would, Christie's phone rang at seven-thirty am precisely.

"Christie sweetheart, it's Maggie, knew you'd be up early, no rest for us girls is there?"

Trying to sound enthusiastic, Christie continued trying to apply her make-up, the phone lodged precariously under her chin. Maggie was the last person she wanted to speak to this weekend.

"Hi Maggs, Mike said you would phone, what you up to?"

"Well I thought you could come over for some supper later. If you can make it for three we can have a drink and a yarn and I'll rustle up some food. I'm going to get Lucy and the kids over too, try to cheer her up a bit."

Christie was reluctant and fumbled for a realistic excuse.

"That's very kind of you Maggs but I'll need to make sure the boys are sorted, I'm not sure yet what their plans are for this evening, I'm still trying to get them out of their bloody beds. I'm not too keen asking Anna to help out again and they might need dropping somewhere and I'm not sure whether we'll be back by three."

Maggie dealt with it in her usual manner.

"Oh I'm sure you'll sort it out, you're such a clever girl. Bring the boys with you, they can chill out in the attic with the TV and X-box, no-one ever uses it these days. See you whenever you can make it sweetheart; ring me to let me know when you're setting off. Bye."

"Bossy bitch," Christie said aloud, throwing the phone onto the bed while trying to erase the smudged mascara. She was cross with herself now.

"How the bloody hell did I let that happen?"

Lucy was also angry with herself, angry that she had shown absolutely no resistance to Maggie's plans for her day. Not that she had any. As she began to clear the remnants of the children's breakfast she glanced at the clock, it was only eight o'clock and the weekend stretched out in front of her like a prison sentence. At least the visit to Maggie's would break the monotony and the children would love it; they loved Maggie's house with its acres of garden, tree houses and attics and of course the ponies. Maggie was also exceptionally good at baking. The excitement of the proposed visit had at least ensured that they went to their rooms to get dressed by themselves.

She poured herself a second cup of coffee and opening the cupboard door she stared aimlessly at its contents. She had no appetite, despite the gnawing ache in her stomach and the pain in her head was getting worse. Closing the cupboard door she opened the fridge. An egg would probably help but then she would have to have bread and she was desperately trying to lose weight, the bread wouldn't help. What she did fancy, she realised with reluctance, was a glass of wine. She reached into the fridge and took a chilled bottle of white from the top shelf, then as it dawned on her exactly what she was doing, she thrust it back. Fighting back the tears she closed the fridge door and leant against it.

"Oh my God" she whispered softly, "I've got to get a grip."

A few hours later, perched on the toilet in Maggie Dunbar's bathroom, Lucy looked around. Maggie's toilet was a reflection of its owner. Clean and tastefully scented, with shiny taps and Crabtree and Evelyn soap, its walls were adorned with carefully selected family photographs, artistically framed and creatively arranged, a tribute to the achievements of Maggie Dunbar. Roses, no doubt from Maggie's garden, rested elegantly on the occasional table which stood beside the toilet, alongside the latest edition of Country Life and Horse and Hound. Hopefully, Lucy ran her finger over the polished wood, but as expected it was dust free. Everything about Maggie bathroom reinforced Lucy's feelings of inadequacy, highlighting her perceived failure as a wife and mother as well as a woman.

Lucy looked at the photographs; the girls winning rosettes, the girls skiing, Maggie riding, Maggie and girls sailing, Maggie with prize sweet peas, Maggie and girls in Sydney, Maggie climbing Ben Nevis for the Hospice, Maggie, Maggie, bloody Maggie. Apart from a single photo of Callum and Maggie on their wedding day, Callum appeared to be missing from this display of self congratulation. Self centred bitch, Lucy hissed under her breath.

Despite not wanting to come over this afternoon, it had actually proved to be a relief. Maggie had brought in one of the girls from the stables to entertain the kids and they had been thrilled at the prospect of a pony ride, tea with home baked cakes in Maggie's tree house and DVD's before bed in the attic. Not having to cook was also an added bonus. The other saving grace was that Maggie had also asked Christie. She liked Christie, as despite her obvious talents, Christie admitted to failings. Failing wasn't on Maggie's agenda.

Lucy flushed the toilet and straightened her skirt, its tightness reminding her that she was putting on weight. Washing her hands with the rose scented soap she studied herself in the mirror. Christie looked lovely this evening, despite trying to convince Lucy that she was knackered and even Maggie looked younger than her forty-five years. Lucy hadn't bothered with any make up, not even lipstick. She looked at her hair, it hadn't been near a hairdresser since Christmas and there were definitely a few more greys. There were a few more lines around the eyes too. She wondered whether Steve still found her attractive, whether he compared her to Christie or even Maggie. She wondered whether he still loved her at all. Lucy dried her hands, making sure to leave the towel as neatly as she had found it and with a deep breath, walked back out to Maggie's kitchen.

With Lucy in the bathroom, Maggie took the opportunity to discuss Lucy's failings with Christie. Maggie, of course, looked immaculate, as if reinforcing her status as commander in chief amongst the wives, and her concern for Lucy's welfare was part of her duty. Opening a bottle of very expensive Sancerre, Maggie poured all three a glass of wine.

"I'm very worried about Lucy you know," Maggie said in a low whisper, "you can see she's not functioning properly, to be honest she's looking a mess. She has definitely put on weight and she's letting herself go, if she doesn't sort herself out soon, she might find herself on her own."

Christie looked at her. "For God's sake Maggie, she doesn't look that bad, a bit tired but her kids are younger than ours, hardly bad enough for Steve to divorce her. He thinks the world of her and the kids, he told me the other night. He said she has been a bit down lately but he's certainly wasn't talking about leaving her. What makes you think he would do that?"

Maggie took a large mouthful of the Sancerre. "Men will only put up with so much before they start looking around," Maggie said knowingly, "and Steve is a good looking guy, he probably gets plenty of offers. If she's letting herself go she's not interested in herself and if she's not interested in herself then you can guarantee she won't be interested in him, if you know what I mean. Men have their needs Christie; they can't go without it for too long."

Christie tried to suppress a laugh. "So just because Lucy's let her hair get out of hand she's not having sex. Come off it, you can't make those sort of generalisations, you sound like a bloody self help book. We've all been there Maggie, it's just a bad patch, as the kids get older things will improve."

"Well that's where I think you're wrong, I think she's going downhill. She looks bloody miserable." But as Maggie finished the sentence she thought about Callum, he looked miserable too and they hadn't had sex for weeks.

As Lucy walked back into the kitchen, Maggie and Christie both looked up. As the conversation had stopped it was obvious that they had been talking about her. Christie looked uncomfortable.

Maggie offered Lucy the wine and she sat down at the kitchen table. Christie helped herself to another olive and with a smile pushed the bowl towards Lucy. Lucy smiled back gratefully. Christie, eager to take the pressure off Lucy, re-started the conversation.

"How are the children enjoying school Lucy, Lily is so cute, I would have loved a little girl, you have no idea what it's like living with four men in the house, toilets are a nightmare." Lucy grinned but before she had chance to answer, Maggie cut in.

"It's the opposite in our house; make up, hair straigtners, girly things really. The girls are all pretty sporty but they still like to look attractive. We've just got a new hairdresser actually, Nigel, fantastic with colour. Who do you go to now Lucy?" Christie felt her stomach tighten, god she was unbelievable. Maggie didn't wait for the answer. "I'll give you his number, he really is fabulous, he did a fantastic job on Carol Smithson and you know what a state her hair was in." Lucy toyed with her wine glass. "Maybe we could get you in on Monday morning, spruce you up a bit, give Steve a nice surprise when he gets back."

Looking up, Lucy glared at her.

"Why don't you just fuck off?"

Maggie looked stunned. Christie took her hand "Are you ok Lucy?"

Lucy took another swig of the wine, confused by her sudden outburst.

"I don't know whether I'm ok Christie," she hissed angrily. "If not going to the hairdresser, getting fat, drinking too much, crying all the time and not wanting to sleep with my husband means I'm not ok then I suppose she's right, I'm cracking up, but a bloody hairdresser isn't going to fix that. If I was that bloody unattractive Maggie Dunbar, Steve wouldn't want to share my bed, but the sad thing is he does. I'm the bloody problem."

Slowly Maggie sat down at the table and looking down she very quietly broke the silence.

"I wish Callum wanted to share mine."

Chapter 7

It was early afternoon by the time the English boys made it to Hotel Internationale and the Scots had wasted no time in soaking up the sun around the pool. White bodies were already feeling the effects of sudden exposure to the sun and a hefty fine had swiftly been issued to El Divo for sporting a pair of vivid green Speedos and to Callum for getting fat. Steve lay back on his lounger and closed his eyes, listening with amusement to the juvenile conversation going on around him, trying desperately not to think of issues back home. He had tried to call from his room earlier but got no answer. Maggie, he assumed, had got her way which at least meant that Lucy would not be hitting the bottle alone. He had decided against phoning her at Maggie's. Suddenly, from the direction of the hotel reception, came the sound of a familiar voice. Cavendish, Steve sighed, he really was a prize tit.

Cavendish led his team into the hotel, looking around with satisfaction at the gleaming marble interior.

"Well boys," he bellowed, pleased with himself, "very nice, very nice indeed."

The rest of the boys, murmuring their approval, followed him to the desk and depositing their cases and golf bags on the floor, proceeded to check in. Glancing at her name badge, Cavendish wasted no time on the receptionist. She was slim and pretty, her dark hair drawn back into a neat bun. He leaned forward on the desk as he spoke.

"The name's Cavendish Avelina, I booked the suite."

Avelina, used to his type, did not respond other than to confirm his booking.

"Thank you Mr Cavendish, could you fill this in for me please, I will need your passport details." And she handed him a form without catching his eye. Cavendish smiled to himself, there would be other opportunities.

His booking complete, Cavendish instructed the rest of the team to meet back down in the bar in fifteen minutes and called Mike on his mobile.

"Mike where are you? I'm in reception."

"Yeh, we could hear you from here you noisy bastard. We're by the pool, where the hell have you been?"

"Plane delayed, usual crap, the others have gone to dump their bags. Get your lot organised and be in the lounge bar in fifteen minutes."

"Only if you ask me nicely."

"Fuck off MacDonald."

As Mike hung up he grinned. It was going to give him great pleasure getting under Cavendish's skin and he knew it wouldn't be difficult.

"Right boys, Cavendish wants us in the lounge bar in fifteen minutes so go and get changed and we'll meet in twenty five, that'll piss him off."

Up in his room, Andy dumped his bag on the floor and looked out of the window. He had a view over the tennis courts and the sea, probably a mile away, was just visible. He felt guilty, Sophie hadn't had a holiday this year and here he was in a hotel he couldn't afford. He rummaged in his pocket and sent a text. *"Sorry. Don't worry. Love you. xx"*

Alone for five minutes in his shared room, Simon called Tracey but she didn't answer. He left a message. *"Hi it's me, just to let you know I've arrived, nice hotel and its bloody roasting. I'll try and call later but you know what it's like. Enjoy the peace, love ya lots x"*

Cavendish removed his socks and shoes and sprawled on the

king sized bed in his executive suite. He called TJ.

"TJ, Myles Cavendish, just confirming I've arrived and we're still ok for tomorrow night?"

"Yes Mr Cavendish sir, everything is booked, your girls will arrive at eleven-thirty pm."

"Good man TJ and what's the chance of sending me a little taster for this evening, say about midnight?"

"No problem at all sir, where should I send her?"

"Call me when she's on her way, I'll sort it out then."

Cavendish loosened his shirt and closed his eyes for a few minutes. Maybe Avelina might have been persuaded with a little more persistence but paying for it was less complicated, it wasn't so difficult to get rid of them afterwards.

A loud cheer went up as the Scots walked into the lounge bar and they greeted each other with firm handshakes and mutual admiration. Drinks were ordered and Cavendish called for quiet.

"Welcome everyone to this twentieth anniversary tour of which I am delighted to be in charge. The plan for the rest of the day is to have a quick nine holes, as we didn't get here on time, and then I've booked a restaurant in town for about eight. The team sheets for tomorrow will be distributed tonight. Now fines are as usual, no pointing or swearing and there will be extra fines for not knowing the words to the songs I sent and any three putts. Worst score tonight wears the red dress to dinner and walks home. Minibus for golf is booked for three so be in reception. Cheers everyone." He raised his glass.

Callum Dunbar's heart sank. He wasn't in the mood for all this.

Back in London, the grey skies threatened rain and Sophie grabbed her umbrella as she set off to Nico's. Not being able to face being alone in the house with her reality laid bare on the kitchen table, she had called Tracey and arranged to meet for lunch. The Italian bar would be busy and she could lose herself in the bustle and conversation of other people's lives. Not that she could afford it. By the time she arrived, Nico's was heaving but the manager, being a good friend of Andy's, had reserved a table on the balcony from which Sophie could watch the door and look out for Tracey.

"Can I get you a drink while you're waiting?" asked the young waiter.

"Yes please, a gin and tonic," smiled Sophie, folding her coat and placing it on one of the chairs.

"Shall I leave menus? The specials are on the board."

"Yes, thanks," she said, grateful for something to look at while she waited. Sophie stared at the menu but she couldn't take it in, she was still in shock at the mountain of debt that was now threatening to engulf her and she really did not know what she was going to do. Facing Andy was going to be the hardest thing she had ever done in her life unless she could find a way of dealing with it before he came back.

"Hi Soph, sorry I'm late," said Tracey, slightly out of breath, "couldn't find anywhere to park, it would probably have been quicker to walk."

Tracey looked fabulous as always, her dark blonde hair tied back, her grey eyes complemented by a silver blue jacket. Removing her scarf she placed her bag under the table and sat down.

"Don't worry, I've only just got here, you look fantastic Tracey, how do you do it with two kids?"

"Well I am not a hard working teacher for a start," Tracey replied smiling, "and I have in fact been to the spa this morning so for what I have just paid I would like to think that people will notice."

The young waiter appeared promptly and smiled at Tracey appreciatively.

"Can I get you a drink madam?"

"Oh yes please, I've just drunk a gallon of water, what have you got Sophie, is that a G & T? I'll have the same please and can we have a bowl of olives please, I'm absolutely starving."

For the first half an hour their conversation skirted around the issue of the golf trip, but eventually Tracey felt brave enough to test the water.

"Have you heard from Andy at all?"

"Not yet but that's probably a good thing, we both need time to cool off."

"Look Sophie, I'm really sorry, I had no idea, you do know that don't you?"

"Yes I know, I just felt so stupid and angry at him for being so bloody spineless, I still can't believe he thought he would get away with it. Am I really so awful that he thought he couldn't tell me?"

"Oh you know what they're like, they're just big kids really and I suppose in a funny sort of way they enjoy a bit of intrigue. Simon felt awful, he had no idea that things were tight for you, Andy never said anything. Are things really that bad?"

Sophie couldn't contain herself, the genuine concern in Tracey's voice piercing through her defences. Her voice shaking, she choked back the tears.

"Yes," she whispered, "they're really that bad."

And as Sophie poured her heart out, the bistro bustled around them, oblivious to the torment of the respectable teacher in the blue dress. Tracey wondered how many other people in the bar were now in a similar situation and how many others, like Sophie, had demons that were starting to check in.

"What are you going to do, are you going to tell him?" Tracey asked, not really sure herself how she would deal with it if she were in that position. "I mean you have to really, surely you don't have a choice. Andy would understand."

Sophie looked up and wiped her eyes with her fingers.

"I don't think I can Tracey, not yet, I'm not brave enough,

I'll just have to work something out, there'll be some organisation somewhere that can help, there always is, there's bound to be one for idiot, debt laden wives who can't face their husbands, there's probably thousands of us. The problem is he thinks it's his entire fault and that's what's making me feel bad but I just can't tell him, I'm such a bloody coward."

Tracey looked at their half eaten meals and at Sophie's tear stained face. What a bloody mess she thought to herself. What a pointless, heartbreaking mess. She waved towards the waiter.

"Come on, let's order a really awful desert and then we'll go back to my place; the boys are away and we can try and think this through. I know it seems like it Sophie but this is not the end of the world, it will work itself out, these things always do one way or another."

Sophie blew her nose, grateful for being able to share her burden, but at that moment her particular mountain seemed far too huge to climb.

Chapter 8

Callum Dunbar was grateful for his single room, at least he could get some work done tonight without being disturbed. He opened his case and took his files out of the back pocket and lay them on the desk, their presence a reminder of his responsibilities. He was tempted to phone Maggie but instead opted for the basic text, *"Arrived safely, hotel good, weather hot, call soon x,"* it was easier. Undressing, he freshened up in the black and white marbled bathroom. He was tired, unenthusiastic and miserable; two more days under the watchful eye of Cavendish would no doubt be purgatory especially as he would have him down as a marked man for trying to call off. He dressed slowly in one of the immaculately ironed golf shirts and cream shorts and then, as he had a few minutes to spare, he picked up one of his files and sat down on the bed. A glance at the first page reminded him that he was on a loser. His head was a mess, his life was a mess, there was no point. In a sudden rage he flung it with force across the room and as the contents scattered themselves upon the floor, Callum Dunbar lay down on the bed wishing that he could go to sleep and not wake up.

With Steve sorting out team kit with Alex, Mike lay on his bed in their shared room flicking through the TV channels. He jumped as his mobile rang.

"Hey Mike, it's Simon. Have you got five minutes?"

"Aye, got a problem?"

"Yes Cavendish, he's a big problem. I thought I ought to warn you about tomorrow night, you know he's got some women booked after the dinner, I've just got a feeling things could get out of hand and some of the boys might regret it, I've known him a long time now, he's bloody dangerous."

Mike was surprised at the frankness of Simon's call, it certainly wasn't usual for anyone to show concern as to the outcome of any tour events, but Simon sounded genuinely agitated.

"I wouldn't worry mate, were all big boys, I'm sure we can all look after ourselves, it's not as if any of us haven't seen a few tits and arses before and the boys will be so pissed they won't know what's going on anyway."

"Well that's just it, that's what worries me, I just think we're asking for trouble, and you can put five Euros in the kitty by the way."

"Look mate, I'll have a word with him and try and find out what he's got up his sleeve but I don't expect he'll give much away. Relax Simmo, Tracey'll never find out, if I see you trying to shag any of those lovely ladies I'll drag you off. Are you sharing or you in a single? A few people seem to be in singles this time, must be nice not having to put up with anyone else's farts. I'm used to Steve's by now though."

Simon realising that the cause was lost and the rest of the conversation now pointless, confirmed that he was in a single and signed himself out of the conversation. He would need to get himself livened up; being sluggish on tour was too dangerous. The water was refreshingly cool as he splashed it over his face in the bathroom, trying to wash away any negative thoughts in the process. This was the first time he had felt like this on the trip and he had no explanation other than a feeling of guilt for something that was to be out of his control. He tried to think positively, he would just have to get on with it and Mike was right, Tracey would never know.

With ten minutes spare, Mike looked over his team sheets for the draw later this afternoon. The pairings looked good apart from the pairing of Callum with Alex. Alex wasn't the best golfer in the world and usually Callum would bring him up but Callum was so bloody depressed the pairing was not looking too productive. He decided to put himself with Callum and Rex could go with Alex. The English team was pretty strong this year and the extra chinks in the Scottish armour could prove costly. Mike did not want to lose to Cavendish at any cost. He would need to keep the boys focused and any chance to send the English boys into an alcohol fused delirium would be seized upon by himself and Steve, expert tour players for the past twenty years. He knew Steve wouldn't want to give Cavendish any chance of winning either, there was no honour in defeat. A beep from his phone signalled a text message.

"Hi, hope all well. At Maggies, big drama, Lucy pissed off, Maggie getting pissed, tears at bedtime probably. Don't tell S & C. Having a lovely time!!! Love you x"

Mike smiled, women were so bloody complicated but at least she seemed to be finding it amusing. He sent a text back.

"Just off to play golf. No one pissed yet. Callum depressed, Cavendish a wanker. Probably tears at bedtime too. Love you x"

Reading the text in Maggie's vast hallway Christie smiled, it was reassuring to see that life wasn't too straightforward for the boys this time either. It was interesting that Mike had mentioned Callum though, not usual for Mike to comment on any of his mates emotional states, what the hell was all that about? Christie walked back into the kitchen. After the shock of Maggie's disclosure the atmosphere had changed slightly as both she and Lucy were hit with the realisation that Maggie Dunbar was in fact vulnerable. After pouring them both a drink, Christie had offered to settle Lucy's kids in front of a DVD in the attic while Maggie went into automatic overdrive and prepared their supper. As Christie sat herself back down at the table she looked at them both. They both looked drained. Lucy, she noticed to her surprise, hadn't actually drunk much more of her wine; Maggie, on the other hand, had finished her third glass.

"Can I help with anything Maggie?" Christie asked cautiously, "there must be something I can do, peel something or set the table?"

Maggie wiped her hands on her apron and tucked her hair back behind her ears. For once she seemed awkward in the kitchen. She opened one of the cupboards as if to look for something and without turning round to face them she said in a matter of fact tone.

"Do you think Callum could be having an affair? Do you think he could have met someone else?"

Lucy and Christie looked at each other, neither of them having the faintest idea what to say. Of course it was feasible but they had never given it a second thought. Lucy was filled with silent admiration that Callum would be brave enough. Surely if Callum had been having an affair Mike would have told her, Christie thought, but then again, men were pretty oblivious to these things. On the other hand, they also protected each other. To break the silence Maggie continued.

"I mean I don't even know if he's on the trip, he could be anywhere. Mike phoned me this morning to see if he had left so he obviously thought he might not come, how would I know if he was seeing someone else?"

Feeling the need for a drink herself, Christie poured herself another white wine and interrupted.

"He's definitely there Maggie; Mike said so in his text to me half an hour ago."

Maggie turned and fixed her eyes on Christie. "Now why would Mike mention Callum in his text? Did he mention everyone else in the team? Mike's probably trying to cover for him."

"Mike wouldn't do that," said Christie indignantly, "Mike wouldn't get involved in all that stuff, he couldn't be bothered for one thing. Look Maggie, he mentioned Callum in his text to tell me that he seemed depressed, he said it in a jokey way but ok, I agree with you something's up. Have you tried talking about it, have you asked him what's wrong?"

Maggie refilled the bowl of crisped roots and passed them around.

"No, and if I'm honest it's because I don't want to really. I keep hoping everything will sort itself out if I just carry on as normal. I just can't believe that he could have met someone else. I mean the ridiculous thing is he's never exactly been Mr Casanova, he'd keep his socks on given half a chance."

As the thought of Callum fornicating with his socks on tumbled into Lucy's head she suddenly snorted, spraying some of her wine across the table. Maggie, for a moment, stared incredulously then, without warning, joined Lucy in a helpless fit of demonic giggles.

Standing in the foyer waiting for the minibuses to arrive, Mike told Steve about his changes to the pairings.

"I just don't think we'll get much out of him unless he comes with me, I could do without it though, I came on this trip for a laugh, I'm starting to feel like a therapist. I've just had Simon on the phone too, worried about these birds that Cavendish's got lined up, doesn't seem to trust Cavendish's judgement. He's terrified that his Mrs will find out I think but what the hell am I supposed to do about it?"

Steve slapped him on the back.

"Come on Clare Rayner cheer up, we're here for a good laugh and a well deserved break. If I thought too hard about what's going on back home I'd be miserable too but I intend to deal with all that when I get back. We are all consenting adults and they all know the rules, if they can't take it that's their problem. Jesus, it wouldn't be a trip without constant torture and abuse would it?"

Mike's phone beeped again and he fumbled in his pocket.

The text was from Christie *"Is Callum definitely with you, don't ask, just yes or no, tell the truth x."* Mike re-read the text. "Jesus Christ," he said under his breath. *"Course he is,"* he replied, *"What the fuck is going on?"*

A large beer was suddenly thrust into his hand.

"MacDonald you can get that down your scrawny Scottish neck, no texting in public especially if it's your wife."

Mike smiled as he looked Cavendish in the eye.

"At least I've got a wife Cavendish. Cheers boys." And expertly he downed the beer to the applause of the rest of the team.

With Lucy and Maggie still in a useless state at the kitchen table, Christie picked up the text. Well at least Callum was there, she thought relieved, although that still didn't rule out an affair. *"Don't worry"* she replied as Lucy and Maggie continued to snort over mutual sexual revelations, *"Both pissed now but no tears – enjoy yourself"*

"MacDonald you tosser, if that phone goes one more time," Cavendish bellowed, "you'll drink the bloody swimming pool. Lads, get him another beer!"

Chapter 9

Back at Tracey's house, Sophie gratefully removed her coat and sank into one of the comfy chairs in the sunny conservatory. The forecast rain had not yet materialised and the conservatory was warm and comforting.

"Excuse the mess," Tracey shouted from the kitchen, "tea or coffee or something stronger?"

"Coffee please," Sophie replied, despite the fact that something stronger was definitely tempting.

Sophie looked around the conservatory trying to find evidence of mess, but the room only reflected the welcome chaos of family life. How she envied it. Through the windows the early summer blooms looked vibrant in the glare of the afternoon sun, but the agitated buzz of an imprisoned bee broke the silence. Sophie unlocked the doors and threw them wide open and watched with satisfaction as the bee edged towards the doors and then flew to its freedom. There would be a way out she said to herself, she would just have to find it.

Tracey took down the cafetiere from the cupboard and placed it on the tray along with the cakes she had grabbed from the local bakery on the way home. She hadn't expected this, and to be honest she felt a little out of her league. Her own life so far had been straightforward and comfortable, normal upbringing, good education, happy marriage, easy childbirth. She'd been fortunate, very fortunate. Life had been kind. Worry had never really entered her life on a grand scale. Any of her worries had always been trivial. In Sophie's case coffee and cakes seemed inadequate but not knowing what else to do she picked up the tray and walked through to the conservatory.

"Here we are," she said chirpily as she placed the tray on the coffee table, "what a lovely afternoon. It's always nice in here even in winter, it always relaxes me. I think it's because it brings you closer to the garden. I hate it when the boys come in here though; I always want it for myself."

Tracey sat down leaving the coffee to brew.

"Your garden is beautiful Tracey. I don't have much time or enthusiasm for it these days although I wish I did. Things haven't quite worked out as I had planned really."

Sophie looked wistfully out towards the garden. Tracey so desperately wanted to help but was struggling for the right words. Leaning forward she pushed the plunger down on the cafetiere.

"How did it start, the credit card thing?" she asked as she added milk to Sophie's coffee.

"Oh I don't know really. I think after the IVF failed again I just sort of lost myself for a bit. Sadly I think I was trying to find myself, turn myself into a woman that was obviously not a mother, oh I don't know really, buying things distracted me, stopped me from thinking about it all. You know the hardest thing has been that I've always up till now been in control. Teaching is about being organised, having everything in order but I couldn't control having a baby and I suppose buying things was some sort of sad reflection of me losing control."

"But did you not realise that things were getting out of control?"

"I didn't want to see it Tracey, I suppose it's a bit like gambling, you get the next fix but it's short lived and before you know it the world comes crashing in." Sophie looked at the cake on her plate but had no appetite for it.

"How did Andy cope with the IVF?" Tracey was now feeling guilty for never having discussed this with Sophie before.

"Oh you know Andy, just gave me cuddles and said it didn't

matter, that we would be fine on our own, think of all the things we could do together without kids, but for me it was like my heart had been ripped out every time the results came through."

"But you know Sophie, men are just not very good at the emotional thing but he would have been feeling it too. Simon deals with these things everyday and he's told me that often the look on the men's faces when he has to break the news, that's harder to bear because they know they have to be strong for their wives. It's not that they don't care, they care but they don't feel able to show it. He'll be worried about work too and in the same way he won't want you to worry about it. You just have to sit down and talk about it and I mean everything, you have to Sophie."

"Yes, I know," Sophie sighed as she watched the bees in the garden, "I know."

On the first minibus to leave, Mike was starting to feel the effects of the two beers forced on him by Cavendish. Bastard, he thought to himself. He had managed to sit himself beside Andy on the bus and the banter between the two teams was gathering momentum.

"My money's on Alex for the frock this evening, I played with him last week and he was bloody useless," shouted Rex from the back.

"Five Euros," cried several voices in unison.

"I would love to see Cavendish in that dress," said Mike, "but unfortunately he's probably playing too well at the moment, he's down to three now, so not much hope of him losing easily."

"Believe me, quite a few of his own team would like to see him in that dress," Andy laughed. "He just needs bringing back to the human race now and again. How's your golf anyway?"

"Not bad, playing off five so can't complain, what about you?"

"Ten now, not played too good lately, not had much time to

be honest, trying to get as much work as I can but it's pretty dire at the moment, having to take whatever I can find really just to get through the worst."

"I might have some work coming up mate, there's a plot I'm looking at in Glasgow, just going through planning, I'll keep you in mind."

"Thanks mate, appreciate it."

Rex shouted again from the back of the bus.

"Is Cavendish shagging anyone at the moment? There must be something we can fine him for. Andy the builder, you must have something on him, come on, give us some ammo."

Andy drew a blank.

"Simon's your best bet, he knows him better than anyone else, try your luck with him. You should have seen him trying to chat up the receptionist, hilarious, she wasn't having any of it though which made it even funnier but he's well used to knock backs. How many wives has he been through now?"

"Two that we know of," chipped in Steve, "but Lucy says he's tried it on with a few of our birds too though she won't let on who. Don't worry boys, they all knocked him back. There must be some mileage in that piece of knowledge. The guy is without any moral substance."

"Too bloody right," agreed Mike.

"Ha," shouted Andy pointing at Mike, "five Euros!"

"Ha," laughed Mike, "five Euros for pointing!"

In the second minibus, Cavendish was holding court.

"I want to see one of the Scottish boys walking home in the dress after this so no one in my team had better let me down. Who wants a tenner on the worst round? My money's on Dunbar, he looks like a loser today, who's in?"

Alex, grateful for not being the subject of Cavendish's derision for once, held his own for the Scottish team.

"I hear you're on for a big fine for some recent extra-curricular activities too Cavendish," he said bravely. "I'm looking forward to dinner this evening watching you squirm for once."

Cavendish smirked.

"If anyone's going to squirm I can tell you right now that it definitely won't be me."

After the third bottle of Sancerre in Maggie's kitchen, tongues were loosening and guards were well and truly down.

"So if you did find out that Callum was having an affair Maggie, what would you do?" Lucy asked, empowered by Maggie's new found vulnerability.

"I honestly don't know, I'd be bloody furious of course," Maggie replied gulping her wine, "but then what do you do, I mean with the kids and everything. I suppose it would depend on whether it was a serious affair or a middle aged crisis fling."

"Is there a difference?" Christie asked, trying to picture her own reaction to a misdemeanour from Mike.

"Well I know at first sight it seems bad but men can be pretty stupid and sometimes they don't think with their heads do they? Having a one night stand has to be more forgivable than a proper affair because that has to be planned and they obviously have some feeling for the woman involved."

"Oh I don't know," said Lucy, "if they have to shag around then there's a problem somewhere, but you never really know what's going on in their heads do you? I often wonder if Steve has been faithful, I wouldn't blame him really if he hasn't as I don't imagine I'm much fun these days and it's not his fault."

"Do you still find him attractive?" Christie asked curiously. "I know Steve still adores you because he told me."

"Why were you discussing me?" Lucy felt quite indignant.

"Because he obviously thought as another woman, I might have some sort of explanation for something he doesn't understand, which I don't, because if we're all honest, I don't think we understand ourselves either."

"Well he could have asked me himself."

"Oh and what would you have said Lucy, come on be honest, you would have said what we all say when we're in a huff and we don't know why, the usual answer being nothing and expecting them to understand. You were actually quite honest Maggie, you haven't said anything to Callum because you don't want to know the answer and Lucy, even when Steve has tried to ask, you don't know what to say because you don't know the answer. Basically the human race is well and truly fucked. We might as well take to drink. Cheers girls."

And as the three of them clinked glasses, a bond was well and truly established.

The evening sun was shining as Sophie walked back up the path to her front door. Jim, her next door neighbour, heard her approach and looked up from his weeding. His garden was his pride and joy and his summer bedding plants were the envy of the more horticulturally minded in the street. Leaning his hoe against his own front door, he rested his arm on the wall, signalling that he was ready for a chat.

"Evening Sophie love, had a good day?"

"Oh not bad Jim, not bad, wish you would do mine too," she said, raising her eyes as she surveyed her own tidy but colourless front garden. "Never seem to get time these days. How's Mavis?"

"Oh the old girl's struggling on, she's got her check up next week so we're keeping our fingers crossed."

Sophie turned the key in the front door.

"Well give her my love Jim, and if there's anything I can do just let me know."

As she went to step inside, Jim stopped her.

"Sophie love, I don't mean to pry but there were two men looking for you earlier, burly looking like, pleasant enough when they spoke to me but in my mind they looked like bailiffs. They hung around for about half an hour until I said you might be away. Thought I better warn you love, are you in a spot of bother?"

Sophie froze. Bailiffs? She hadn't even considered the possibility. Bailiffs were something that happened to other people, not people like her.

"Well no Jim," she stammered, "I don't think so, there must have been some mistake. Maybe they were just trying to sell something."

"It was you they were after love, you sure you aren't in any bother and you wouldn't be the first you know."

Sophie made an attempt at a smile.

"No, no Jim, honestly, none at all. Did they say they would be back?"

"Well my love, if its bailiffs they'll be back, those buggers never give up, until you pay em of course. Look if you need any cash just come to me first, don't let those ruthless devils into your house, they'll be away with the lot, I should know, my old mum had the bailiffs in every other week when we was kids, bastards didn't give a monkeys whether we were starving or not."

"Really Jim, I'm sure it's all a mistake, honestly there's nothing to be concerned about but thanks anyway. Oh, I think that's the phone, I'll see you soon Jim."

"Righty oh," Jim said to the closing front door, "but don't forget where I am."

Jim went back to his hoeing with a heavier heart. He had seen that same look on his mother's face fifty years ago, the shame, fear and hurt pride. It still haunted him. Poor love.

Behind closed doors, Sophie slumped to the floor, shaking violently. All she knew was that she had to get out of the house. She had no intention of being here when they came back. Picking herself up, she ran upstairs and frantically grabbed a random selection of clothes. She couldn't think straight. Opening

Andy's wardrobe door she rummaged through his pockets hoping to find some cash. The bank had threatened a stop on her own account, the joint account would probably still pay out but with Andy away that would no doubt have taken a hit, despite the fact that he was being subsidised. Instinctively she grabbed a sleeping bag and pillow and stuffed them into a black bin bag. She had no idea what she was doing or where she was going.

As she closed the door behind her she garbled an explanation to Jim.

"That was my friend Tracey on the phone. She's not well and needs help with the kids. Keep an eye on things for me Jim will you please?"

Jim was no fool.

"Course I will love. Now you be careful, it'll all work out, it always does."

"Yes, yes, I'm sure she'll be well again soon. Thanks Jim."

As Sophie drove away, Jim wondered whether he had been right to warn her, running away never sorted anything out. "Don't do anything stupid love," he said to the disappearing car, "Don't you do anything daft."

On the first tee, Mike watched in despair as Callum sliced his tee shot into the water on the right. Cavendish, for once, restrained himself but added insult to injury by nailing his drive straight down the middle of the fairway.

"May the best team win then boys," he said with a wink as he strode off arrogantly down the first fairway, "I just hope you haven't put on too much weight for the dress Dunbar."

Chapter 10

At the fourth, Mike pulled Callum aside. He was all over the place and Mike was getting annoyed.

"Jesus Callum," he hissed, "pull yourself together, you're playing like my mother, get a grip will you."

Blanking him, Callum didn't respond and Mike could tell by his body language that he didn't care. Out of the corner of his eye he could see that Cavendish had witnessed this exchange and was furious that Callum had given him the satisfaction of watching them crumble under pressure. Getting desperate, Mike tried a different tack.

"Come on mate, you can play better than this, you've got to pull yourself together, don't give that tosser the satisfaction of watching you walk back."

Again Callum made no attempt at a response.

"Oh what the fuck," Mike sighed in exasperation as he walked away. "Do what you want."

The fourth was a short par three. Cavendish chipped in his second shot for an impressive birdie; Callum three putted for a six.

Back in the Golf Club bar, Cavendish collected in the cards but didn't bother checking them. He'd already made up his mind who would be wearing the dress; he couldn't believe that anyone else could have played as atrociously as Dunbar. Cavendish was pleased with himself, Dunbar had always been a smug bastard, big house, fancy superior wife, three perfect children, blah, blah, blah. He had absolutely no intention of showing him any mercy apart from the fact that it was now getting too late to make him walk back, especially if he wanted to have the opportunity of giving him a hard time in the restaurant, and if he was honest, something about Dunbar's demeanour suggested that if he allowed him to walk, he might not turn up at all. Cavendish called for quiet.

"Well it gives me an immense amount of satisfaction to announce the lucky recipient of the gala frock for this evening's dinner – a worthy winner, and as he played like a girl this evening he should do it justice, if he hasn't got too fat to fit into it. Dunbar, the dress is yours."

As Cavendish forced the red, sequinned dress over Callum's head and topped it with a blonde wig, to whoops and cat calls from the rest of the group, Steve and Mike felt uncomfortable. Usually the sight of a fellow tour player in a state of embarrassment was hilarious but tonight the sight was pathetic, and as Callum stood on the table and downed three consecutive beers to strains of *Lady In Red*, his public humiliation was in his own mind complete.

"Have you ever thought about having an affair Maggie?" asked Lucy mischievously, "because you horsey types are supposed to be randy as hell."

Maggie didn't flinch but instead took her time answering, much to the amusement of the other two. Her hesitation promised an interesting answer. Staring across the kitchen she fingered the stem of her wine glass.

"Well I must say that on occasions I have found other men attractive and there was a stable hand at the Mountley Stud who brought me out in a hot sweat, but I was old enough to be his mother. To be honest, I don't think I could be bothered. Mind you most of the women at the stables are at it like rabbits."

"Must be all that bouncing up and down," Lucy chipped in. "It would be such an effort though wouldn't it, having an affair. There's a woman at the playgroup I go to and she seems to be having it off with everyone apart from her husband, he works offshore from what I can gather, and she tells everyone about it. Apparently, last week, she shagged her dentist. She's ugly as sin too. I've no idea how she manages it, although most of the other women think she's making it up. God I'd have to go back to having my bikini line waxed, have a Brazilian or whatever they call it now. I was in Debenhams the other day and they even have knickers now especially for them. They have this strip of material down the front, tiny really and they are still charging a fiver a pair." Lucy stood up in an attempt to demonstrate the dimensions of the knickers.

"Especially for what? What are you talking about Lucy?" Maggie slurred.

"A Brazilian, a bikini wax that just leaves a strip of pubic hair down the middle, they call it a landing strip." Christie giggled, enjoying the look of disbelief on Maggie's face.

"And you have to stick your arse in the air while they wax all the hair out from between your buttocks. Or you can go the whole hog and have it all off, a Hollywood they call it."

"Oh my god," gasped Maggie, "surely that must be absolute agony. Do men find it attractive? I mean they must do if women are prepared to torture themselves to that extent. I can't believe I've never heard of it before. It does sound a bit perverted though, a bit school girlie if you know what I mean."

"It probably wouldn't be a popular feature in Homes and Gardens Maggie," laughed Christie.

"Do you think if I got one Callum would find me attractive again?" Maggie asked in a serious tone.

"Maybe we should text him and ask him," laughed Lucy mischievously, picking up Maggie's mobile from the table. Sensibly, Christie prised it from her hands and placed it out of reach.

"I'm sure it's got nothing to do with you having a hairy fanny Maggie, in fact I am sure everything will sort itself out."

Christie got up to put the kettle on. "Does anyone want coffee?"

Luckily the restaurant owner had had the foresight to ensure that the table was in its own alcove at a reasonable distance from the other guests. Drinks were flowing, fines were in abundance and Cavendish was in his element, forcing drinks down other's throats while avoiding it himself. He wanted to be in a reasonable condition for later, he wanted value for money. Suddenly a tapping on a wine glass quietened the group. Steve Sinclair stood up.

"I would like to propose that our tour leader be issued with a fine," he said loudly. The rest of the group cheered and banged their hands on the table in a primitive display of approval.

"It has come to our attention that our tour leader has acted in a dishonourable manner and that on several occasions he has made unsolicited and inappropriate advances to a number or our womenfolk." The rest of the boys began to boo and hiss.

"A crime such as this demands an appropriate fine as well as an apology. I propose that the accused forfeit the pleasure and freedom of ordering his own drinks for the remainder of this evening, as well as pay the bill for the rest of the team. He will also be asked to drink from the glass of redemption until it is empty, after which he will apologise to his fellow brethren. Those in favour raise your hands."

The room erupted into roars of approval along with the obligatory banging of tables. Steve placed a vile looking drink in front of Cavendish. This had not been on his agenda.

"Accept your punishment Cavendish for your monstrous crimes."

Cavendish stood up, slightly rattled by this unexpected turn of events. Bastard Sinclair, he should have known he would have something up his sleeve. He looked around the table, they were all enjoying this. The drink looked lethal but he realised he had no choice. Picking up the glass he raised it to the expectant mob.

"I accept my punishment for crimes I have committed and humbly apologise for my misdemeanours, although in my defence, I would like to question the accusation of unsolicited advances, as if I recall, on at least one occasion, my advances appeared more than welcome. Cheers." And winking at Steve, he drained the glass in front of him.

Steve stared back at him in a silent rage. Was he winding him up or was this anything to do with Lucy's behaviour? Surely she wouldn't be attracted to an animal like Cavendish. His head reeling, he sat down.

With Sinclair expertly dealt with and the mobs attention moving elsewhere, Cavendish took his usual opportunity to sneak to the gents and expertly vomit up the contents of his stomach.

Christie poured the coffee and handed round the tin containing Maggie's homemade biscuits. The Brazilian conversation was ongoing.

"Christie you're the glamorous one, have you ever had one?" asked Lucy.

"Oh for God's sake you two, if you are both so fascinated why don't I book you both in for a good stripping tomorrow and get it over and done with. That'll surprise Steve more than a haircut Lucy. No I have not resorted to the Brazilian, although I do have my bikini line waxed regularly. To be honest, I am not brave enough to raise my arse to a complete stranger. I try to keep myself tidy though."

"Bit like gardening really," Lucy laughed.

"But it must be itchy when it grows back and what about in growing hairs, surely that can't be conducive to an exciting sex life, a fanny that looks like a plucked chicken." Maggie was obviously fascinated. "Let's get the laptop and have a look on the internet, I want to know if it's a realistic option."

Christie looked at Lucy. "Now look what you've done, you

know what's she's like, she'll be on a mission now."

"Can't wait to see the new photo in the toilet though," Lucy whispered, "arse in the air -Maggie's First Brazilian."

This time it was Christie who tried not to choke.

Cavendish checked his watch, eleven-thirty. As requested his mobile rang, informing him that his order was on her way to the hotel.

"Right boys, I'm heading back, big game tomorrow. I've paid the bill so any more drinks you're responsible MacDonald, but if I were you, I would get that useless girly git back to his room before you have to carry him. What the hell's wrong with him anyway?"

Cavendish gestured towards Callum, now a pitiful sight, blonde wig askew, his legs splayed open as he slumped in his chair.

"Do you honestly think we'd tell you, you bastard," Steve interrupted savagely, standing in between Cavendish and Dunbar, fists clenched. Mike pulled him away.

"Leave it Steve, just leave it," he said gently, "let's get him back to the hotel."

Cavendish didn't move, but for once he felt slightly nervous. Maybe he'd pushed it too far with Sinclair this evening, he'd obviously hit a nerve.

"I'll see you in the morning boys," he offered almost courteously as he left the restaurant "Sleep well".

Steve was absolutely raging.

"I loathe that bastard sometimes. Do you realise what he was insinuating this evening, he basically said in front of everyone that he had shagged Lucy," he said incredulously.

Mike was desperately trying to calm the situation. He hadn't expected this turn of events.

"He was just winding you up Steve, you had him on the spot and he didn't like it, that's all."

"Do you think she would though?"

"Would what?"

"Sleep with Cavendish, she couldn't have could she? He's such an arsehole. Maybe that's why she says she hates him, because he's had his fill and moved on."

"Look mate, I am sure he's winding you up, forget it. Lucy's not daft, she hates him because she sees him for what he is, a prize prick. Come on, take an arm, let's get Sue Ellen here back to the hotel."

"Oh my God," squealed Maggie, "oh my God, look at that, I had no idea about any of this, where have I been? I'll have to ask some of the girls in the stables, oh I am actually tempted you know, what do you think girls? Shall I go for it?"

"Why not go for the full Hollywood and just have it all off," suggested Lucy, "that would shake Callum up a bit."

"Or terrify the living daylights out of him," murmured Christie.

"Well I might just do that," Maggie laughed, "and then maybe I could do a demonstration at the WRI."

Lucy raised her glass. "To Maggie's fanny," she giggled, "and all who sail in her."

Chapter 11

Cavendish left the more hardy of the group in the hotel bar and headed through to reception. Avelina was on duty again as he asked for the key to his suite.

"Your guest is waiting in the lounge bar sir," she said courteously. There was no judgement in her voice, but her eyes told a different story.

"Thank you Avelina," he replied conceitedly, "please ask her to come up in about ten minutes and send me up a bottle of good champagne, there's a good girl." He went to pat her on the hand, but she was too quick for him.

"Will there be anything else sir?"

"That will be all my lovely – have a good evening." Cavendish took the key and whistling headed for the lift.

"So what are you going to do with your life Lucy?" slurred Maggie, as with concentration she attempted to butter an oatcake. "You're a bright, attractive girl, what would you like to do? Come on, there must be something, we all have our little fantasies, don't we Christie?"

"Like the stable boy at the Mountley Stud," Lucy giggled, "what a great headline that would make; Maggie Mounts stable boy at Mountley – pony club in uproar. How old did you say he was?"

"I don't know, I never asked, but he was definitely too young. Anyway, that is getting out of the question Lucy Sinclair, like you always do."

"Your kids are still quite young Lucy, there's plenty of time, don't worry about it." Christie smiled sympathetically.

Lucy swirled the wine around the glass. "Maggie's right though, I do need to find something. I am in a rut and to be honest it's getting worse. I am a pretty miserable cow these days and it isn't Steve's fault, it's easier to blame him though than look at my own failings."

"What failings, well apart from being bloody miserable," grinned Christie.

"Oh everything. I'm crap at cooking, but that's probably because I don't like it, my house always looks like a bomb has hit it, I'm getting fat, I sadly enjoy daytime TV, I drink too much, how many more do you want?"

"Yet with all those failings, you still have two lovely children and a gorgeous successful husband that loves you to bits," sighed Maggie, "you must be doing something right. How can you not want to sleep with him though, I mean he is pretty gorgeous Lucy. I wouldn't throw him out of my bed, if he wasn't married to you of course and I wasn't married to Callum and he found me attractive, which he probably wouldn't."

"I think she's had enough," whispered Christie to Lucy.

"Yes he is attractive and I'm very lucky and I don't know why I don't want to sleep with him. Maybe I'm just bored. Maybe I need a fling with your stable boy Maggie, that could liven things up. Do you have his number? "

"No I don't, and that is not the answer young lady," replied Maggie, drunkenly wagging her finger in Lucy's direction.

"Or maybe you and I could have a fling Maggs, a lesbian tryst. Now I bet Callum would find that interesting. Most men do, now why is that I wonder?"

"Lucy I do not fancy you. I'm just going to have to get you out a bit more, broaden your horizons, free the Lucy within," evangelised Maggie. "You will be a new woman."

"God help me," muttered Lucy. "Christie, I think it's time for bed."

Cavendish ran the shower and stepped in, the steaming water removing any trace of the restaurant and the dust and sweat of nine holes. He liked to feel clean even when he was paying for it. He tilted his head back and let the water run over his face. The evening had actually been shit and the reaction of Sinclair had unnerved him. He realised that some of them despised him, but fuck em, he didn't care. Tomorrow night would be entertaining though, he knew it wouldn't take some of them long to forget their matrimonial vows. Stepping out of the shower, Cavendish wrapped himself in the complimentary white towelling robe, and as he walked from the bathroom, there was a gentle knock on the door. Striding over to the door, he looked through the peephole. She looked young, early twenties he guessed, pretty rather than the harsh airbrushed attractiveness of the average tart. He opened the door.

"Mr Cavendish?" she asked politely, her brown eyes looking directly into his own.

"Please come in, make yourself at home," he smiled, as she walked through the door. A ding from the elevator signalled that the champagne was on its way, and leaving the door ajar, he watched her as she walked around the room. She was elegantly dressed, simple black dress, the obligatory high heels, her glossy, black hair gently waved. The porter placed the champagne bucket on a table in the middle of the room and expertly poured two glasses. Rewarded with a handsome tip, he left the room. She was sitting now, legs crossed on the large leather sofa and Cavendish could see a hint of stocking top. She looked good. He handed her a glass of champagne.

"Do you have a name?" he asked.

"Catalina," she answered without smiling, "in Romania, it means pure."

So she was Romanian, he had guessed eastern European, but wasn't sure. He took a swig of his champagne. Catalina followed suit and then stood up, eager to get on with the job in hand.

"So Mr Cavendish, how can I entertain you this evening, is there music? Would you like me to dance for you? I am a good dancer Mr Cavendish. Would you like to watch me dance?"

Cavendish smiled and walking over to the wall, he switched on the music. Dimming the lights, he settled himself in the large white leather chair and watched as Catalina began to sway. Slowly, she unbuttoned her dress and allowed it to fall to the floor, revealing her red underwear. She moved her hands as if to unclasp her bra, but Cavendish stopped her.

"Keep it on," he sighed, "I like it left on."

Catalina continued to dance suggestively and Cavendish was content to watch her move. As she came closer, he asked her to turn around and lean forward,enjoying her cry as he slapped her hard on her buttocks. He slapped her again, this time leaving a hand print. He felt her tense. He pulled her round to face him and he could see in her eyes that she was afraid. "What's wrong Miss Romania, you not enjoying yourself?" Roughly he pushed his hands inside her bra and pulled back the fabric to reveal her nipples. He pinched them hard between his fingers until she cried out again, her cries inducing a sudden eagerness. "Get down on your knees," he demanded suddenly, and as she dropped down to her knees he grabbed her hair and roughly forced her head between his legs.

Still in his dress, Callum Dunbar stood drunkenly beside the hotel swimming pool. He could still hear them in the bar, loud, smashed, their laughter reinforcing his misery. He traced the light on the purified water and watched it shimmer in the delicate ripples fanned by the light on-shore breeze. He could smell the chlorine as it intermingled with the scent of jasmine and honeysuckle that hung on the balmy night air. He had read somewhere that drowning was a peaceful way to die, that is if you surrender and don't struggle, open your mouth and invite the water in. If you surrender, death comes quickly. It would be an unfortunate accident, another stupid Scotsman having too much to drink. He stepped into the water, felt the coolness, the muffled silence. He could hear his own heartbeat; feel the silky fabric of the red dress as it clung to his legs. He opened his eyes but he couldn't open his mouth. He prayed to God to let him open his mouth.

"You can use the shower if you wish," Cavendish said courteously, "help yourself."

Catalina picked up her dress and walked towards the bathroom.

"Nice tattoo," Cavendish smirked. "What does it say?"

"Ionathan," she replied robotically.

"Is that your pimps name? Do they brand you these days?"

Catalina turned to look at him. There was no hint of emotion.

"Ionathan is my son, his name means *Gift from God,* and he is five years old."

Cavendish said nothing, as she turned again and walked away from him into the bathroom.

Leaving the noise of the bar, Mike watched in confusion as Callum stepped into the pool. He still had his drink in his hand, he didn't jump, he just stepped in. The water hardly registered his entry as he went under. As realisation suddenly dawned, Mike dropped his drink and running towards the pool, jumped in after him.

"What the hell are you doing?" Mike gasped, as somehow he found the strength to drag Dunbar out of the pool. He could hardly speak, the shock and exhaustion messing with his brain. Mike watched as he lay there, coughing up the water he had tried desperately to swallow. The pool was almost still again, all evidence of the drama erased apart from a slice of lemon floating casually on the ever decreasing waves.

"Are you drunk or did you seriously just try to top yourself?"

Mike shuddered, as the cold and horror of the situation worked its way through his body. Callum was silent. Mike looked down at him, the red dress now clinging to his body. He looked pitiful. The silence was deafening, despite the singing still coming from the bar. The whole situation was surreal. Suddenly Callum began to sob.

"I can't face them Mike, I don't want to see the way they look at me when I let them down. If I die they'll never know I was a useless failure."

"Jesus Christ, Callum, I don't believe this, nothing can be this bad. They might have to face a few hardships, but believe me, Maggie wouldn't want you dead, you stupid bastard. Think what it'll do to them, they need you for God's sake."

"No they don't, they don't need me, they need what I provide. They don't need me, no one ever needs *me*, no one ever thinks what I might need. I know how they'll react, they'll resent me, hate me for being a failure. Christ, I can't even manage to kill myself properly."

"Come on, get up," Mike said, desperate for some form of normality. Callum didn't move.

"I said, get up. You are not going to lay here and wallow in self pity, you are going to get up Callum Dunbar and face it, even if I have to drag you up, you are not going under, do you understand me, you are not going to give up."

Lucy and Christie were giggling helplessly as they helped Maggie into bed.

"Do you think we should make her drink some water? She's going to have one hell of a hangover in the morning." Sensibly, Christie was relatively sober.

"Do her good," smiled Lucy with some satisfaction. "It's probably been a very long time since Maggie Dunbar was legless and I am enjoying every minute of it."

Back in the hotel room, Mike helped Callum out of his wet clothes and ran the shower. Neither of them spoke. Through the open window Mike could hear strains of *Flower of Scotland* being bellowed out from the bar, the raucous laughter only adding to the pathos of the heartbreaking situation. Mike helped Callum into the steaming water and closed the shower door. Laying a fresh towel on the chair outside the shower he closed the bathroom door and walked through to the bedroom. He was cold himself, but it could wait. He stood for a moment looking out over the swimming pool. It was quiet now, as though nothing had ever happened. How he wished nothing had happened. Mike started to shake, and with Callum safely enclosed in the shower, he picked up the phone and called Christie.

Chapter 12

Anna, Christie's au pair, looked at the bedside clock. It was past midnight. Why was the phone ringing? Picking up the phone in Mike and Christie's room, she answered cautiously.

"Christie, it's Mike."

"Mike, it is Anna, Christie is at Maggie's house. What is wrong, has something happened?"

"Oh I'm so sorry Anna, no everything is fine, I'll try her mobile. Everything ok there, boys not giving you any trouble I hope."

"No more than is usual, I think they not scared of me anymore Mike. No everything is fine."

"That's good. Sorry again to wake you, I'll see you soon. Thanks Anna."

Mike tried Christie's mobile.

"Christie, are you awake?"

"Bloody hell Mike, I am now, what time is it? What's wrong, what's happened?"

"Callum's tried to kill himself."

"What?" she gasped, as she sat bolt upright, trying to keep her voice down. "You can't be serious, how?"

"Walked into the swimming pool, pissed as a fart of course but he knew what he was doing. Luckily I saw him. He's in the shower now, so I can't speak too loud."

"Bloody hell, what are you going to do?"

"I don't know, put him on a plane and send him home if I can get one. I don't really know, I can't think straight. I need you to talk to Maggie, break it to her gently, apparently he's about to get the chop at work and couldn't face telling her, so if you can soften the blow and send her to meet him at the airport."

"You make this sound very simple Mike, you're right, I really don't think you're thinking straight. Will he be ok to travel alone? I mean he might do a runner or something if he's that depressed. Maybe Maggie should fly out. Look, let me talk to her in the morning and I'll call you or I'll arrange the flights. Maggie's completely plastered tonight, out cold, she thinks he's having an affair."

"Oh well, there's always a silver lining. I'll call you early in the morning, not looking forward to dealing with Cavendish; he's being a right bastard. At least I won't forget this trip in a hurry. Oh and keep it quiet, don't tell anyone else."

"Lucy's here. Have you told Steve?"

"No, but I will, once I find him, so it's ok to tell Lucy. Right better go, speak to you in the morning."

"Ok, I still can't believe it, poor Callum, poor Maggie. How am I going to tell her?"

"You'll be fine. We'll probably have a good laugh about this one day."

"Oh I don't think so, only a man could say something as stupid as that. Look after him Mike, I love you."

"Me too babe. Speak in the morning."

Sophie turned off the radio in the car. She needed to sleep but she didn't feel safe. She had thought that the twenty-four hour supermarket car park would be the safest option with its lights and traffic, but as the number of shoppers had dwindled, so had her confidence. She looked at the clock, twelve-twenty am. Her back was stiff and her head ached. She wanted to go home. She jumped as the lights flickered on the car beside her, triggered by the automatic car key of another midnight customer. He was young, cigarette in his mouth, jeans hanging way below his waist, exposing a pair of vivid pink boxers. He clutched a six pack of beers under one arm, a packet of disposable nappies under the other. Sophie wondered whether he was the father, whether he should be responsible for bringing up a child. As if reading her thoughts, he glared back at her as he started the engine, revving it too many times, before making his fuck off, screeching exit. She felt exposed now without cars on either side, vulnerable. Another car pulled up, opposite this time, a smart Audi. She watched as a woman got out of the driver's side; she looked elegant, high heels, a cream Mac. She was blonde, her hair piled up into a classic knot. Sophie couldn't tell her age. She wondered who she was, was she married, single, a mistress maybe, a hooker. She wondered whether she was going home or going out, wondered whether her life was as complicated as her own. She looked at the clock again. She couldn't stay here all night. Urgently she fumbled in her bag for her phone and dialled.

"Hello," said a sleepy voice eventually.

"Dad, it's me Sophie, can I come home?"

Steve was still in the bar when his mobile rang. He stepped outside to the poolside.

"Mike. Where the hell are you? I thought you'd snuck off to bed you sly old bugger."

"I bloody wish, look get yourself up to Callum's room, we've got an issue."

"What sort of issue? He's not puked has he because I can't stand the smell of puke."

"Just get up here, I need your help."

Steve realised through his alcoholic haze that Mike wasn't joking and leaving his drink on the empty poolside table, he headed towards the lift. When he got to the room, Callum's door was slightly ajar, and tentatively, Steve pushed it open and peered inside. Mike ushered him in and closed the door behind them. There was no sign of Callum, although Steve could see that the light was on in the bathroom.

"He's only tried to top himself in the bloody swimming pool," Mike whispered, "just as well I saw him, stupid git, he's in the bathroom drying off."

"Fucking hell, you sure it wasn't just an accident? He was pretty pissed."

"Yeh and pretty pissed off too obviously. He stepped into the fucking deep end Steve, I watched him, he thought about it, and then stepped in. He cried like a baby when I got him out, thinks Maggie would rather have him dead than unemployed."

"He's got a point; I'd consider shooting myself rather than face her."

"Oh come off it, she's not that bad. I've phoned Christie who happens to be conveniently staying at Maggie's with Lucy, she's going to tell her in the morning when she's sober."

"Is Christie pissed, that's Lucy for you, bad influence she is."

"Will you shut up and listen. Maggie's pissed, not Christie, I have no idea about Lucy. Maggie thinks Callum's having an affair."

"Poor old Maggs. So what's the plan? Bloody hell, I'm not exactly sober myself." Steve steadied himself and sat down on the bed.

"Well I think I'd better be on suicide watch and share our room with him and you can sleep in here. Thing is, we really ought to let Cavendish know that he won't be playing, maybe two of us, as someone will have to keep an eye on him until we either get him on a plane or Maggie gets here. Maybe we should get Simon in here, he's a doctor. Give him a ring, my phones on the bed. Fucking hell, I came here for a laugh, some fucking trip this is turning out to be."

Simon had snuck off to his room as soon as Cavendish was off the scene and was aimlessly flicking through the TV channels when Steve called. He could tell that Steve was pissed but agreed, with some reluctance, to go over to Dunbar's room.

Throwing on some clothes, he turned off the TV and stepped out into the corridor. As Simon closed his door, Catalina was letting herself out of Cavendish's suite and as he walked towards her she looked up and her eyes caught his. Her mascara was smudged. Cavendish had obviously had his money's worth. She looked away and Simon sensed her embarrassment. He could see that she was eager to be away as quickly as possible. She looked so vulnerable. Poor cow, he thought to himself, what a way to spend your life being shagged by the likes of Cavendish.

Christie couldn't sleep. How the hell was she going to tell Maggie? Well at least he wasn't having an affair. Was this easier to deal with though, she wondered. Maggie was a tough old bird. She would have been a land girl in the war or driven ambulances, fearless in the face of adversity, stiff upper lip and all that. This was different though, and she had seen another side to Maggie this evening. She had no idea how she was going to take it. Christie picked up her phone and decided to look for flights. She couldn't sleep, she might as well try and do something useful.

Steve was waiting for Simon in the corridor outside Callum's room and as he arrived he signalled to him to be quiet.

"What's going on?" Simon whispered.

"Dunbar's tried to drown himself in the swimming pool; Mike pulled him out but thinks you should see him because you're a doctor. We can't leave him on his own can we? Mike's gonna share a room with him and hopefully we can sort out how we're gonna despatch him in the morning. Mike's Mrs is going to speak to Maggie. Fucking marvellous eh? Just what you need on a well earned trip with your mates. God, I'm pissed, just as well I didn't have to pull him out." Steve leaned against the wall for support.

"Are you taking the piss?" Simon was still trying to absorb the information.

"Nope, I wish I fucking was. He's sitting on the bed now with Mike. Go on in Dr Spock and see if you can sort him out, I've got to go and see Cavendish."

"You can't tell Cavendish," Simon gasped, "there's not a sympathetic bone in his body."

"No, I know that, but I have to let him know that two of us can't play in the morning so he can sort it out. It's not fair on everyone else to have a shambles at the last minute. I'll sort him out, you go and sort the Little Mermaid. The bloody dress is ruined by the way, it was dry clean only."

Steve knocked on Cavendish's door. There was no response. He knocked again, louder this time. Steve took his phone out of his pocket and dialled Cavendish's mobile.

"Cavendish, open the bloody door will you, we have an issue."

Cavendish was not happy.

"Piss off Sinclair, I am not talking to you now, I'm shagged out."

"Well lucky you but the boys won't be too happy in the morning if you are two players short and you haven't got it sorted by breakfast and I let it slip that you knew the night before. Come on Captain Cavendish, you have responsibilities now open the fucking door."

Reluctantly Cavendish let him in. Steve eyed the empty champagne bottle.

"Was it worth it you sad git? And what's that under your eyes, is that moisturiser? Are you wearing eye cream, you bloody ponce Cavendish."

Cavendish couldn't be bothered to answer, he was wary of Sinclair.

"Right Captain L'Oreal, we have an issue, the result of which is that we are two players short tomorrow. One will be out permanently and the other will be back in, hopefully by the afternoon."

"Don't tell me, fucking Dunbar," Cavendish hissed, "useless tosser, what a waste of space he is, I knew he'd screw things up."

Aided by the amount of alcohol he had consumed and the events of earlier in the day, Steve snapped, and grabbing Cavendish by the throat, pushed him up against the wall.

"If you hadn't forced him into coming in the first place and made his life a fucking misery, he wouldn't have just tried to top himself. Do you hear me you callous bastard, Dunbar has just tried to kill himself. You will rearrange the schedule tomorrow but you won't breathe a fucking word to anyone else. As far as you know he has issues at home. If you breathe one word I'll make sure that you never come on this trip again, do you hear me?" Cavendish nodded and Steve let him go. Cavendish rearranged his dressing gown.

"Who's the other call off?" Cavendish asked, clearing his throat. He hadn't expected this.

"Mike probably, he's sorting out how to get him home, not sure whether we're sending him on a plane or Maggie's coming out."

"Maggie's coming out here?"

"Yes Myles, Maggie his wife. Dunbar has a wife and family and he has just tried to kill himself, fucking brilliant eh. I hope you're fucking pleased with yourself."

Cavendish looked visibly upset. "Oh God," he said suddenly, sitting down on the sofa and burying his head in his hands, "I don't believe this."

Chapter 13

"Where the hell has everyone gone? I thought this was a boy's trip," Rex Haig slurred, leaning back in one of the leather armchairs in the bar. "Everyone's gone to bed, even the tour leader. The tours going to the dogs I tell you, we're all getting old. What do you think Davie, you randy old bugger, are we getting too old for all this?" The bar was quiet now apart from the clinking of empty glasses as the all night barman went calmly about his duties.

Davie Sutherland, as usual on tour, was plastered and lay with his feet up on the leather sofa.

"I bet Cavendish is shagging, that's why he's not here, he's always shagging, the lucky bastard."

"I couldn't shag anything right now, God I'm pissed, not that I would want to shag anyone other than my lovely wife." Rex grinned inanely and raised his glass to no one in particular. "How's your love life Davie boy, how is the gorgeous Priscilla?"

Davie smiled. "The gorgeous Priscilla is still gorgeous but unfortunately I am not, and at this moment she is probably shagging someone more her own age. I couldn't keep up with her mate, I'm going to have to find someone my own age. I'm past clubbing. I'm seriously starting to think I need a wife."

"Maybe you should try one of those dating sites, I bet you get some howlers on them." Rex had closed his eyes and his drink rested precariously on the arm of the chair.

"I've already looked, your Mrs was on it but we weren't compatible."

Rex didn't rise to the bait and didn't bother opening his eyes.

"My Mrs isn't compatible with anyone, not even herself."

"Talking of lovely wives, did you hear about Andy the builder? Didn't even tell his Mrs he was on the trip till Simmo's Mrs dropped him in it accidentally. Simmo had to go round to stop her killing him. The poor bastard hasn't got any work."

"He's not the only one mate, most of us are on the edge, some of us are bound to hit the deck sooner or later, it's probability isn't it? Being an estate agent isn't very profitable at the moment. I'm not exactly Mr Popularity with Rachael for this trip; I'll be hiding the credit card bills when I get home. We should have seen it coming really, shouldn't we mate, but we didn't and now we pay the price for our gluttony, debauchery and excessive living. But don't worry, Dave and Nick's big society's going to save us from ourselves. And where is Andy, he was here a few minutes ago?"

Davie signalled towards the pool bar. "Outside I think having a fag with Alex, Alex will be giving him the marriage guidance chat, the sharing, caring shite that he usually comes up with. Do you know I'd like to marry Alex, life would be so simple. He even tidied our room before we came out, it's like sharing a room with Mary Poppins."

Rex finished the last of his drink. "Talking of Mary Poppins, have you learnt all Cavendish's songs? We're supposed to know them for tomorrow and I only know the Elvis ones."

"Well you're in deep shite too then, like the rest of us, although I bet Alex knows them. Alex," Davie bellowed from the sofa, "Alex, get in here and give us a rehearsal, we need help with the Lonely Goatherd!"

Mike and Simon helped Callum into a pair of shorts and t-shirt, the silence was overwhelming and Mike was finding Callum's reluctance to speak disturbing.

"You can share with me tonight mate, we'll head over to my room and I'll get the kettle on. Steve's going to sleep in here. We'll sort everything else out in the morning."

Mike decided it would be too much to tell him that he had contacted Christie. That would best be left until he knew what Maggie wanted to do.

Callum looked at him. "Thanks Mike," he said quietly.

Steve sat with Cavendish in his suite, the immediate priority of sorting out the pairings had calmed the situation.

"One of our boys will have to play for your team, it's the only option," Cavendish said quietly. "You can have Simon if you like, seeing as he knows what's going on, and he's a pretty average player."

"Fine by me," Steve replied, "and hopefully we can get Mike back in, although that screws things up again, being one short. I'll pull out of the afternoon if I have to."

"We might be able to get a stand in at the golf club, someone'll be looking for a game, leave that to me in the morning." Cavendish picked up the draw sheets and folding them, placed them beside his phone on the table. Steve could see that he was disturbed.

"I had no idea that he was that depressed Sinclair, I would have lain off him."

"Would you though? You didn't give him half a chance Cavendish, you're an arrogant bastard, but to be fair none of us expected this. We're all pretty evil when we want to be, we've all dished it out in our time, I've never given it a second thought that it could have any consequences. Anyway we are still on tour and it's up to you to make it work. I'm knackered, I'm going to bed, what time do you want to meet?"

"Breakfast at seven-thirty?"

Steve looked at his watch; it was already two-fifteen am.

"Jesus, I am getting too old for this."

As Sophie turned into the drive of her father's house, she could feel the tension in her chest, her emotions a complicated mix of guilt, shame and relief. She remembered the time she had come home with a letter from school for hiding in the toilets to miss PE, the letter that had to be signed by her parents and returned the next day. Her dad had dealt with it calmly and sensibly, had phoned the school and charmed Miss Muller into submission. PE had still been purgatory, but her dad's words of wisdom had enabled her to face her fears and get through it. Now here she was again, a grown woman needing help from her dad. The light was on, welcoming her home. As she turned the engine off in the car, the front door opened and her dad stood there in his dressing gown. As soon as she looked at him, the floodgates opened.

In his bathroom, Cavendish stared at himself in the mirror. Sinclair was right, he was an arrogant bastard. A lonely, sad, arrogant bastard. His wives had said the same each time they divorced him and each time he had put up another barrier, another line of defence. The day his father had killed himself had been the final fence in a racecourse of fences, erected to deflect the loneliness of an un-parented childhood, spent in a boarding school amongst the affluent but emotionally deficient. His mother's affairs were legendary amongst his peers, beautiful but insane, she had picked her way through most of his father's friends, goading him into his early demise, the only thing over which he had any control. Leaning over the wash basin, Cavendish clenched his fists but as usual the tears wouldn't flow.

The window was still open in Mike's room as he and Callum walked in, and drunken strains of Lonely Goatherd could be heard from the bar. Mike smiled and went to close the window.

"Leave it open Mike," said Callum quietly, "I love this one."

Lying awake, Christie heard the bathroom door on the landing close. Getting out of bed, she opened her door slightly and waited to see who, like herself, couldn't sleep. She heard the toilet flush and the door opened. To her relief it was Lucy.

"Ppssst Lucy," she whispered, "Lucy, get in here."

Lucy was startled, her eyes were still half closed and her mouth felt like sandpaper. What on earth was Christie up to? Christie dragged her into the bedroom and closing the door behind her, put on the bedside light.

"Are you properly awake?" Christie asked, staring at Lucy, trying to ascertain whether she was in a fit state to deal with the news.

"Well I am now, what time is it?" Blinking in the light, Lucy pulled her dressing gown tight around her. She was cold.

"I have no idea. Look you have to listen because something terrible has happened."

Lucy looked startled, a myriad of possible scenarios flashing through her mind.

"Oh my God, has somebody died?" she asked quietly.

"Nearly, oh Lucy, Callum tried to kill himself. Mike phoned me, we have to break it to Maggie. Mike fished him out of the swimming pool and he and Steve are trying to sort him out while keeping it from the rest of the guys."

"Oh my God," whispered Lucy again as she sat down on the bed, "why the hell has he tried to kill himself, my God, it's awful, poor Maggie, how are we going to tell her?"

Christie looked anxious.

"I have no idea. Mike said Callum is about to lose his job and couldn't face Maggie. Well he'll have to face her now won't he? I have to phone him in the morning as we think it might be best if Maggie flies out and brings him home. I've looked up flights, we can get her on an early one but she'll be feeling awful. I'm going to have to wake her soon or we'll never get her organised."

"How could he do that, I still can't believe it," sighed Lucy.

"People don't think straight do they when they're scared, fear's a terrible thing, it can take you over. One of my school friend's tried to kill herself once because she failed her English exam and didn't want to tell her mother because she was such a pushy bitch. Sounds ridiculous now, but believe me, it wasn't at the time. So sad though, that he felt he had to kill himself rather than face Maggie. I have no idea what'll happen now. How do you think Maggie'll take it?"

Lucy shrugged her shoulders.

"I really don't know. You know, if you had asked me yesterday morning I wouldn't have had much sympathy, because well, Maggie's Maggie, you know what I mean, but after last night I realised that she's just the same as the rest of us, same hang ups just hidden behind a brilliant facade. I really don't want to have to tell her."

"Neither do I but we'll have to. The saving grace is that we are here and she doesn't have to find out with a phone call. What time is it?"

Lucy looked at the bedside clock.

"Twenty past two, what time shall we wake her?"

"I can get her on a flight at eight forty-five so we'll need to get her up at five. Oh god, I really don't want to have to do this."

In Mike's room, both men lay in their beds in the darkness. Neither spoke but both knew that the other was trying to make sense of the evening's events. The darkness brought some comfort but both of them realised that the dawn would soon be shining its gentle light on a very harsh reality.

Chapter 14

The kitchen was warm and Sophie gratefully accepted the mug of tea that was offered. Vic had let her cry without asking any questions, instead offering his arms, a tissue and sweet tea. Drying her eyes, Sophie sat down at the kitchen table and took the mug between her hands.

"Are you hungry, I can make us some toast, bit peckish myself now?" Vic enquired gently. "Get your coat off and I'll make us something to eat. I can make my eggie toast if you like?"

Sophie smiled and shook her head.

"No thanks Dad, just normal toast please."

"I thought you liked my eggie toast, I always made it when your mum was ill."

"We were just being polite Dad, that's why we used to cover it in brown sauce, to make it edible. We ate it because we didn't want to upset you. Charlie used to try and feed his to the cat but even the cat rejected it."

Vic looked slightly crestfallen.

"Well bugger me, I thought you all liked it. Oh well, make yourself useful and get some plates out of the cupboard behind you, there's butter and jam in the fridge. I still can't believe you didn't like my eggie toast."

Vic popped two slices of bread into the toaster and looked at his daughter as she busied herself in the kitchen. It didn't seem five minutes ago that she had left home. Where had twenty five years gone? He was touched that she had come home though, glad that she felt she still could, and more than anything, it felt good to be needed again. He hadn't felt needed since Joyce had died; it was good to have her home.

As the waiter brought over another round of drinks, Andy stood up.

"Sorry guys, I've had enough, I can't drink anymore, I'm off to bed."

"Come on Bob the Builder, just one more, go on, shame to waste it," slurred Rex, his eyes half open.

"Yeh come on," grinned Davie, "better get your fill while you can, cos your missus won't be letting you out for a while when you get home. Go on, don't be such a poof, get it down your neck."

At the thought of Sophie, Andy felt a pang of guilt. The drinks in the hotel were expensive and here he was, pissing money they didn't have down the toilet. He looked at Rex and Davie, both so drunk they could hardly speak, let alone stand. How they were going to play golf in a few hours time was anyone's guess. Andy picked up the glass from the tray and raised it towards them.

"Cheers boys, see you at breakfast if you're still alive. Cavendish will be delighted when he sees the state of his opposition. I hope I'm playing against you."

Alex looked worried.

"Mike's gonna kill me, I'm supposed to be keeping an eye on these two, look at the state of them."

"Alex, you don't stand a chance my son. I'd get to bed if I were you, you're wasting your energy and your teams gonna need as much energy as it can get."

And grinning, Andy left them in the bar, emptying his glass into the first available plant pot on the way out.

As Sophie buttered her toast she started to feel embarrassed. Her dad had let her cry, just as he had always done, and now she was going to have to tell him the truth. The tea and toast was the softner, the preamble, the freezing before the injection. The next bit was going to hurt. As Vic sat at the table, he hummed a little tune as he always did before confrontation. Sophie recognised the signal.

"So," he said gently, "what's up, have you fallen out with Andy?"

"No, not really," she sniffed, "although he's probably going to fall out with me when he gets back from his trip."

Sophie didn't look up, but instead took another piece of toast from the rack.

"Go on," Vic prompted.

"Well money's been really tight, Andy's hardly had any work and to be honest Dad, we are really struggling."

"But you're earning good money, have you stretched yourselves too far like the rest of your generation?"

Sophie took a deep breath, and holding back the tears, continued to stare at the unbuttered toast.

"Yes I suppose I have, if you include a massive amount of credit card debt that Andy doesn't know about. Oh Dad, he has no idea, he thinks we're struggling because he hasn't got enough work but we'd be fine if I wasn't putting most of my wages into repayments. I've not been facing it but I had bailiffs at my door yesterday, that's why I'm here. I'm too scared to go back in case they come again. I don't know what to do and I'm terrified of telling him."

Vic looked at his daughter, she was ten years old again, scared, vulnerable and in need of his help.

"Well running away isn't going to help is it? So I want the truth, how much do you owe?"

"A lot," Sophie said, covering her eyes with her hands.

Vic remained calm.

"How much is a lot? Come on Sophie, I can't help you unless I know what I'm dealing with."

"About £24,000."

"I see," Vic said quietly. His first house hadn't cost that much.

"What have you spent £24,000 on; I am presuming you have a mortgage as well?"

"Crap, that's what I've spent it on, useless crap that I don't need and yes, we have a mortgage, a huge mortgage, but we might not have one for much longer when we go bankrupt."

"These bloody banks," Vic muttered, "bloody irresponsible, letting people borrow more and more money until they've got you where they want you, take you to your limit and then take you down."

Vic got up from the table and put the kettle on. How the world had changed. His own generation had been terrified of debt and to the best of their ability had lived within their means. It hadn't been easy, but generally everyone had lived by the same philosophy. If you couldn't afford it, you didn't buy it. How everything had changed so quickly and who was to blame, he didn't know. What he did know was that somehow he had to get his little girl out of this whole crazy mess. Taking a hot water bottle out of the under sink cupboard, he filled it with hot water, tightened it and dried it with the tea towel his grandson had given him for Christmas. It was covered in the self portraits of Alfie's nursery class. Alfie had drawn himself with three eyes and a big smile. Vic didn't envy him; three eyes would probably come in useful in this messed up modern world that he would be more than glad to leave behind.

"Right, off to bed and get some sleep and we'll sort things out in the morning. Sleep will help us think a bit more clearly. I know it seems like it love, but it's not the end of the world, we'll get it sorted. I just wish you'd told me or Andy earlier. Come on, off to bed, you look awful."

"Thanks," Sophie sniffed, "you know how to flatter a girl, can't see what Mum saw in you."

Vic grinned. "They were fighting over me, I can tell you, she was lucky your mother."

Sophie hugged him.

"Yes she was Dad, she was very lucky, and so am I."

Lying in Callum's room, Steve picked up his mobile. He wondered whether Lucy would be awake yet and whether she knew what was going on. Would he have been able to tell Lucy if his business had gone under? Course he would, how could he not. What had possessed Callum ? How could he not tell his wife? Mike had looked shaken, he was a good bloke Mike, he only ever saw the best in people. He would hate this. Cavendish had surprised him though, he had actually looked upset when he left him, maybe he was human after all. He looked at his watch. What time was it? Lucy might be awake. Christie would have told her by now, women couldn't keep anything to themselves. They'd be in their element trying to sort out the unfolding drama, like witches round a cauldron, delighted that their husbands lives weren't quite as straightforward as they liked to believe and equally delighted that they were now involved in the trip. He was glad they were there for Maggie though, women were good at that sort of thing. Steve sent a text. *"Are you awake? If you are call me please"*. Closing his eyes, he drifted off into a drink fuelled, exhausted sleep.

Having turned off the air conditioning, Andy's room was warm. Opening the window, the cool sea air was refreshing and he left the curtains open in the hope that the morning light would wake him. He looked at the clock on his mobile, two fifty-five am, four hours for sleep. He set the radio alarm for seven. Checking his messages, he was disappointed that Sophie hadn't contacted him. Usually she sent him a text and she hadn't replied to his last one. He thought they had left on reasonable terms but maybe he had read it wrong. She really had been upset when he left, maybe he shouldn't have come. Poor old Soph, it hadn't been easy for her. Kids would have made a difference. At the moment though, Andy was glad that they didn't have any. Knowing he had to support kids as well would be even worse. It was too late to call her now. He would try in the morning before breakfast. It would probably be the last chance for a while. Once the golf kicked off tomorrow, communication would be impossible and he couldn't afford any hefty fines. Andy lay his mobile beside the bed and got undressed. It was still warm in the room but the hotel was now quiet. He wondered whether Alex had managed to persuade Rex and Davie to call it a night or whether they were now comatose in the bar. One thing was certain, things were looking up for the English boys tomorrow with two of the Scots best golfers on the ropes. Cavendish would make mincemeat of them.

Unusually, Cavendish was unable to sleep, the darkness calling forth too many unwelcome memories; memories that he had hoped to keep well and truly filed away. He hadn't seen his mother for years, not since he had left school and erased her from his contact list, vowing to make it on his own without her help. Why was he thinking of her now? His father's suicide had ensured that any insurance premiums were null and void, leaving him without financial help. Had he hated his wife so much that he had forgotten that he had a son? Could hate do that to you? Had he even thought how it might affect him? Dunbar, on the other hand, had a wife and kids that loved him, how could he even think about it? How selfish was that? Fucking hell, Cavendish said aloud to himself, everything's such fucking shit.

Chapter 15

Tracey had slept restlessly, and giving up on a bad job went downstairs to get a drink, in the hope that a change of scene would help her get back to sleep. She had been excited at the prospect of time to herself this weekend but in the middle of the night, alone in the house, she realised that she felt slightly vulnerable. Pouring the filtered water into the kettle, she switched it on and took out a chamomile teabag from the cupboard. Too many coffees with Sophie had probably put paid to a good night's sleep, along with the fact that she was also feeling a little guilty for not asking Sophie to stay the night. The thought had crossed her mind, but her selfish desire to have time to herself had ruled it out. In the end she had done nothing constructive with her time, she should have asked her to stay. It was too late to do anything now. She would have to phone her in the morning. With the boys away she could make lunch. Tracey wondered if Simon was asleep. His obligatory text had said all was well but that of course meant nothing, for all she knew he could be up to anything, although he had never given her any cause for concern so far. Simon was a terrible liar and she always knew if something was troubling him. She was convinced that he would never manage an affair. The influence of drink and the peer pressure from the rest of the lads, especially Cavendish, however, always made her uneasy. Simon, she was convinced, could be easily bullied and Cavendish had been an expert over the years at forcing drinks down his throat. Cavendish had been a constant throughout their married life, having been at university with Simon and Simon's stag night organised by

Cavendish had almost resulted in the wedding being called off. Tracey had tolerated him over the years, entertained numerous girlfriends and a couple of wives, none of whom lasted long, and even invited him for Christmas rather than see him by himself, as despite all his shortcomings, Tracey did in fact feel sorry for him; a motherless, unloved boy who really had lost his way. He really could be such a wanker though. Picking up the Saturday supplement from the kitchen table she took it, along with the chamomile tea back to bed. She had noticed a good recipe which would do for lunch tomorrow.

Simon couldn't sleep at all. He had had a feeling about this trip but had not expected anything like this. Callum was in a bad state and the sooner they got him home the better. He would speak to Maggie tomorrow and offer some medical advice. How the hell this trip was going to continue he didn't know, but the boys would crack on as they always did, brushing any setbacks aside. The match would take place in one way or another, Cavendish would make sure of it. Nothing would stand in the way of his moment of glory. Simon just wanted to go home.

Having settled his daughter into bed, Vic went back down to the kitchen and re-boiled the kettle. He was awake now, sleep wouldn't come easy. He hadn't expected this when she had phoned to come home, a fall out with Andy maybe, the pressures of not being able to have kids must put a strain on any marriage, but this? This was sheer stupidity. Vic sighed to himself, Andy was a good man, a hard worker, his only fault that he was probably too nice, too nice for his own good if that were possible. He'd obviously let Sophie have a free rein with money but he supposed that was how it was these days. He was disappointed with Sophie though, he thought he had taught her better than this, but then women were very complicated. To be honest he had never really understood Joyce, even after forty years of marriage. She had certainly had her funny ways, most of them a mystery to him. He gave the teabag a stir in the teapot and poured himself another cup of tea. He had loved Joyce though and he missed her terribly. Bloody selfish of her to go before him, although she would have been worried sick if she had seen the mess her daughter had got herself into. Poor Joyce had suffered with Sophie throughout her miscarriages and then carried her through the traumas of the IVF. Vic had watched as Joyce's own heart had been broken by her feelings of inadequacy, the despair of a mother unable to help her child. This was different though, this problem could be solved, but Vic knew it had to be solved the right way. He was adamant that his daughter would learn a few valuable lessons.

There was a pale pink glow in the sky as Christie looked out of the bedroom window. Everything was still, apart from the swishing tail of one of the ponies, silhouetted against the morning light in the east paddock; an early riser like herself but with far less on its mind. The grounds, along with everything else in Maggie Land were perfect, straight lines, immaculate lawns, all in order. Stones didn't dare stray from the gravel pathways and weeds did not bother to rear their heads amongst the tasteful stonework of the stable courtyards. Christie wondered whether God had felt a similar satisfaction on the seventh day when he had looked down upon his creation and whether he felt any sense of despair at what a mess his creation had become. Despite the chill, Christie opened the window and the cool, crisp air made her shiver. A blackbird was singing its heart out on the fence below. Everything was perfect, the archetypal calm before the storm.

Rummaging in her bag for her hairbrush, Lucy noticed that her phone was signalling a message. It was from Steve. Quickly she opened it, but realising that it had been sent more than an hour ago, she decided against phoning. In the dim light of the bedroom Lucy replied. *"Just about to wake Maggie. Terrified. Hope to get her on early flight. Look after them. Call me when you wake up. X"*

For some reason unknown even to herself, she couldn't tell him that she loved him.

At four forty-five am, Lucy and Christie stood together outside Maggie's bedroom door. Having debated the necessity for brandy, they had sensibly opted for black coffee, given the amount that Maggie had consumed earlier. Christie held on to the mug for comfort. Neither of them wanted to open the door. Reluctantly, Christie turned the handle and Lucy followed her inside. Maggie was sleeping like a baby and the snoring emanating from the large king sized bed made Lucy smile. In a different situation it would have been hilarious. In the darkness, Christie fumbled for the bedside lamp and the sudden blast of light caused Maggie to stir and turn over. Christie put the coffee down on the bedside table and placing a hand softly on Maggie's shoulder, shook her gently.

"Maggie," she whispered, "Maggie, wake up, please Maggs you need to wake up, it's me Christie, Maggie you have to wake up."

Maggie stirred and Christie shook her a little harder.

"Maggie, can you hear me, it's Christie, come on, you have to wake up."

Maggie opened her eyes and stared at Christie, blinking in the glare from the lamp. She looked at the two women, fully clothed beside her bed and her heart missed a beat. Instantly, despite her alcoholic haze, she knew something was seriously wrong.

Chapter 16

The bedside alarm pierced the silence and Steve slammed his hand down on it with a force that sent it shooting off the bedside table. His head was thumping and his throat was raw. He was sweating. God he felt like shit. Covering his eyes with his arm he lay there taking stock of his physical condition. He needed water and painkillers, if he could find them. Slowly his brain recalled the events of earlier and he remembered that he was, in fact, in Callum's room. Whether he had brought his bag with him, he had no idea. He couldn't actually remember getting into bed. Unfortunately, the events of last night had not been a dream.

"Oh fuck" he said aloud to himself. "What a fucking nightmare."

Making an effort to sit up, he opened one eye and fumbled around for his phone. Looking at the screen, he struggled to focus, but as expected there was a message from Lucy. He dialled her number, he knew she'd be waiting for him to call. His call was answered immediately.

"Steve is that you?" Lucy garbled. "Oh my God, this is so awful. Is Callum ok? Are you ok? I still can't believe it. What actually happened? It's terrible."

Steve's voice was hoarse. He was desperate for water.

"Morning sweetheart," he croaked. "Yep, you're right, it's all pretty shit. Callum's ok I think, Mike's sharing a room with him, didn't want to leave him by himself obviously."

"Well you don't sound too good, how much did you have to drink last night?"

"A bucket load. It's a boys' trip Lucy, that's what we do, well

96

we did. I have no idea how we'll get through today without letting the rest of the guys know."

"Are you all still going to play golf? How can you when this has happened?"

Lucy sounded incredulous. Steve chose his words carefully.

"Well it's best the others don't know isn't it, best for Callum and Maggie? As far as I'm concerned, the fewer people who know the better. What's happening with Maggie? How did she take it? Is she on her way?"

Lucy sighed, recalling the traumas of a few hours ago. It had been awful.

"Badly, what do you think? She's stunned actually, although she said she knew something was up with him. It was so awful having to tell her. Christie's taken her to the airport, I'm here with the kids and I have to phone the kids' school and let them know that she's had to go away. Thank God they weren't home this weekend. Is it bad for Callum Steve?"

"To be honest Luce, I don't know. It's been a shock to us too, we had no idea. He's hardly said a word since he's been here. Cavendish was giving him a hard time yesterday and it must have pushed him over the edge."

"I told you he was a bastard," Lucy said triumphantly. "I don't like you going away with him, I hate him."

Steve wasn't convinced. He was still smarting from Cavendish's innuendos.

"A lot of women find him attractive though," he said, fishing.

"Well I don't, he's revolting, shame it wasn't him who tried to kill himself, there'd be no loss there."

"Woah, that's a bit harsh. Callum jumping into the pool wasn't Cavendish's fault, he was possibly a contributing factor, but it wasn't his fault."

"In your opinion, anyway look after Maggie when she gets there, I am worried about her. I keep trying to put myself in her position."

97

"You'd probably be delighted if I jumped in the swimming pool."

"Steve that's a terrible thing to say, you know that's not true."

"Do I?"

"Oh come off it." Uncomfortable, Lucy changed the subject.

"Christie is calling Mike with the flight details so he can fill you in, she thought about flying out with her but Maggie said she would be fine."

Steve sighed.

"Well I'd better sort myself out and go and find them. Oh God, I feel terrible."

"Well serves you right, I don't have any sympathy for self inflicted pain."

"Don't know why you're being so superior, from what I hear you had a few last night yourself, but Christie said you were having a good time until all this happened."

"Yes I was actually, I hate to admit it, but I was and to be honest I do have a little bit of a headache myself."

There was a brief silence before Steve spoke again.

"Lucy, I do love you, you know. I just want you and us to be happy again but to be honest I don't know what to do. We have to try and sort things out, for all our sakes."

"Yes I know we do and we will talk about it when you get back."

"Promise?"

"Yes I promise."

"I'll hold you to that. Right better go and make myself presentable. I'll phone you later when Maggie's arrived and let you know what's happening. Bye darling, love you, kiss the kids for me."

"I will, look after yourself."

Steve hung up. Why couldn't she tell him that she did in fact love him too.

At Glasgow Airport, Christie ordered coffee and croissants and carried the tray over to the corner table where Maggie was sitting quietly. Despite the emotional roller coaster of the last few hours, Maggie still managed to look fabulous, although her dark glasses were hiding her puffy and slightly bloodshot eyes.

"I think you should try and eat something Maggs, you'll need something in your stomach, it's a few hours flight and you know how awful the food is especially in cattle class."

Maggie took a sip of the coffee and added a sugar. The croissant remained untouched.

"When did I take the paracetamol?" she asked quietly. "My head is throbbing."

Christie looked at her watch.

"I think you can have more in about an hour. Do you want me to get you something stronger? Look, there's a chemist over there."

"No my sweet, you've done more than enough, the paracetamol is fine. This is why I don't drink much Christie, I can't stand the pain."

Christie felt relieved as Maggie hinted at a smile.

"Mike's going to meet you at the other end, are you sure you'll be alright?"

Maggie patted Christie's hand and gave it a small squeeze.

"Don't worry my darling, I'll be fine. It takes a lot to bring me down."

Christie smiled.

"Please phone me if you need to talk Maggs, honestly, if you need anything, just call."

"Thanks Christie, you have no idea how much I appreciate it."

Mike bolted out of a fitful sleep. He had hardly slept at all, terrified that his charge may make an attempt to escape. As he looked over towards Callum, he realised that his fears had been unfounded. Callum was asleep. Stupid bastard. Part of him wanted to punch him for messing up a good trip but the other half felt desperately sorry for his mate. He had looked like a broken man lying beside the swimming pool. How had it happened that none of them had seen it coming? Were they that unapproachable as friends that he thought they wouldn't understand? And would they have understood or would they just have slapped him on the back, handed him a pint and told him it would all work itself out? Probably. That's the way it was usually done and this was the bloody result.

Mike re-read Christie's earlier text confirming Maggie's arrival time; they had a couple of hours to sort themselves out. The second text was from Cavendish.

"Have booked a suite for Dunbar and Maggie in Hotel Olympia. It's paid for. Thought they might need some privacy."

Bloody hell, Mike thought to himself, he's probably feeling guilty but it was still a great gesture. It would certainly help matters and make it easier to keep things quiet. Mike texted back.

"Thanks mate. Appreciated." Grateful, he forwarded the text to Steve.

Cavendish opened his window and walked out onto his balcony. The air was cool and refreshing and the hotel was quiet apart from the occasional scraping of furniture on the marble floors as the cleaners went out about their business. Cavendish looked down over the swimming pool. Idiot, he said to himself, what a bloody stupid thing to do. His derision, however, was short lived, as scanning the pool bar, his eyes settled on two figures, sprawled on adjoining sun beds. Rex Haig and Davie Sutherland had obviously not made it to their beds last night.

Bloody marvellous, Cavendish grinned, rubbing his hands with satisfaction, advantage England.

Chapter 17

To her relief, Maggie had managed to grab a window seat. She felt more secure tucked up against the side of the plane and the window gave her the opportunity to avoid conversation if the need arose, although thankfully, the pasty-faced woman sitting next to her had shown no inclination to chat. The over-bottle tanned hostess had offered drinks and Maggie had opted for a Coke, the icy sweetness tasting like nectar in her dehydrated state. Christie had kindly bought her a magazine and she flicked through it aimlessly, hoping for a distraction. Today, however, the glossy pages made no sense, nothing made sense. She closed the magazine and looked out of the window. Blue sky and white clouds; it was how she imagined heaven would look as you stepped through the pearly gates, if, of course, you got there in the first place. Maggie felt devastated. What had possessed him to try something so utterly selfish, how did he think she would cope without him and what about the children? How could he say he loved them and then attempt something so unbelievably brainless, just like that, with no warning? Christie had said that he was worried about work but why couldn't he tell her? She was his wife, for God's sake. Obviously it didn't say much for their marriage. The sudden glare from the sun as the plane changed direction caused her to close her eyes, and she leant back against the headrest. Thank God he hadn't managed it. What she was going to say when she saw him she had no idea; her husband had become a stranger to her and she was now in uncharted territory.

Andy called Sophie. He was desperate to talk to her before the golf got under way. If he didn't catch her now he knew it would have to wait until tomorrow. No answer. He tried her mobile. Answering service. Where the hell was she? Giving up he threw the phone on the bed and headed for the shower.

The news of Cavendish's hospitality was well received by Steve, who had been troubled by how they were going to keep Maggie and Callum away from the rest of the boys. At least it would give them some space. Unfortunately, an even more pressing problem was the state of Rex and Davie, who were still out cold beside the pool. He had known they couldn't be trusted and Alex had obviously failed miserably. Knocking on Alex's door, he was annoyed.

"Alex, are you awake? Come on we've got a team to sort out."

Alex unlocked the door, he was showered but not dressed. Steve walked over to the window and signalled towards the pool.

"I've just seen your room mate; he's out cold beside the pool with his playmate. I thought you were in charge?"

Alex was irritated.

"Oh bugger off Steve, he's a law unto himself, you know that. There was no way I was gonna get them out of the bar, they were hammered by midnight. If you were so worried you should have hung around a bit longer instead of wimping out."

Steve resisted the temptation to divulge any information.

"Well get your clothes on and help me wake them up. Cavendish will bloody love this. What about the rest of the team, any other fallers?"

"How would I know," mumbled Alex, "I'm not the bloody captain, where is he anyway, shouldn't he be up by now?"

Steve fumbled for an excuse.

"He's up but he needs to sort out a hitch. Dunbar's got a problem. He's going home so we are already one down, maybe two temporarily, so with those two tossers out cold, we are pretty well stuffed. We might as well hand over the trophy at breakfast and be done with it. I hate losing, but losing to Cavendish really pisses me off."

Cavendish straightened the collar on his team polo shirt and admired himself in the mirror. The team colours were slightly radical, he admitted that, but the Scots would no doubt appear in yet another variation of bloody tartan. At least he had shown a little originality. Splashing himself with cologne, he stared at himself. He was looking forward to the game and looking forward to taking the trophy back to England.

The well directed contents of an abandoned ice bucket brought Rex and Davie to their senses.

"Jesus Christ," spluttered Davie, "what are you doing you stupid bastard?"

Steve was unrepentant.

"Get up, we've got to be on the first tee in an hour, go and get showered and be at breakfast in thirty minutes."

Davie and Rex shivered, arguing was pointless. They had no idea what time it was.

"The only saving grace," Steve continued, "is that you only slept with each other, come on hurry up we've got a few team issues already, we need you at breakfast in thirty minutes."

As Davie and Rex staggered off, Steve's phone rang. Mike sounded anxious.

"Steve where are you?"

"Down beside the pool waking up Rex and Davie, Alex's with me, Jamie and Dougie are up and at breakfast. What are you thinking?"

"Well from what I can gather, Maggie's due in mid-morning so I'll miss the first game, can't really ask anyone else. I'll meet you in the restaurant in fifteen minutes; Callum said he'd be fine. Did Davie and Rex go to bed last night?"

"Well yes, if a sun lounger counts, they're still pissed so don't expect any miracles."

Mike sighed. "That's all I fucking need, see you down there."

Sophie ignored the mobile, it would be Andy, but she didn't want to speak, she couldn't face lying. She would text him in an hour or so when the golf was in full swing, he wouldn't be able to reply then. She could hear Vic moving around in the kitchen, she should be getting up. Instead, she pulled the covers over her head and closed her eyes.

As Mike pulled on his team polo, his phone rang.

"Mike, Simon here. Look, why don't I sort out Callum, I'm really not worried if I miss this morning, that would make the teams even."

Mike was taken aback.

"No don't worry mate, it's our problem, we'll sort it."

"But you're the captain. Come on, seriously, I'm happy to and as I am a doctor I would like to talk to Maggie when she arrives. I'll clear it with Cavendish. I'll be over in ten minutes."

As Mike hung up Callum opened his eyes.

"Mike I am so sorry, look I'll be alright now, you don't have to stay with me. I know it was stupid but I'm not about to do anything again."

"Well I don't know that do I and I'm not taking any chances. Look mate, Maggie's on her way, she'll be here in a couple of hours. We've got you a room in another hotel where you can have a bit of time. Simon's coming here to sort things out."

Callum sat up, he was agitated.

"Maggie's coming here, you told Maggie. What did you do that for?"

Mike lost his patience.

"Because quite honestly Callum, we didn't know what else to do. How do you think I felt pulling you out of that pool? I'm not going to forget that too easily I can tell you. One of my best mates tries to kill himself and he couldn't ask me for help, of course I phoned Maggie, and if she didn't care about you she wouldn't be on her way right now. So shut up and do as you're told before I top you myself."

Chapter 18

Red eyes and shaking hands were in abundance at breakfast and delicate stomachs were struggling with the mountain of food on offer. Incredibly, the Scots were first down, dressed in stylish Oscar Jacobsen purple trousers and classic navy polo's.

"Nice kit," slurred Davie, admiring himself in the reflective glass doors. "I would definitely wear this again; last year's kit was shite. Priscilla wet herself laughing when I put it on. That's probably why she dumped me."

"The only reason she dumped you," retorted Alex, "was that you were playing up a division, out of your depth mate."

Swaying slightly, Davie grabbed the back of a chair for support. "Jesus, I need to sober up, how long have I got?"

Alex sighed. "Not long enough, Mike and Steve are not happy I can tell you, you'd better pull something out of the bag. Oh for God's sake, will you look at that lot?" Alex was looking towards the entrance of the restaurant.

As Andy and the rest of the English team walked over to their table, Rex raised his sunglasses for a better look.

"What the hell are you guys wearing? You look absolutely ridiculous. Will they let you on the course dressed like that?"

Andy couldn't help but smile because he did indeed feel ridiculous, his red hair clashing disastrously with the scarlet polo and red and white striped trousers. In fact they all looked ridiculous. Even Cavendish was struggling to carry it off, despite his aviators and Gucci loafers.

"Words forsake me boys," Steve smiled, "Cavendish you look like a complete knob."

Cavendish was undeterred.

"Red is the colour of winners Sinclair, St George, Tiger Woods, Man Utd," he boomed. "Red is for those who want to leave their mark, to stand out. Unlike your dreary Scottish heather blend. Navy as we all know is for losers, blue is for sad, blue is for wet, navy is for wet, sad losers."

For once, Sinclair thought he might have a point.

"Wait till the sunburn kicks in boys," shouted Davie, "and your faces go red as well, you'll clash darlings. You look like barber's poles."

Cavendish smiled. "The only red faces will be yours Gok Wan when we lift that trophy, anyway enough of the jovial banter, I need my breakfast. Is everyone here?"

"More or less," said Steve quietly, as Mike appeared in the doorway.

Cavendish tapped a glass with one of the teaspoons. "Quiet," he bellowed. "Right, everyone eat and aim to be in reception ready to go in fifteen minutes, we need to get a shift on. Mike can I have a word please?"

Mike was slightly taken aback at the use of the word please, he wasn't used to any form of civility from Cavendish, but it did at least indicate that he was aware of the gravity of the situation. Mike sat down and Cavendish handed him a black coffee.

"Simon told me that he's sorting out Callum and Maggie, which leaves you and Sinclair free to play. A much better option I think. I've told my lot that Dunbar has to go for family reasons and Simmos sorting out his travel. To be honest, I think they're all too hung over to take much in. The pairings have been re-done so everything should go to plan."

Cavendish took a mouthful of coffee and buttered a croissant.

"Are you ok MacDonald?" he said quietly. "You don't look that great to be honest."

Mike gave a wry smile.

"Not every day one of your best mates tries to do away with

107

himself is it. I knew something was up, but Jesus, he didn't have to do that. Stupid bastard."

Mike ran his hand through his hair and looked out of the window towards the pool. Cavendish added jam to his croissant.

"No one ever sees it coming mate," he whispered. "The only good thing about this whole bloody mess is that he never managed to do it, and that hopefully, his kids will never have to find out."

Mike stared at Cavendish, who concentrating on his croissant, wouldn't catch his eye. He could see he was hurting too. Maybe he was slightly human after all.

Back in London, Vic placed a mug of tea on the bedside table and drew back the curtains in his spare bedroom.

"It's no good hiding under there my girl, that's not going to solve anything, is it? Come on, drink this tea and get yourself up. We'll have a good breakfast and then have a chat about what's to be done. Come on, up you get." And he patted the bump under the duvet playfully.

"It's a lovely day," he continued, "sun shining, blue sky. You can give me a hand later, put some bedding plants in and make yourself useful."

Sophie reluctantly removed the duvet from her head and blinked in the glare of the morning sun streaming in through the window. This had been her bedroom once, but little evidence of her occupancy remained, apart from the small dressing table and a couple of photos.

"This room was always nice in the morning," she mumbled, sitting herself up and adjusting her pillows. "Thanks for the tea Dad."

She looked around the room. Her mum had had it decorated not long before she died, wanting a nice room for visitors, and she had done a good job. It was pretty, without being fussy, and with the sun streaming in, the rose-pink glow was comforting.

After she'd gone though, there hadn't been many visitors.

"Where are the bedding plants for, back or front?" Sophie asked casually, trying to bring herself back to the present. Vic was staring out of the window, enjoying the sun and watching the postman as he criss-crossed the street. He looked perky this morning, the sun was obviously bringing out his good side.

"Back mostly," he said as he turned his attention back to the room, "and a few tubs and baskets. Trouble is, your mum was the expert at the baskets. I just shove em in and hope for the best. I keep doing them for her really."

Sophie smiled at him. "Probably gives her a good laugh seeing what a pigs ear you make of it. I like them too though; it makes the house look welcoming and cared for."

Sophie picked up the tea but strangely she didn't fancy it. She still felt nauseous and the thought of facing up to the tasks ahead wasn't helping. Vic could see that this wasn't going to be easy.

"Right come on, let's not waste the day. I've put clean towels in the bathroom. I'll see you downstairs."

With the children dressed, fed and dispatched to help with the ponies, and the phone call made to Maggie's children's school, Lucy was alone in Maggie's kitchen. She was tired now, tired from the lack of sleep from last night, on top of years of tiredness that early motherhood can bring. As she cleared the wine glasses and bottles, she smiled to herself as she recalled some of the banter around the table, and tried to remember the last time she had laughed so much. It had been a long time, too long. Somewhere along the line she had lost herself, at no point in particular, but each time she had placed her responsibilities over the needs of herself, she had buried herself a little deeper. Walking out into the hall, she caught sight of herself in the vast Art Deco mirror. The woman looking back at her was a frump, a miserable cow, who had no reason to be miserable other than the fact that she had forgotten to care for herself too. How the hell Steve was still with her she didn't know. "Get a grip," she hissed at the reflection, "and get a bloody haircut." As she walked back into the kitchen, the phone rang.

"Lucy, it's Christie, I'm ten minutes away, put the kettle on, I'm desperate."

Lucy was delighted to hear Christie's voice.

"How did you get on? Did she get away ok?"

"Yeh, no problems. Poor Maggs, I don't think she really knows what's going on. It's such a shock and the hangover didn't help, but I'll tell you everything when I get back. I've still got to check on my kids, although they're probably still be asleep if Anna's got any sense. Check out the fridge Luce, I could do with a fry up, I'm starving."

Sitting in Mike's room with Callum, Simon phoned room service and ordered up two continental breakfasts.

"I'm not sure I want anything," Callum said quietly, as he buried his head in his hands. He looked and felt wretched.

"Well I've ordered it now and you might change your mind when it arrives. Did Mike bring your case here or is it still in your room?"

Callum shrugged his shoulders.

"I don't know, I don't remember unpacking. I don't know, I think that's it on the floor."

Simon opened the case that was lying beside the bed. It was beautifully organised.

"I bet you didn't pack this yourself. Bloody hell, I'd be scared to touch it."

Callum gave a hint of a smile. "That's Maggie for you. God what am I going to say to her? Why did Mike have to call her? I can't face her Simon, I can't."

Simon sat beside him on the bed.

"Look mate, Maggie loves you and she's on her way right now because whether you realise it or not, you do in fact, need her help. It won't be too easy for her either you know."

"Well let's see if she loves me when her whole life goes pear shaped. Believe me, Maggie's not the type to stay with a loser."

Simon got up to open the door for room service. He had no intention of speaking for Maggie and Callum wasn't in the frame of mind to listen anyway. Maybe she would leave him, but either way, he wasn't about to try and predict the outcome.

Maggie Dunbar looked at her watch. Forty-five minutes to landing. As she looked out of the window, silently, from beneath her Versace sunglasses, the tears began to flow.

Chapter 19

Tracey checked her phone for texts from Simon. Nothing. Cavendish was obviously making life difficult. She looked at the clock, they'd be on the course now, she wouldn't be hearing from him till tomorrow. Instead, she called Sophie. Getting no reply from either phone, she sent a text.

"Hi there. If you fancy lunch give me a call. Hope everything Ok. T x"

Pouring herself another coffee, Tracey picked up her laptop and headed through to the small sitting room she attempted to use as a study. The room collected the morning sun and was already warm. Leaving the laptop unopened, she instead picked up a magazine and flicked her way through the glossy pages. Her book was half done, it had been for three months now and at the moment it wasn't going anywhere. Her writing, like her life, appeared to be drying up.

Tracey was right, the boys were indeed on the golf course, and with pairings and rules set, they had managed to tee off on time for the first round of the day. Usually this would have taken the form of a fourball, but with two players out, Mike and Cavendish had agreed that sixteen players would play in pairs and the two of them would play singles, with the afternoon session still taking the singles format. The customary side bets had been placed, and three holes into the round the English were up in two with the Scots up in one. Cavendish was two up on Mike.

"What time is Maggie due in?" Cavendish asked, as they walked to the fourth tee.

"Eleven-twenty I think. I'm actually relieved Simon's going and not me, not sure I'd have been that great. I'm not looking forward to seeing Maggie. What the bloody hell do you say?"

"Look MacDonald, you pulled him out of the bloody pool, saved his life and got hold of his wife. I think you've done your bit for now so just forget it, please, just for today, try and enjoy your golf and give me a bit of competition. Stop being so bloody selfish."

Mike turned to look at Cavendish, and realising that Cavendish was trying to be funny, patted him on the back.

"Right then, you're on. Twenty Euros says I win."

"Easy pickings," smiled Cavendish as he shook his hand.

As Simon and Dunbar took a taxi to the airport, Simon wished that they had organised it better, but being unable to contact Maggie, he had no choice but to take Callum with him to the airport and then take them both on to the hotel. The best option would have been for Maggie to take a taxi to the hotel, but it was too late now. Neither he, nor Dunbar, were looking forward to the meeting, neither having any idea what to expect from Maggie. Simon didn't know Maggie that well, other than the yearly get together when she usually held court and terrified the rest of the wives, but from the conversations he had had with her, he had liked her. Her enthusiasm for life he had found infectious. Yes, she was competitive and slightly scary, but he had always thought her heart in the right place. When she had held the get together at her place, the weekend had been fabulous. Nothing had been too much trouble, she had cared for everyone. This would have knocked her sideways. Callum, on the other hand, was terrified. He felt like a schoolboy being taken to the headmistress for doing something he now knew to be stupid and irresponsible, but that at the time seemed the only option. In his mind's eye, he tried to imagine the look she would give him, the look she reserved for those she considered lacking or inadequate. To be fair she had rarely used it on him, but it was in her armoury and he felt desperate.

Steve Sinclair was not a happy man, being two down after five holes against Chris Smith and Fats Mitchell, probably two of the worst players on the tour. Usually he played pretty well with a hangover, but not today. Today his golf was shite.

"I think I heard your phone beeping," said Vic as he walked into the kitchen, "would that be a text?"

"Probably," Sophie replied unenthusiastically, "I'll check it when I go back up."

Vic realised that she probably wanted to avoid any contact with Andy, but he pressed ahead.

"Have you heard from Andy? How's he getting on? Could do with a holiday myself but it's not quite the same organising something just for me. When's he back?"

"Tuesday lunchtime. I can't say I'm looking forward to it."

Vic picked up the half-eaten breakfast from the table. "Good food wasted that, what's wrong with it?"

"Nothing, I'm sorry, I'm just not feeling like eating at the moment."

Vic had to agree, she did look pale; pale and tired. This had obviously been hanging over her for a while.

"Well you can't go on not eating, it's not good for you. Maybe you should see a doctor love, just to make sure everything is ok."

Sophie shook her head. "I'm fine Dad. I know it's just the worry of it all. I expect as soon as I've faced the music, I'll feel a bit better. So what's the plan?" she said, getting up from the table and changing the subject.

Vic handed her a tea towel. He wasn't going to give up that easily.

"Well firstly you can help with the drying up and then we'll take a drive over to your place and get all the paperwork so that

I can have a look at it and try and work out where we stand. Once we've done that, we'll get out in the garden and get those bedding plants in."

Sophie looked at him, a look of fear in her eyes.

"We can't go back to the house, what if the bailiffs are there? I'm sorry, I'm not going back."

Vic took her hand.

"Yes we are, we are going back. We won't be there long, and if they're there and I have to pay up to stop them going in, I will. You could do with a change of clothes too by the look of you. Come on, get this finished and we'll get going. We could get lunch at that nice garden centre near the roundabout."

Up in her room, Sophie checked her mobile. To her relief, the message was from Tracey.

"Thanks but dad not too well so staying with him for a few days. Thanks for yesterday. Will be in touch X"

"Oh God," she said quietly, as she lay back down on the bed. She felt awful, but whether she felt sick or not, there was no way she was going to get out of this one.

At the turn, Mike was back to all square and the Scots had clawed their way back to one match down over all. Sinclair was still struggling but had managed not to lose anymore holes and was still two down. Mike and Cavendish had no idea how the rest of the guys were playing but Cavendish was happy that Mike had managed to get himself together. If he won, he wanted to win against decent competition and Mike was a good bloke and a good player. Hopefully, the dinner tonight would cheer everyone up and the Scots boys could try and put last nights events behind them. Cavendish had hoped that the twentieth anniversary tour would be one to remember and unfortunately, for all the wrong reasons, it was failing to disappoint. Tonight though, he hoped he could turn it around and at least send most of the boys home happy.

In the toilet at the airport, Maggie Dunbar washed her face and reapplied her make-up. She had to hold it together and a flawless mask gave her confidence. Her hands were shaking as she applied her mascara, but she took a deep breath and blew out slowly through her mouth, calmly trying to breathe out her tension as she had been taught in her yoga class. She stared at herself in the mirror. She looked different. Checking her lipstick and replacing her sunglasses, she took another deep breath as she opened the door and walked back out into the busy airport. Everything would be different now. Her life would never be the same again.

Chapter 20

As the taxi arrived at the airport, Simon turned to Dunbar.

"Are you ok?" he asked softly.

Dunbar nodded. Simon took a deep breath.

"Look you stay in the taxi while I go and find Maggie, unless you want to come in and get a drink or something?"

Dunbar shook his head. "I'll wait here thanks."

"Well don't go disappearing on me, hopefully she's not been delayed. Have you got your mobile or is it knackered?"

"No, it's here, I just haven't got it on."

"Well put it on, just in case. Right I'll be back in a minute hopefully."

The airport was busy and Simon took out his phone. Mike had given him Maggie's mobile. Calling her number he looked around for arrivals. His call was answered quickly.

"Hi, Maggie Dunbar."

"Maggie, its Simon Lewis, I'm here at the airport, where are you?"

"Oh hello Simon, I was looking for Mike. I'm just coming through arrivals, I should be able to see you any second, where are you?"

"Under the big clock, screen thing, don't worry I can see you now," he said, waving.

As Maggie walked towards him, Simon instinctively held out his arms and Maggie accepted their comfort gratefully.

"I am so sorry Maggie, I really am. No one had any idea there was anything wrong."

Maggie pulled away and rummaging for a tissue, she lifted

her glasses and dabbed at her eyes.

"Me neither Simon, I really can't believe he could do such a thing. Where is he now?"

"Waiting outside in the taxi, he's terrified of facing you."

Maggie sighed.

"It doesn't say much for me does it. Am I really that bad Simon?"

Simon smiled, struggling for an answer.

"The thing is Maggie, he's obviously suffering from depression, so I'd suggest that you organise for him to see his doctor as soon as he gets back. In fact, I would phone him from here, let him know the situation and get his advice. I can talk to him if you like. Cavendish has organised you a room at another hotel which he says you can use until you're ready to fly back. The only people who know what's happened are Mike and Steve, myself and Cavendish."

"Thanks," whispered Maggie, "it's very good of Cavendish, very kind."

Simon smiled. "He has his good points; we just don't see them very often. Right come on, give me your case. It's time to face the music."

And with another deep breath, Maggie took Simon's arm and headed for the taxi.

As Sophie drove up to her house, her heart was pounding. How many of her neighbours had noticed the bailiffs she wondered; if she saw them here now she would keep driving, she didn't care what her dad said. As she drove past the house everything seemed ok, no men in dark suits lurking in her doorway, but taking no chances she looked for a parking space a little further down, just in case. Turning off the engine, she looked at Vic.

"Well so far so good," she said quietly. "Let's hope I can get in and out without any incident."

Vic opened his door.

"Look I'll deal with any bailiffs, come on, let's go and get all the bits and pieces and get it over and done with."

As they walked up the garden path, Jim glanced out of his window. He was relieved to see Sophie, relieved that she appeared to have taken the sensible option and got herself some help. He'd been worried all night. He liked Vic; they had a lot in common. Vic would help her sort things out.

In the kitchen, Sophie picked up the notebook and file of unpaid bills and handed them to Vic.

"Take these, I'll just go and pack a few things and then we can get out of here."

Vic laughed. "For goodness sake girl, you're acting like you're on the run."

"Well it feels like it and it's not bloody funny. I feel awful."

"Believe me missy, you're not the only one in debt, everyone in the bloody country owes too much money. You've just let it get a bit out of hand and you'll have to get it sorted."

"Yes I know," Sophie said between gritted teeth, as she ran up the stairs feeling an urge to throw up again, "believe me I know."

At lunch in the clubhouse bar, the English were one up overall. Mike and Cavendish had finished all square, as had Alex and Andy. Davie had somehow managed to win two up but Rex and Steve had both lost. Steve was furious.

"I can't believe I played such shite golf," he said, taking a beer from Mike, "I played like an absolute pussy, couldn't hole a putt, I couldn't do anything. Bloody miracle we were only two down. Just as well Jamie played well. Jesus Christ."

Mike sat down and took a swig of his beer.

"We're only one down; it can all change this afternoon. Cavendish has got one of the members here to play in place of Callum so that Simon can get a game; Cavendish is going to make the draw in a minute. It's not over yet mate, not by a long shot. My only worry, is that Davie's probably sobered up and he obviously plays better pissed. Tommo said he played a stormer. Think I'll go and spike his beer."

Steve smiled. "Can't believe they won and we lost to Smithie and Fats. It pisses me right off."

"That must be at least twenty Euros in the pot from this table," laughed Andy as he pulled up a chair.

"Someone's not a happy bunny!"

As Steve and Mike handed over the cash, Cavendish called for quiet.

"Right everyone, well played this morning, nice to see things so tight, makes for a bit of cut-throat competition this afternoon. Lunch will be ready in ten minutes but I thought I would do the draw now for this afternoon. Singles of course, so no hanging about or we won't get finished and we don't want to be late for the party tonight."

He picked up the glass containing the names of the English players and pulled out the first name.

"Smithie," he said in a serious tone, then drawing one of the Scottish names, "Smithie... will play Alex."

Steve whispered to Alex. "Hope you have better luck than me, please don't let him win twice, we'll never here the last of it."

"Simon," boomed Cavendish, looking around the room. "Simon plays Mike."

The draw continued with plenty of heckling and good humoured banter, until Cavendish was drawn out of the glass. "Myles," said Cavendish, grinning inanely, "Myles, will play Sinclair."

Shit, Steve said to himself, that's all I need.

Tracey picked up her laptop and turned it on. She had no enthusiasm to write. Looking for a distraction, she opened *Facebook* and signed in. Skimming over the page on the screen, she was amazed at the amount of time people spent on it, and how much of their lives they seemed happy to share. Tracey rarely contributed, acting more as a voyeur than an active participant. She had no idea who half the friends of friends were or how they managed to appear on her page. Even her so called friends really had little interest in her life, and she had no interest in theirs. Real friends phoned each other as far as she was concerned. She was about to exit when one of the conversations caught her eye, Sarah Thompson, that was Tommo's wife. Scrolling down she devoured the conversation that had obviously taken place last night. Sarah was apparently delighted that Tommo was away and was extolling the virtues of *Randolph's,* the new bar in Chelsea that she was planning to frequent with a few friends this weekend. If Tommo planned to enjoy the lap dancers on offer on his weekend away, then she would be looking for entertainment of her own. Two could play at that game.

Tracey went cold. No wonder the bastard hadn't phoned.

Chapter 21

"What do you think'll happen now?" asked Lucy, as she spooned coffee into the warmed cafetiere.

"What do you think she'll do?"

Christie shrugged her shoulders.

"I have absolutely no idea. What would you do?"

"Don't know really. I think Steve would tell me if he had a problem, although I suppose I like to think he would. You never really know with men though do you? They don't like talking about things at the best of times. To be quite honest, I think Steve loves himself far too much to try and kill himself."

Christie smiled.

"Mm, I don't think Mike would either, but you're right, you never know. Maggie's got a lot to lose though hasn't she? I mean look at all this; this place must cost a fortune to run. I wonder if it really is that bad. Poor Callum, he must have been worried sick. Did you phone the school?"

Lucy poured two coffees.

"Yes, didn't go into any detail, just said that a relation was ill and Maggie had had to fly abroad for a few days. The school was fine about it. Thank God though that the girls were away, Maggie won't want them to find out. What about your boys? You probably need to be getting back."

Christie looked at her watch.

"I know, just as well Anna helped out, I'll need to give her a big tip for this one. Have you heard any more from Steve?"

Lucy shook her head.

"Not since this morning. He sounded pretty shaken, although

his hangover wasn't helping. I couldn't believe they were still playing golf but I suppose he's right, the fewer people that know what's happened the better. I don't suppose I'll hear from him again until tomorrow, now the golf's under way, unless he can escape from Cavendish for five minutes. Steve said that Cavendish had given Callum a hard time yesterday; I bet he pushed it too far. He said it wasn't his fault but you know what he's like, he's an arsehole."

"An attractive arsehole though," smiled Christie mischievously.

Lucy looked astonished.

"You can't be serious, he's a complete pig."

"Mmm, but still very attractive in that bad boy way. Come on, you can't deny that he has a certain something. He's got a fabulous arse and there's always something slightly erotic about men you know you should avoid at all costs."

Christie winked at Lucy as she finished her coffee.

"Go on, admit it, you fancy him really."

"I seriously do not, I can't stand the man. Do you know he asked me back to his room at Davie Sutherland's fortieth? He's supposed to be a friend?"

"Did you go?" Christie continued playfully.

"I hope you're joking, course I didn't."

"Well at least he asked. You should be flattered, shows you've still got it babe."

Lucy sighed. "He would only have asked me to get back at Steve, they don't exactly see eye to eye do they?"

"Well that's where I think you're wrong, because despite what you may think, you are actually a very attractive woman Lucy Sinclair and the sooner you get your head around it the better."

Lucy blushed. She didn't deal well with any form of flattery.

"I know Steve still fancies me but I just don't seem interested at the moment. The last thing I want to do when I climb into bed at night is have rampant sex. Steve's always up for it, he'd have sex three times a day given half a chance, but somehow, after a day of wiping bums and noses and everything else, that to be honest is pretty bloody boring in my life, I can't just turn it on. The only thing I want to do when I get into bed is sleep."

Christie smiled at her.

"Trust me Lucy, you are not the only one, despite what Cosmopolitan may say. Most married women feel like you do for quite a lot of the time. Men and women are completely different, men can get it up at the drop of a hat can't they, it's a physical thing. For us women it's a bit more complicated, you know that. It's a bit more of an emotional thing and you're in the tough time right now, your whole life is taken up looking after your kids who need you every minute of the day. It's hard to turn into some raving nymphomaniac as soon as the bedroom door is closed. Bloody hell, the times I've lay there mentally preparing tomorrow night's dinner while Mike's giving it laldy, trust me it'll come back eventually."

Lucy laughed.

"But how the hell do you get it back? I mean it just doesn't happen like that does it, you know after all the excitements worn off and you've seen them having a crap on the toilet. There's just no mystery any more is there? It's the mystery that's exciting, and when they do such disgusting things like fart in the bed you want to bloody kill them, not shag them. Oh I don't know, I'll have to think of something."

Christie finished the last of her coffee. "Well I think you should shave your fanny and send him the photo before he gets back, that'll rev you both up a bit."

"What?" cried Lucy. "Are you serious?"

"Definitely. There's nothing like a bit of phone sex to spice up your life. Right, what time is it? God I'd better get a shift on. Are you heading back too?"

Lucy looked out of the window; the kids were playing contentedly in the tree house.

"I'm actually in no rush, so I'll tidy up and head home in a while. The kids are happy out there at the moment and one of the girls said they would take them for another pony ride so I'll head back later. Actually, I might try and find Maggie's hairdresser's number and give him a ring. Do you have the number for the Brazilian waxing?"

As Simon and Maggie walked out of the airport, Simon stopped her.

"Look Maggie, do you want me to get another taxi and you two head to the hotel by yourselves?"

Maggie felt embarrassed and slightly flustered.

"No Simon, of course not, you've done enough already. I don't want you having to fork out for another taxi as well. No, I won't hear of it. You sit in the front, it'll be alright."

At that moment, Simon would have paid anything to take another taxi.

Simon let Maggie open the taxi door herself, he didn't want to catch Callum's eye. He especially didn't want to intrude on what would inevitably be a painful moment. Instead, he jumped quickly into the front seat and engaged himself in conversation with the taxi driver, desperately trying to block out any conversation coming from the back seat. The back seat, however, was ominously quiet.

The twenty minute journey to the hotel felt like a lifetime to Simon, as the tension hanging in the air in the taxi became overpowering. Simon found himself grasping for any topic of conversation, and on discovering that Simon was a doctor, the taxi driver seized on the opportunity to divulge details of his wife's recent operation, which in his mind had been completely bungled by the health authorities. For once, Simon was happy to oblige, his sole aim to fill the taxi with anything but silence.

In the silence, Maggie took hold of Callum's hand and held it tight. She knew he wouldn't be able to say anything right now. It could wait until they were alone.

Tracey stared at her *Facebook* page. So, there were lap dancers were there, Cavendish up to his usual tricks again. She wasn't stupid, lap dancers and too much booze would only mean one thing. He would have known too. Cavendish would have told him what had been organised, he would have known before he went. She wondered whether Sophie knew or any of the other wives for that matter. Obviously some of them did.

"Bloody lying coward," she hissed at the screen. "How could you? You just bloody wait."

Up in her bedroom, Sophie packed a small case enough for a couple of days until Andy got back. She would have to text him soon as she knew he'd be starting to worry. She looked at herself in the mirror, her dad was right, she looked pale and drawn. An afternoon in the garden would actually do her some good. Opening her wardrobe she took out her large wash bag and walked through to the bathroom. She hadn't even taken a toothbrush when she had rushed out yesterday; she would take a bath later and try and freshen herself up a bit. Rummaging in the bathroom cupboard she took out the basics; cotton wool, cleansers, moisturisers. She tried to think what else she would need. She picked up a box of tampons. Would she need these, when was her last period, when was she due? As she stared at the packet she tried hard to work out how long it had been since her last period. She and Andy had been away for the weekend and he had been pissed off because her period had started. How long ago was that? She counted back and as the realisation dawned that it had been ten weeks ago, Sophie let out a tiny gasp of disbelief.

Chapter 22

Steve watched helplessly as Cavendish canned yet another long putt into the hole. Cavendish was on form and there was nothing Steve could do. For every putt that Cavendish sank, Steve lipped out. Things were not going to plan. Steve was still smarting from Cavendish's remark at dinner last night, and the thought of Cavendish having any type of relationship with Lucy, was gnawing away at the back of his mind. He'd wanted to stuff him this afternoon, but he was failing miserably. Retrieving his ball from the cup, Cavendish resisted the urge to gloat, despite being three up with seven to play. He could see that Sinclair was on the edge, he didn't need to say a word. As they walked off the green, Cavendish continued an earlier conversation.

"So did you have any idea that Dunbar was going under? He must have said something."

Steve tried to recall if any of his recent conversations with Callum had hinted at a problem.

"Not a clue anything was wrong until you called us on the way to the airport. He didn't come out the night before but he blamed that on Maggie. He was a nightmare at the airport, hardly said a word. According to Lucy, Maggie said he'd not been himself, she thought he was having an affair."

Cavendish snorted. "Fair play Maggie for thinking he was capable. Can you honestly see Dunbar having an affair, the fat bloater?"

Steve didn't really want to think about it.

"Simon said they didn't say a word to each other on the way to the hotel, said he'd never been so grateful for a conversation with the taxi driver about his wife's medical history. Do you think Maggie will leave him?"

Steve looked at him.

"For God's sake give them a chance, I wouldn't think Maggie knows what the fuck is going on at the moment and neither do I to be honest. Just give it a rest will you, I don't want to discuss it."

"Ok, ok," Cavendish replied, raising his hands in surrender, "I'll change the subject. I'm so bloody glad I'm not married any more, too much fucking hassle as far as I'm concerned."

As Steve watched Cavendish hammer the ball down the fairway, he had to agree with him.

Davie, despite sobering up, was still playing well and he and Andy were enjoying themselves as they both chipped onto the eighteenth green. Taking his putter out of the bag, Davie was getting excited at the thought of the night ahead.

"Tommo says that the entertainment tonight will be top drawer. He was at one of Cavendish's functions a few weeks ago and the girls were gorgeous. Apparently one of the guys got a right bollocking for going home with whip marks on his backside."

"Bloody hell, if I go back with anything on my backside it'll be curtains for me, I'm on parole as it is."

Davie laughed. "Fair play mate, trying to lie to your missus, top marks for bravery."

"Bloody stupid more like, I'm not looking forward to going home. She hasn't contacted me since I've been here, I could be on the way out for all I know. She's probably got her bags packed already."

"Join the club mate, that's all my women ever do."

"I'll marry you mate, when Sophie chucks me out, as long as you don't want any kids."

"Don't worry, I wouldn't want your kids, they'd be crap at golf."

"Is that a yes then?"

And laughing at all square, they walked off the eighteenth green and into the bar.

Tracey was still fuming. She'd have Sarah's number somewhere; they'd had dinner over there a few months back. Finding the number she made the call.

"Sarah, it's Tracey, Tracey Lewis, how are you?"

"Oh hi Tracey, fine thanks, what are you up to?"

"Oh enjoying the peace with the boys away and my kids are also away, which is why I'm phoning. I saw on *Facebook* that you were planning a night out tonight and just wondered if I could tag along, if it's ok of course, please say if it's not."

Sarah laughed mischievously.

"Course it's alright, the more the merrier. Just because those stupid buggers are away, doesn't mean we have to stay in and weep and wail. While the cats away and all that. Not ideal going out on a Sunday night but I'm not working tomorrow. Randolph's is fab, not cheap, but you can usually wangle a few free drinks especially when you look as gorgeous as you do. You'll love it sweetie. Why don't you glam up and come here for cocktails and munchies at seven?"

For a moment Tracey hesitated.

"Thanks, that will be great, see you at seven."

On the way back to the house, Sophie had run into the chemist on the pretext of getting paracetamol, and now she was perched over the toilet trying to pee onto a piece of white plastic. She couldn't believe she was even thinking that she was pregnant, it was madness, as well as unbelievably bad timing. Putting the tester on the side of the bath, she washed her hands and looked at her watch. She'd give it another minute. Slowly, she put down the lid on the toilet seat and sat down, head in hands, her heart thumping. A minute later, hands shaking, she picked up the tester and as the unthinkable, crazy, realisation dawned, she burst into tears.

Maggie tipped the porter and smiling courteously, closed the door after him. The suite was palatial; Cavendish had indeed been very kind. Callum had walked out onto the balcony and Maggie could see him, hands in pockets, silhouetted against the sunlight. The net curtains swayed gently in the warm breeze. He hadn't said a word; he hadn't even looked at her. Walking out onto the balcony she stood beside him.

"Callum darling," she whispered gently, as if talking to a small child, "we have to talk."

Callum stared straight ahead. He didn't want to talk, mainly because he didn't know what to say. There was too much to say. He hadn't planned on having to say anything at all. Years of denying himself any self indulgent emotions didn't make for easy conversation.

"Callum," Maggie continued, taking his hand, "please look at me, I need you to talk to me, I need to understand what's going on. Please Callum."

Callum looked at his wife and as he acknowledged the look of fear in her eyes, he crumpled sobbing onto the floor.

Steve watched as Cavendish's putt dropped into the hole. The bastard had played well, he deserved the win. Steve took off his cap and shook Cavendish's hand.

"Well done mate, well played," he said, acknowledging the fact that he'd been outclassed.

"Just hope the rest of my team have done better than me."

Replacing his cap, Cavendish smiled.

"Let's hope not. It's our turn Sinclair. You lot have won it too many times, it's nice to share you know."

"Bollocks," laughed Steve, "come on I need a drink."

In the bar, the boys had wasted no time in tucking into the booze.

"I don't think I need to ask who won," shouted Mike to Sinclair, "I could tell it was all over as you walked down the eighteenth. You need to get your body language sorted you know."

Steve threw his cap onto the bar and signalled the barman.

"Body language is the least of my worries, my golf's been absolute pish. I need a drink. So what's the damage? Please don't tell me Cavendish has won."

"Fraid so, we were all pish. Even if you'd won it wouldn't have made any difference. It's worse for you because you lost to him. Anyway forget about it now, it's party time. Time to get pissed!"

Tracey looked at herself in the mirror. She looked good, and much younger than her 40 years. The knee length black dress was flattering. It was elegant, without being tarty. As she stepped into the red and black stilettos, she marvelled at how heels flattered the legs and instantly made a woman feel sexy. Two could indeed play at this game.

Chapter 23

Staring at the two blue lines, Sophie stayed rooted to the toilet seat. She had waited for this moment for so long; dreamed of it, visualised it, prayed for it even. How the hell could she be pregnant now when all the longing, waiting and praying was over? She looked away and then looked again at the tester. There was no mistaking the result. Standing up, she looked at herself in the bathroom mirror. Finally, her wildest dreams had come true. She was going to be a mother. What a shame her own mother wasn't here to share it with her. Gingerly she placed her hand on her stomach and began to stroke it gently.

"Well sunshine," she whispered softly, "you've got one hell of a sense of timing."

"Right," bellowed Cavendish, as the boys stumbled out of the minibuses into the hotel foyer.

"We'll meet back in the bar at seven-thirty, gives us time to spruce ourselves up. Dinner is booked for eight, anyone falling asleep and not making it on time will get serious punishment."

Cavendish strode out of the foyer and headed towards the lift. Avelina was on duty and called to grab his attention.

"Excuse me, Mr Cavendish, there is a message for you."

Cavendish smiled at her as he accepted the piece of paper. She really was quite beautiful.

"Shame, I thought you'd changed your mind on my offer of a drink."

Avelina didn't smile.

"You can be sure Mr Cavendish," she answered politely,

"that I will never change my mind. Have a good evening sir."

Cavendish watched her as she walked away. He loved them when they played hard to get. As he walked into the lift he looked at the piece of paper. It was a message from Maggie Dunbar, asking him to call her if he got chance tomorrow. Poor old Maggie, he thought to himself, as he added her number to his contact list. It's not going to be quite so easy now is it your ladyship?

As Cavendish left the bar, Steve called to Mike and Alex.

"Fancy a quick one before we head up? If I have too long up there, I'll fall asleep. What you drinking?"

Mike wasn't keen. As far as he was concerned, forty winks seemed like a good idea, but Steve was insistent.

"Go on then, I'll just have a bottled beer. I need a shower, so I'm not hanging about. Alex are you having one?"

Alex looked at his watch.

"Might as well, Davie's just gone up, so he'll be in the shower already. I'll have the same as Mike."

Steve was still bitter about losing, but Cavendish had been decent company on the way round. His parting comment had touched a nerve though. Steve had thought about it as he'd put his clubs away. What was it he'd said? It was nice to share, that was it. Share what? Trophies or wives? Surely Lucy wouldn't sink that low. The whole bloody issue was really starting to get under his skin.

Mike raised his glass.

"Well boys, here's to a good night, let's hope we all survive the bouncing boobie ball this evening. I'll tell you what; I plan to get really hammered to lead me well away from any temptation. Unlucky Alex, you've got Davie to contend with."

Alex shrugged his shoulders and took a swig of his beer. He had no intention of looking after Davie.

"I'm not responsible for him any more now the golf's over, but it'll really piss me off if he starts shagging in our room because you can bet your life he won't be content with having just one of them, sad bastard that he is."

Steve grinned.

"Actually him and Cavendish have got a lot in common, shag anything. You can always go in with Steve, I've got Dunbar's room now. Mike's got the key."

Alex turned to Mike.

"What actually happened to Dunbar anyway, was it family or something?"

Mike glared at Steve for bringing it up.

"Yeh, sort of, he didn't really go into detail. Right I'm off to get a shower and a quick shut eye. Don't let him get too pissed before dinner; he's got a solo to do."

Mike patted Steve on the back. Alex rolled his eyes in exasperation.

"Do I look like Mrs Fucking Doubtfire? What is it with you lot? If he falls asleep he's on his own."

Having got the kids into bed, Lucy phoned Christie. Christie sounded tired.

"Hiya Luce, how's it going?"

"Fine thanks, I haven't been back long but the kids are asleep and I've got a slushy dvd and a big bar of Galaxy, diet starts tomorrow. I don't think I'll be late in my bed."

"Yeh I'm planning an early night, I'm exhausted after last night. The boys are knackered too after their rugby, so early night all round I think. I've got work in the morning, which I could really do without. Have you heard anything from Maggie? I haven't heard a thing."

Lucy sighed.

"No, me neither, we'll just have to wait I suppose. Anyway, she'll be proud of me as I've organised Steve's mum to pick up from nursery tomorrow and I've booked myself in for a haircut and makeover. Maggs was right, I do need a bit of an overhaul."

Christie was pleased.

"And what about your fanny? Hope you're going for a bit of topiary as well; short back and sides, maybe a few highlights?"

Lucy giggled.

"Well yes I have actually, not sure yet how far I'll go, but anything will be an improvement on the privet hedge that's lurking down there at the moment."

"Go on, I dare you, go for the Hollywood, then you can have Steve's name written in Swarovski crystals. What do they call it, a vajazzle?"

"What?" shrieked Lucy, "are you taking the piss? Anyway, I'll text you when I've done the deed."

"Look forward to it. Have fun and I'll speak to you tomorrow."

Lucy hung up, she felt more alive than she had done in the last three years and she had no desire for a drink. Maybe it wasn't too late to rescue the real Lucy after all. Picking up her mobile she sent a text to Steve.

"Ps I love you too."

On the way back to their rooms, Simon had caught up with Cavendish and again was trying to raise the subject of the after dinner party.

"Do you really have to have the lap dancers Myles? It'll only cause trouble and you know it."

Cavendish, his blue eyes sparkling, grinned his usual grin, the one which meant he had no intention of changing any of his plans, especially this one, as he had absolutely no doubt that he was about to put the pussy amongst the proverbial pigeons.

"Look Lewis, if these boys want to play, let them play. If they don't, they can bugger off to bed. Either way they have a choice. It's not all about you, you know, just because you're scared to death of your missus."

Simon stopped as they reached his room.

"It's nothing to do with that, you're just looking to cause trouble, you bloody well know you are."

Cavendish walked off.

"I can't help it if I like a bit of mischief. Come on man, loosen up for Christ's sake, it's a boys trip not a frigging Saga holiday."

A beeping horn signalled the arrival of her taxi and Tracey gave herself one last look in the hall mirror. Pursing her lips, she wondered whether the lipstick was too red. It wasn't her usual colour, she was maybe too pale to carry it off. Maybe she should put her hair up for a little more sophistication. Her mobile signalled a text. Simon. For a brief second she wondered what on earth she was doing, a married, forty year old woman intentionally dressed like an upmarket hooker, but before she could change her mind, she grabbed her bag, slammed the door, and headed for the taxi.

Chapter 24

The kitchen was warm from the oven, and Vic realised as he laid the table that he was tired. He'd forgotten what it was like to have to think about anyone other than himself, and the worry of Sophie's situation was obviously taking more out of him than he realised. It was good having company for dinner though; he hoped she'd actually eat something this evening. The potatoes were just about ready when Sophie walked into the kitchen.

"How's the headache love, are you feeling any better? Can you manage a spot of dinner, just a roast chicken and a bit of veg?"

Sophie didn't respond but instead held out the plastic tester. Vic looked blank.

"Do you know what this is Dad?" she asked quietly. Vic didn't answer. He felt confused.

"It's a pregnancy tester Dad and the blue lines on it mean I'm pregnant, I'm actually bloody pregnant. I thought I was feeling sick with all the worry, but I'm pregnant!"

"Are you sure love? I mean after all this time."

"Well it says in the leaflet it can be wrong if there's only one line, but not if there's two, I can't believe it myself, it just seems impossible. Poor Andy, he won't know what's hit him."

As the realisation dawned, Vic smiled.

"Well bugger me," he said as he walked over and took her in his arms, "just goes to show you never know what's round the corner. And there's poor old Andy, totally oblivious, poor sod. Are you waiting till he gets back to tell him?"

Sophie laughed.

"Yep, what do you think I should give him first, the good news or bad news?"

"Poor bugger," laughed Vic. "He has no idea what he's coming home to."

Simon tried phoning the home phone. Where the hell was she? He hadn't heard from her since yesterday. He tried texting Max, maybe he knew where his mother was. Simon threw the phone on the bed and with little enthusiasm ran the shower. Well at least he wouldn't be fined for clearing off after dinner; although it was probably better he stayed to make sure things didn't get out of hand. In the shower, he wondered what Tracey was up to. Maybe she was sulking because he hadn't called her earlier or she could just be out with Sophie. That shouldn't stop her texting though. As he dried himself off, his mobile beeped. The text was from Max.

"Spoke mum pm, sed goin out on raz. Chill dude"

Thanks mate, Simon muttered to himself. Thanks for bloody nothing.

"Can I get you a drink darling, a G and T or something else?" Maggie opened the door of the mini bar and looked inside.

"If you want a proper G and T I could phone room service, we need to think about ordering dinner anyway. Do you want to look at the menu?"

She was still finding the silence unnerving. Callum was sitting on the balcony, he'd hardly said a word apart from saying he was sorry. He was refusing to talk about work, refusing, in fact, to talk about anything and Maggie was beginning to feel helpless, and now, slightly irritable. Simon was right, he was obviously suffering from some sort of breakdown and getting him help as soon as possible was the only option. Getting no response, she poured two gin and tonics and took one out onto the balcony. Briefly she wondered whether gin, a balcony and a depressed husband were a bad combination but really she had no idea what else to do. Callum muttered his thanks as she placed the drink on the table beside him, he still couldn't look at her.

"Here, have a look at the menu, see if there's anything on it you fancy. The sea bream looks nice."

Callum took the menu but made no attempt to give it any attention. Taking a seat beside him, Maggie took her mobile out of her pocket and sent a text to Christie asking her to investigate flights back. The sooner they got help the better. Any form of conversation, even by text, was welcome and she hoped that Christie would get back to her soon. As she looked over at Callum, she could see that he wasn't going to make a decision. Her patience was starting to wear thin. Taking the menu from his hand she walked over to the phone.

"I'll order for you then, whether you eat it or not is up to you."

Maggie ordered two sea bass then picking up the magazine that Christie had bought her, returned to her seat on the balcony. It was getting dark, but the air was still balmy and fragrant with the scent of jasmine. In any other situation the evening would be perfect. She jumped as her phone beeped. The text said unknown. Opening it, she realised it was from Cavendish.

"Maggie, Cavendish making contact as requested. Bit tied up tonight but will call tomorrow. Hope everything ok. Call if you need anything."

Gratefully Maggie replied.

"Thank you so much for everything. Things very difficult. Would be good to speak tomorrow if you have 5 mins. Maggie"

The next text was from Christie.

"Hope u ok. Had a quick look at flights, not looking good for tomorrow, may have to be Tuesday. Leave it with me. Call if u need me. Keep chin up. XXX ps Lucy having haircut!!!"

Smiling Maggie texted back.

"Top or bottom??"

"Both" came the reply.

"That's my girl" texted Maggie triumphantly.

Andy took his dinner shirt from the wardrobe and held it up. It was pretty creased but it would have to do. Cavendish would be giving him plenty of stick anyway. He might as well start as he meant to go on, with the first fine for the most slovenly appearance. As he did up the buttons, his mobile beeped. "About bloody time," he said aloud to himself as he opened the text from Sophie.

"Sorry for not being in touch. Staying at Dad's. Have a good time. I love you xxx"

Sitting on the bed Andy sent a reply.

"Thought you'd left me but glad you haven't. Sorry for being such an idiot. Don't worry, we'll get through this I promise. Try and call you tomorrow. Love you too xxx ps we won!"

Getting out of the taxi, Tracey realised that she probably wouldn't know many of the other women, but possibly that was a good thing under the circumstances. As she rang the doorbell, shrieks of laughter could be heard from inside. The party already appeared to be in full swing. With her usual enthusiasm, Sarah opened the front door. She looked fantastic in a figure hugging silver dress which showed off her more than ample cleavage and her platinum blonde hair was piled up dramatically. The term goddess sprang to mind. Tracey was beginning to feel like the black widow in comparison.

"Tracey darling, you look absolutely gorgeous, I love your shoes and your skin is just glowing. What's your secret, do tell?"

Without giving her time to answer, Sarah whisked her through to her vast kitchen.

"Come and meet the slappers, you'll love them, so glad you could make it sweetie, I'm so sorry, I can't believe I haven't invited you before."

"Well I invited myself really," Tracey laughed nervously, feeling slightly overwhelmed by Sarah's exuberance.

"Quite right darling, sort of thing I do myself. If you don't ask you don't get."

As they walked into the kitchen, all eyes turned to Tracey. Slappers they certainly were not, every woman in the room looked fabulous.

"Girls, this is Tracey, a fellow abandoned wife with intent. Tracey, I'll let the girls introduce themselves and don't worry, they might look dangerous, but it's all a facade. Champagne?"

Tracey accepted gratefully, but as she took her first mouthful, she had a feeling that she may have made a slight mistake.

Chapter 25

As Steve and Mike walked through the foyer, Avelina smiled at them.

"You look very nice in your kilts, very smart," she said warmly, "and is it true what they say about Scotsmen and kilts?"

Mike grinned at her, "and what would that be young lady?"

Avelina blushed, suddenly wishing she hadn't been so forward. Steve kindly put her out of her misery.

Using his best Sean Connery accent he teased her.

"I'm afraid we can't tell you Monneypenny," he winked, "it's top secret, if we did we'd have to kill you."

She laughed. "I think it must be true then, how funny. Everyone is in the bar at the moment but your room for dinner is ready whenever you are. Have a good evening gentlemen."

Mike thanked her as they walked through to the bar; the bar was busy, most of the guys seemed to have arrived on time. Mike looked around.

"Bloody hell, guess who's not here?" he asked Steve.

"Who?" replied Steve, handing him a beer and glancing around the bar.

"Davie and Alex, bet they've fallen asleep useless tossers. I suppose I'd better phone them, here hold this."

Mike passed his beer to Steve and took out his phone. As he walked back out into the foyer, Steve again looked around. All the boys seemed on good form, the golf had been good despite the hiccups, and they all looked set for a good night. Cavendish, as usual, could be heard above everyone else and Steve watched him as he held court. There was no denying it, he was a good looking bloke; his blond hair and angular features were striking and he exuded confidence. Steve could see why Lucy might find him attractive, despite her protests. He couldn't keep a woman though, thought Steve, with some satisfaction. Despite his obvious charms, they never hung around for long.

"Can you believe they'd both fallen asleep, you'd think they'd have thought to set alarms," said Mike retrieving his beer and taking a well earned swig. "I told them to get their arses down here in five minutes, bloody useless."

Steve finished his beer and ordered another.

"Wonder how Maggie's getting on, have you spoken to her? I suppose I should have but I've been avoiding it."

"Me too, Christie sent a text saying Maggie was finding it a bit difficult and that she was trying to sort out flights, but no more than that. We'll have to get in touch in the morning. Let's not think about it now, I want to have one night of this trip without any bloody hassle. Bloody hell, you knocked that back, here, get another one in while I finish this."

As Steve ordered another beer, Simon joined them.

"Any news on Callum?" he asked quietly. "I presume they're still here?"

Before Mike could answer, Steve jumped in.

"Jeremy Kyle doesn't want to talk about it, he's having a night off," he answered, nodding his head towards Mike, "wants one night on the trip without counselling duties. We're assuming no news is good news and we'll give Maggie a ring in the morning, if we survive tonight that is. I'm not as good at keeping up with it as I used to be and I'm already in trouble, I don't know any of those bloody songs all the way through."

"I wouldn't mind if we didn't have these bloody girls coming," Simon muttered. "Why can't we just get pissed and fall over like we usually do? If Tracey finds out I won't be allowed next time."

Mike laughed.

"I don't think I've ever seen anyone look so shit scared, come on mate, you're bloody forty not four, and it's not as if you're planning a gang bang is it? Davie'll shag for all of us anyway, I wouldn't worry about it, and how do you think Tracey's gonna find out?"

Simon didn't need to answer as Mike and Steve's attention was suddenly taken by the entrance of Davie and Alex. A loud cheer went up as they walked into the bar. How they'd managed to get themselves looking half decent in less than ten minutes, was nothing short of a miracle.

"Well let's give a big boys trip welcome to the star crossed lovers," boomed Cavendish, who as usual, hadn't missed a trick. Thrusting a drink into their hands, he grinned. "First fine of the evening, get these down your necks, come on down in one then twenty press ups."

"You are such an unbelievable wanker," hissed Davie as he handed the drained glass back to Cavendish, "I'll have you back later you bastard."

Cavendish smirked as he counted them both through the press ups.

"And where's Bob the Builder? Here Bob, you can take this drink for looking such a complete mess, has that shirt ever seen an iron?"

Andy as usual took it in good humour.

"I'm a builder mate, why would I need an iron? Cheers boys, thanks for everything."

Cavendish turned to Simon.

"Don't suppose his Mrs was in the mood for ironing before he left," he laughed. Simon turning away didn't reply. Cavendish, obviously irritated, slammed his drink down on the bar.

"Oh for fuck's sake, are you still sulking about tonight?"
Simon stayed silent.

"Oh bugger off will you, why don't I just tuck you into bed

with a cup of cocoa and a nice dvd. How did you turn into such a bloody woman?"

Thankfully, an announcement from the waiter that dinner was about to be served, diffused the situation and Cavendish, striding off, led his fellow men to their fate.

By the time their taxis arrived, Tracey had already consumed far too much champagne and not enough food. The girls were proving to be good fun and with the help of the champagne, music and banter, Tracey was now in the mood for a good night out.

"Can you tell I've got no knickers on?" a stunning redhead called Lara asked her as they were checking their make up in the hall mirror. Turning, she aimed her perfectly rounded backside at Tracey, smoothing down the deep purple halter neck dress over her obviously size 8 frame.

"Well I can't," giggled Tracey, "but then I'm not looking at your arse trying to work it out. Put it this way, it's not obvious. That colour looks fabulous on you by the way."

Lara looked pleased with herself.

"Thanks, we redheads often find our colour palette a bit limiting. So is your husband on the same trip as Tommo, this sleazy golf trip?"

Tracey felt a stab of anger. She had never ever thought of it as a sleazy golf trip, up until now. Obviously some of the other wives knew more than her, and that hurt.

"Yes, I'm afraid so, they're all pretty pathetic, especially the guy in charge, Myles Cavendish. Do you know him?"

Lara grinned. "Do I know Myles Cavendish?" she answered mischievously, "three quarters of the women in this room know MC, and I'll leave you to guess what MC stands for amongst this lot."

Tracey was taken aback. Was she being serious?

"But I thought all the girls here were married," she asked quietly.

"And your point is?" laughed Lara. "Look don't worry, they haven't all shagged Big Myles. Sarah hasn't for a start, although it wasn't for lack of trying on Myles's part. I think he's got a thing about married women."

"And do any of their husbands know?"

"Look sweetie, most of our husbands work abroad, I'm sure they're not in every night knitting their Christmas presents. It's harmless fun, that's all. What goes on tour, stays on tour, isn't that what the boys say? What the eye doesn't see, oh you know what I mean. All I can say is, that if your hubby's on a trip with MC, it certainly won't be a dull one, so you might as well enjoy yourself too. Come on, let's get the first taxi and then we get first choice at Randolph's."

"First choice for what?" asked Tracey as she grabbed her handbag.

"The men you idiot, most of the men in there are gorgeous."

Chapter 26

With the boys all assembled in the dining room, Cavendish tapped loudly on one of the glasses to get everyone's attention.

"Seating plan," he bellowed, "is alternate Scotland England, and no sitting next to anyone you've played golf against, gives everyone the opportunity for different chat. Gentlemen, please take your seats."

It took a full five minutes for everyone to sort themselves out into an arrangement that suited Cavendish, but once satisfied, he again called for quiet.

"As you know gentlemen, this is the finale to what has so far been a great anniversary tour, and I would like to thank you all for your attendance and for some great golf. This evening, however, is not a time for speeches and self congratulation for the English team and its victorious captain, it is time for gluttony, depravity and debauchery, all of which many of you have become adept at over the last few years. Dinner will be served in about five minutes, to be followed by some very sophisticated entertainment."

As whistles rang out across the room, Simon glared at Cavendish. Cavendish ignored him but unusually decided against humiliating him in public.

"There will of course be new fines, for which some will be paid for in drink, and others in good honest cash. Simon, you can collect any fineage in cash, and Tommo, you can get the drinks. All cash will go into the kitty which will help pay for the lovely ladies who will be entertaining us later this evening."

"Ok. Fines will be as follows. No swearing or pointing, fine five Euros. You will also all take on the name of your first pet, if you didn't have a pet, use the name of your first girlfriend, pretty much the same thing anyway. Anyone using the wrong name will be fined five Euros. My name, before anyone asks, is Pebbles. And finally, the songs. I will make random selections of songs and the singer throughout the evening. If you make a pigs arse of it, its drinkies time. Any questions? Good. Well cheers boys, and remember, what goes on tour, stays on tour."

Steve was sat between Tommo and Simon. Tommo was always on good form, although a bit like Davie, he was a loose cannon. Anything could happen when Tommo was around. Some of his antics had become the stuff of legend over the years.

"So what's your name pal?" asked Steve, pouring them all a glass of wine. "I'm trying to think of my first pet, I think it was a rabbit, but I think we ate it, not sure if it had a name. I think I had a mouse called Tufty."

"Well Tufty it is then," laughed Tommo. "I didn't have a pet but my mum had a budgie called Clint after Clint Eastwood, will that do?"

Even Simon managed to crack a smile. "We had a cat called Winifred, how boring is that?"

Tommo turned to Rex and shook his hand.

"Tufty, pleased to meet you."

"Olga, pleased to meet you too, Davie's name's hilarious, its Willy, how appropriate is that? I'll never remember all these. Cavendish will though, he's got a photographic memory."

Tommo held out his hand.

"Unfortunately Olga, that's your first fine. Our illustrious tour leader is now called Pebbles!"

Randolph's was crowded but Tracey, Lara and Virginia managed to find a table near the bar. Lara was right, the place was indeed full of gorgeous men, but with the champagne high wearing off, Tracey was beginning to feel a bit out of her depth. It was a long time since she'd put herself in this position, certainly not since she'd been married. What disturbed her the most, was the obvious thrill she was getting from the interest already being shown in the three of them from several quarters. What the hell she was going to say if anyone started to chat her up, God only knew.

"I told you the men in here were gorgeous," laughed Lara triumphantly. "I'm glad we got here first before Sarah and that ample cleavage of hers. Tracey what do you think? That guy over there, pink shirt, grey tie, gorgeous. Let's have a couple of bets on his name and what he does for a living."

As Tracey looked over, Mr Gorgeous turned and caught her eye. Blushing and embarrassed, she looked away. He was with a couple of other guys, both of them pretty attractive, and it was obvious that they were discussing the three women who had just walked in. Tracey wondered if they were married, whether any of them had a wife like her tucked away safely at home. But she wasn't though, was she? She wasn't tucked away safely at home; she was out participating in this very dangerous game, hoping to be chatted up by someone who could be someone else's husband.

Virginia was first to place her bet. A tall, olive skinned brunette, her husband was on business in New York and she'd made no bones about the fact that she was game for some extra-curricular activities.

"My guess is that his name's Matt and he's a pilot," she said seriously, "and I don't think he's married."

Tracey and Lara stared at Matt, who was fortunately in conversation with the other guys.

"Oh I don't know," replied Lara, "I think he looks like a Richard, but not sure what he does. I would say he runs his own business, something in property. I've actually no idea, I'm never any good at this game, I'm always so wrong. I don't think he's married either. What do you think Tracey, your turn?"

Tracey also had no idea and was reluctant to catch his eye

again. She took another sip of her champagne.

"I think he's called Mark, and he's a dentist, and he's married."

"Why do you think he's married?" asked Lara. "I can't see a wedding ring."

"Why wouldn't he be, all the best looking ones are aren't they, married or gay? To be honest, I have no idea either, I just wanted to be different. So how does this work then, how do we find out who's right? Please don't tell me you go and ask them?"

Virginia laughed and poured more champagne.

"Don't worry we won't need to. Give them ten minutes and they'll be over, trust me. They'll be discussing tactics right now, look, they're all having a little discussion now, watch, they'll look over anytime now, oh there we go, not very subtle. I wonder what the opening line will be."

Lara leaned forward and said in a deep husky voice.

"Shall we chat or shall we carry on flirting from a distance?" That's what this American guy said to me last time I was in here. Don't you just love the bullshit men come out with?"

Tracey laughed.

"It can't be easy though can it, knowing your putting yourself up for rejection every time you ask someone if they want a drink."

"I totally agree. The stupid thing is, we know what they want, and they know what they want, but they can't win either way," replied Lara. "If they try and come out with something clever, we think they're talking shit, but if they came straight out with it and said can I buy you a drink and hopefully that'll lead to a shag, we'd give them a good slap."

Virginia stopped her.

"Well we're about to find out, here they come."

"Good evening ladies. My friends and I were just wondering if you would like to join us for a drink. I see you're drinking champagne, can I order another bottle?"

150

He was indeed extremely handsome and Tracey was mortified that he appeared to be addressing the question to her. To save her blushes, Lara was quick to reply.

"That would be lovely, the champagne is excellent. I'm Lara by the way, and this is Virginia and Tracey."

"Well, delighted to meet you all, my name's Simon. Let me organise a bigger table and more champagne and we can all get to know each other."

As Lara and Virginia swooned, Tracey was suddenly guilt ridden. Of all the bloody names in the world he had to be called Simon. Another Simon, probably someone else's Simon. Would her Simon hang around in bars chatting up random women? She knew he wouldn't, but right now he probably had his face buried in some slappers tits, and with that thought satisfying her that he had started it, she gratefully accepted another glass of champagne.

Cavendish was on good form, the songs were proving a challenge and once again he was enjoying being able to force alcohol down everyone else's throat apart from his own. Simon was the only one who'd managed to avoid the fine, having learnt every word of Copacabana. Winifred bloody well suited him as a name; he was behaving like an old woman and really starting to piss him off. The last thing Cavendish wanted was for Simon to be sober when the girls arrived. There wasn't an immoral bone in the guy's body. He was a great friend, but tonight of all nights, Cavendish really wanted him out of the way.

Chapter 27

Sophie handed Vic a mug of tea and sat beside him on the sofa. Vic had sat with her earlier and worked through the details of her debts. Together they'd outlined the facts and phoned some of the credit card companies, who had surprisingly been very helpful, and Sophie felt as though a very large weight had been lifted just by owning up to and sharing her problem. But she still had to face Andy, and even though she had the news of the pregnancy, she wasn't really sure how he was going to take it. The thing was, she'd never really discussed the issue of being childless with him. He'd hugged her and comforted her and said the right things each time the IVF had failed, but really that was as far as it went. She didn't really know what he thought. It had always been about what she wanted. Her biggest fear was that he wouldn't be prepared for such a huge change, especially with their financial situation now being so precarious. Would he really want to be a father now?

"What you thinking love? You worrying about what you're going to say to Andy?"

"Mmm," replied Sophie, "I just don't know what he's going to say. What if he's not pleased about the baby, I don't think I could bear it."

Vic took her hand and squeezed it gently.

"Aah he's a good bloke your Andy, a really good bloke, it'll be fine love."

"I hope so Dad, I'm beginning to wonder if I really know him at all; I don't think he knows me that's for sure. We've been living alongside each other for years, but if I'm honest, I don't think we're really that close. I don't know what it is; we just don't really discuss things. I really don't know how he's going to take any of this. Did you discuss things with Mum?"

"What sort of things?"

Sophie shrugged her shoulders.

"Oh I don't know, things, you know life. Did you ever discuss what you both wanted from your lives? Did you both have the same plan for the future? The sort of things that couples should discuss."

Vic remained silent for a few moments before answering quietly.

"No, I don't think we did love. We just trundled along like most couples do. I don't think I ever asked your mum what she wanted and she never asked me. I just assumed she was happy, she never said she wasn't. That's the way it was for our generation. I don't know why I never asked, but then your mum never complained. To be honest, it never crossed my mind."

Sophie felt guilty. Vic was obviously finding the subject upsetting.

"Sorry Dad, I shouldn't have asked, but I don't think much has changed. Me and Andy never talk about anything, well anything important, in fact, I have no idea what we do talk about. We just seem to go along parallel lines, never meeting in the middle."

Vic squeezed her hand again.

"Well you'll have to meet in the middle on this one love."

Sophie sighed, that's what she was worried about, for as far as she was concerned, it was looking likely to be more of a head on collision.

Maggie was starting to despair. Callum had probably uttered about five words to her this evening and only because he'd had to. They were now lying in the darkness in one of the twin rooms, Callum opting for a single bed in order to distance himself as

153

much as possible, his back pointedly facing towards her. Maggie looked at the digital clock beside the bed. It was only eleven and she couldn't sleep. Getting out of bed, she put on a dressing gown and shutting the door behind her, walked to the fridge in the small kitchenette and helped herself to a whisky. Whisky wasn't her usual drink, but her mother had sworn by its magical powers in times of crisis. Adding a couple of ice cubes and a dash of water, she took a sip and instantly felt the warmth of the liquid strangely comforting. It was too late to phone anyone. Christie and Lucy would be asleep and it wouldn't be fair to wake them after all they'd already done for her, and the men would be enjoying their dinner and certainly wouldn't be accepting calls. She hoped Cavendish would contact her in the morning, just for a bit of support and conversation. Simon had been nice too. It had been reassuring having a doctor around. Hopefully she could speak to him as well, as to be honest, she was getting a little uneasy about travelling alone with Callum. Standing on the balcony, Maggie took another mouthful of whisky and breathed in the scented summer air. How had her life suddenly taken such an unexpected turn and how the hell had she, Maggie Dunbar, not seen it coming? Was she strong enough to deal with this? She had to. She knew that, for the sake of the girls, she had to hold it together. Whether she could save her marriage she had no idea, but for the very first time in her life, the formidable Maggie Dunbar realised that she would need to ask for help.

"Right Tufty, you're on," shouted Cavendish across the ever increasing noise. "Lonely Goatherd. Go on, up on the table. Willy help him up."

"Arsehole," hissed Steve, not giving a toss about the fine. "I knew he was saving the worst one for me."

Davie was well and truly plastered, and slapping him on the back, encouraged him up onto one of the chairs. The rest of the boys started clapping and an ohm pa pa rhythm was soon established, with most of them bending their knees in time, holding onto imaginary lederhosen straps. Steve had no idea of the words apart from the first line.

"High on a hill lived a lonely goatherd," he bellowed, the boys joining in with the yodelling.

"La la la la something about a maid heard, le oh do ley whoo whoo."

Cat calls and laughter rang out around the room as remnants of food were fired at Steve from all angles.

"Crap, Tufty, absolutely crap, no one has only managed two lines this evening or one and a half to be precise. St Winifred's School Choir over there managed the whole song. Clint, double fineage, three flaming sambuccas, he deserves everything he gets."

Steve struggled down from the chair and flopped down onto another, waiting for his punishment. He couldn't care less about the fines, it had been a great night and he was ready for his bed. Hopefully, the slammers would send him smoothly into oblivion.

Sitting themselves down at the new table offered by gorgeous Simon, Tracey, Lara and Virginia were introduced to the friends.

"Ladies this is Geoff, and this reprobate here is Rick, don't worry I'll protect you from him."

"Oh let's hope not," giggled Virginia. Tracey was mortified. Had the woman no shame?

The three men smiled. Simon poured the champagne.

"Cheers, nice to meet you," he said smoothly.

Lara took a mouthful and then playfully leaned forward, allowing Simon a clear view of her polished cleavage.

"So Simon, we've been having a little wager. We got your name wrong, although Richard was one of the names and the handsome reprobate here is called Rick, so we were close, but we had a little side bet on what you did for a living. So you can now put us out of our misery and tell us what you do and don't you dare go making anything up."

Simon obviously found this very amusing as raising his eyebrows he grinned mischievously.

"So what did you come up with? I'm intrigued as to what category you placed me in."

"Well," interrupted Virginia, "I thought you were a pilot, Lara thought you were a property person, running your own business or something, she didn't really know actually, and the lovely, sweet Tracey here thought you were a dentist."

Rick and Geoff laughed.

"How respectable, why on earth would you put me as a dentist?" Simon smiled looking at Tracey.

Tracey blushed again under his gaze. She had no idea why she'd put him as a bloody dentist.

"I don't know, it was as good a guess as any. I could just as easily have said a builder, I didn't really think about it. I thought you looked quite respectable."

"Oh I adore builders," sighed Virginia, "there's something incredibly sexual about manual workers, please tell me you're a builder, are any of you builders?"

Simon shook his head.

"Sorry to disappoint you Virginia, no builders I'm afraid. Although I do get involved with plenty of tools on a daily basis."

Rick snorted. "In a manner of speaking Lara, you weren't too far out on the owning a business and I suppose he's a bit like a dentist, he gets to look at plenty of cavities."

Rick winked at Simon. The three girls looked curious.

"So what business are you in?" asked Tracey.

Simon leant back and placed his arm arrogantly on the back of his chair.

"Porn," he grinned, once again looking at Tracey. "I produce porn. Hardly respectable Tracey I'm afraid, but it bloody pays well."

Chapter 28

By the time the entertainment arrived, most of the boys were pretty well gone, and as the girls walked into the room, they were met with drunken cheers from those who could still focus. Cavendish was the exception; having as usual, carefully controlled his own alcohol intake as well as everyone else's apart from Simon's. Simon was still proving to be a fly in the ointment. As the music started, Cavendish watched him as the girls began their parade around the now dimly lit room. Arms folded, the look on his face said it all and Cavendish realised that his staying was designed purely to piss him off. Simon knew that if he left, life would be a lot easier for Cavendish.

Simon looked around the room. The boys were undoubtedly pissed and most of them were now looking bemused and a little awkward as they resigned themselves to possible further humiliation at the hands of Cavendish's hookers. The girls were all extremely attractive, but Simon was disturbed by how young some of them looked. He wondered whose daughters they were and whether anyone missed them or cared about them. How the hell had they had got themselves tied up in this shit?

Davie Sutherland, as expected, was the first to get involved, offering absolutely no resistance to one of the girls as she sat astride his lap. Loosening his tie, she removed it and tied it seductively around her bare, slim, suntanned waist. Gyrating herself on Davie's lap, she slowly unbuttoned his shirt and removing it, cast it to the floor. Davie needed little encouragement. Unhooking her black sequinned bra, he tossed it across the room and buried his face in her breasts, while allowing one of the other girls to remove the tie and tie it loosely around his neck. The girls were quick, and with encouragement from the rest of the room, Davie was soon on his hands and knees being led around the room like an obedient dog. Tommo, not wanting to miss out, grabbed one of the other girls and lay back on the floor, watching as the young brunette stood astride him and removed what little clothing she had on. Tommo squealed in delight as she slowly and seductively lowered herself onto his face.

Steve was almost asleep, the slammers having done a pretty good job.

"Are you not enjoying yourself?" said a soft voice in his ear. "Wake up, you're missing the party."

Opening one eye, he was aware of a hand running lightly up the inside of his thigh and a gentle nip on his earlobe. Disorientated, he sat up and realising where he was, removed the girls hand from under his kilt.

"Sorry, no offence, you're very nice but I'm not interested," he slurred, his mouth dry.

Despite the alcohol, Steve took in the scene around him. He hadn't expected things to go this far, even Alex seemed to have been lured to the dark side. Nearly everyone in the room was half naked apart from Cavendish. Mike and Simon were the only ones who seemed to have slipped away. Turning back to the girl sitting beside him, he once again started to apologise.

"Sorry, I'm very drunk; I'm just going to head off to my bed."

"Shall I come with you?" she asked sweetly, "help you get to sleep. Look I have your key."

Simon made a grab for her hand but she was quick and she held the key behind her back.

"How did you get that?"

"It was in your bag," she said, pointing to his sporran.

"Well I'd like it back please. Look I'm married, I'm not interested."

The girl smiled. "Well let's pretend I'm going with you, I would like to get out of here too. I'll give you your key back when I get to the door. Here, I've got you a soft drink, drink up and then we'll go."

Steve sighed, he could do without this but gratefully he took the coke on offer.

"Fine, help me up then."

As Steve stumbled towards the door aided by Catalina, Cavendish smiled with satisfaction.

"Result," he shouted out raising his arms to the heavens, "what a fucking result."

"Porn!" giggled Virginia, the only one of the three women able to speak. "How delicious. You don't look like a porn star though, shouldn't you have a moustache and lots of bling."

"If he was living in the seventies," laughed Lara. "When was the last time you watched a porn film?"

Simon interrupted.

"Sorry girls, I don't act, I produce. My company distributes, most of it's done online nowadays, easy money. Rick here has an online betting business and Geoff here prats about with racehorses. Doesn't make any of us very respectable really, are you disappointed in us Tracey?"

Tracey returned his gaze. She could tell he thought her prudish.

"You obviously fulfil a need," she answered, taking another mouthful of champagne. Simon smiled and leaned towards her. Running his finger down her bare arm he blew gently into her ear.

"And what about you, do you have any needs?" he whispered softly. "I'm very good at supply and demand."

"Don't look round now, but isn't that Simon Lewis's wife, she's on the table in the corner, nearest to us, three couples.

Look, it's definitely her, I remember her from the staff party."

Susie Jamieson had worked with Simon for the past three years, and her unfulfilled desire for his attention was made all the worse by his obvious disinterest in anyone other than his wife. Jules, her long suffering flatmate, knew every detail of Simon's life, and despite all the warnings, Susie had refused to let go of the belief that one day Simon would wake up and realise that they were, in fact, meant for each other and that he'd been married to the wrong woman for the past fifteen years.

"Simon's away this weekend, he's gone to Portugal on a golf trip," she whispered.

"Yes, I know, you told me. So what are you trying to suggest?" Jules replied, knowing exactly where Susie was going with this one.

"Well they all look very cosy don't they, look at the way the guy in the pink shirt's looking at her. Where's my phone?"

Jules was horrified.

"What are you doing?"

"Taking a photo, I'm sure Simon would love to know what his darling wife gets up to while he's away. Oh that was perfect, just as he kissed her. Well they look more than just good friends to me, look at that!"

Triumphantly Susie showed the photo to Jules.

"Right, give me your phone," Susie said, grabbing Jules's phone off the table. "I'll send this photo to you and you can send it to Simon, he won't know your number."

Jules was furious.

"You can't do that, that's awful Susie, it's so underhand. It'll end in tears, these things always do."

"Yeh, well maybe, but at least they won't be mine this time. Sorry Mrs Simon Lewis, but finally your time is up."

Simon, having deposited Mike in his room, was heading back to the dining room in the hope of saving some of the other lads from themselves before it was too late. As the lift opened, Simon was horrified to find Steve being propped up by Catalina. He recognised her instantly.

"Steve, what are you doing? Are you mad?"

Steve, struggling to hold himself steady, grabbed onto Simon's shoulder.

"Don't worry mate, she's just taking me to my room, I was too pissed to walk."

Catalina smiled innocently.

"I'll take you mate, I've just put Mike to bed."

Steve staggered again.

"Nah, nah, I'm alright. She wants to go home too, don't you sweetheart. I just want my bed. Go back to the party Simon, honestly I'm all right."

Chapter 29

Picking Andy up off the floor in the function room, Simon helped him to find his clothes. Andy had no idea where he was, but the marks on his buttocks were going to take some explaining when he got back. Poor bastard, he was in enough trouble as it was. Cavendish was so bloody thoughtless. Hopefully Sophie would be curtailing her sexual favours for a while and allow him to keep his arse under wraps.

"Come on Bambi, let's get you back to your room. Are you sharing, I can't remember?"

Andy's legs buckled under him and Simon managed to get him to a chair.

"Did you hear what I said? Have you got your key?"

Andy looked up at Simon and mumbled something about his trousers. Simon who was clutching the trousers, fumbled in the back pocket and retrieved the key. There was absolutely no chance of getting him into his clothes. Hopefully, they wouldn't meet anyone on the way back to the room.

"Right come on mate, stand up, you're too bloody heavy, you're gonna have to try and walk. Oh bugger, that's my phone."

Simon sat Andy back down on the chair and took his phone from his pocket. It was a message, but he didn't recognise the number. Opening it, he took a few moments to digest the contents and then silently put the phone away.

"Come on mate, time to go," he said quietly, "I need my bed."

Catalina handed Steve the key and watched him as he tried to insert it into the lock.

"Let me do it," she said persuasively. "You're not doing very well are you?"

Quickly she opened the door and walked inside. Steve was annoyed. He knew he didn't want her here, but he couldn't string two words together. Catalina took his hand.

"Look I'll make sure you're ok and then I'll go, I promise." Walking over to the bed she pulled back the covers and gestured to him to lie down. The room was spinning now. He was beginning to feel nauseous.

"Come on, get yourself into bed before you fall over again and I'll get you another drink."

Taking off his shirt and shoes but leaving his kilt on, Steve lay back on the bed.

"I don't want a drink; I want to go to sleep," he mumbled.

"I'll help you fall asleep," Catalina whispered soothingly, dimming the bedside light, "here let me stroke your head, there now, off to sleep, there's a good boy."

Within two minutes, Steve was snoring. Quickly, Catalina stood up, and reaching inside one of her black boots, pulled out a mobile phone.

"Catalina here, quickly, room 174, I'll leave the door open."

Very gently, Catalina lifted Steve's kilt and folded it up onto his chest. It was true what they said about Scotsmen then. Very quietly, the door opened, and one of the other girls from the function came in and closed the door behind her.

"Have you got the camera?" asked Catalina slightly breathlessly. She was nervous now. Her friend nodded. Climbing onto the bed, Catalina removed her top and sat astride Steve. Lifting his hands carefully, she placed them on her breasts and let her head fall back.

"Quick, take as many as you can," she whispered. "Can you see his face?"

"Yes but you can tell he's asleep, turn his head the other way."

Catalina moved up over Steve and sat just above his face. It would be obvious from his kilt who it was, the photos probably wouldn't go much further than his inbox anyway if he was sensible. Finally Catlina moved down, and taking his limp dick in her hands, began to massage it gently. Even if she could get a slight response it would do the trick. Steve moaned slightly and as she felt him stiffen she lowered her head and took it inside her mouth, just long enough for them to get the final few shots.

Satisfied with their work, Catalina dressed herself, apart from her knickers, and looked at Steve. He was nice, maybe she'd picked the wrong guy. He was, after all, one of the few prepared not to cheat on his wife. That made him a good target though and she needed the cash. If she played this right, she could get herself away from this shit hole of a life before it was all too late. Undoing Steve's sporran, she took out his phone and scrolled through his contacts. She knew his name, where he worked and his e-mail address; she'd got that from a friend of hers who worked at the hotel. This time she was looking for his wife. As expected there weren't many numbers for women and most of them were under a surname. Lucy, what about Lucy? That looked a possibility. Taking down the number, she returned the phone to the bedside table and leaving her knickers lying suggestively on the floor, she and her accomplice let themselves out.

Simon sat down on his bed and took out his phone. It was Tracey all right, she looked stunning. There had to be some mistake though, who was she with? He couldn't see the guys face. And the message?

"While the cat's away..." who would have sent it? How could she do this to him? They were happy, well he thought they were. She'd told him she loved him before he went away. Nothing made sense. He called her number, bloody answer phone. He sent her a text.

"Nice one Tracey, glad to see you're not missing me. Call me if you can drag yourself away, if you want to that is"

Lying down on the bed he closed his eyes, he was shaking. He couldn't get the image out of his head. He just couldn't imagine Tracey with someone else. How the hell could she do this to him? What the fucking hell had he ever done to deserve this?

The arrival of Sarah at Randolph's was timely and Tracey was glad of an excuse to free herself from the attentions of Simon. Gorgeous as he was, she had absolutely no intentions of allowing him to fulfil her needs, the slimy arrogant bastard, and making her excuses, she headed for the ladies. As she sat down on the toilet, her phone beeped. Please don't let it be one of the kids, she sighed, she couldn't handle that right now, especially with the amount of champagne she'd consumed. Rummaging in her bag, she found her phone and looked at the screen. Simon. Well he could bloody well wait; she really didn't want to speak to him right now. He was probably only phoning her because he was feeling guilty. Well he could piss right off; she wasn't going to contact him. She'd bloody well make him sweat until he got home.

Cavendish was pleased with himself. The evening had lived up to his expectations and England had regained the trophy. Bloody marvellous. Davie, Tommo and Rex were out cold on the floor in various states of disarray, somehow he'd have to get them half decent before the staff came in the morning. He had no chance of getting them to their rooms. Simon had been a right pain in the arse though, fussing around like a bloody mother hen, putting the boys to bed before they could be led into any temptation. Not that any of them would have been capable anyway, they were all too pissed. Steve had been the real dark horse though, he wouldn't have put money on that one, the sly old bastard. So much for Mr Happy Families.

Chapter 30

"Right Dad, I'm off to bed," said Sophie, "I'm absolutely exhausted. Are you staying up a bit longer?"

Vic shook his head, yawning.

"No, I'm ready for my bed too, it's been a long day. You need to look after yourself now, plenty of rest. What about work, are you going in tomorrow?"

Sophie looked guilty. She was never usually one to take days off work but she really couldn't face it.

"No, I think I'll call in sick and then try and get an appointment with my doctor, although chances of that are pretty slim, you have to be dead before anyone'll see you these days. Trying to get past those bloody receptionists is like being interrogated by the Gestapo."

Vic laughed, as Sophie took his hand and helped him up out of the sofa.

"Do you want a hot drink to take to bed love? It'll help you sleep," he said kindly.

"That would be nice. I'll go and get the hot water bottles, you get the kettle on. I wonder if Andy's still standing. I hope he hasn't got himself too drunk. He said he thought it would be a bit quieter this year and that they're usually pretty tired after two days of golf. I'm just hoping he'll come back in a good mood."

"Oh I'm sure he will love, I keep telling you, he's a good bloke, your Andy."

By the time Tracey returned from the toilets, Sarah and the rest of the girls had arrived and were wasting no time in catching up on the introductions. Virginia couldn't wait to fill in all the details.

"Right girls, this is Simon, isn't he absolutely gorgeous, and this is Geoff, strong silent type, and this naughty little Irishman here is Rick. He has such an adorable accent, he could read out the bloody Ten Commandments and you'd wet your knickers."

Rick smiled as Virginia continued.

"And you'll never guess what Simon does? Go on, have a guess, you'll love it."

As the girls came up with various suggestions, Simon laughed. He was very good looking, thought Tracey, but also extremely dangerous. It was incredible though, how dangerous men could be so attractive. Maybe it was the risk, or more than likely the challenge of trying to be the only woman able to tame them. Women were so stupidly competitive. Cavendish was another fine example of a dangerous man, or though sadly for Cavendish, Tracey was convinced that he actually longed to find the right woman. He just didn't know how to go about it, poor sod.

"Porn," squealed Virginia excitedly, "he makes porn, how amazing is that?"

With the excitement of the revelation over, some semblance of normal conversation resumed and Simon didn't hang about in continuing his pursuit of Tracey. Offering her another glass of champagne, he joined her at the now very crowded bar.

"So I'm guessing you're married," he asked, acknowledging the wedding ring. "Where's the lucky man this evening? I certainly wouldn't be leaving you alone for very long."

Tracey wasn't having any of it, the champagne now fuelling her confidence.

"There's no need to come out with such crap, you're wasting your time trying to seduce me. I'm just here for a night out with the girls because my husband's away for the weekend. I'm not

167

here looking for a shag so you may want to try elsewhere."

Simon smiled, and resting his arm on the bar, looked her up and down admiringly.

"So why are you dressed like that then?"

"Like what?" Tracey answered indignantly.

"Like you're on the pull. If you didn't want to be chatted up you could have worn a pair of jeans and wellies, although you'd probably still look gorgeous. Come on, women dress themselves up to be chatted up, admit it; you didn't put the shoes and lipstick on for your friends. Where's your husband anyway, is he away on business?"

Tracey felt uncomfortable. He was right. She had dressed provocatively and now she felt stupid.

"He's away on a golf trip with some friends, he goes every year."

"Oh the good old boys trip," he smiled knowingly.

"And what's that supposed to mean? It's a golf trip. They play golf and have a few drinks."

Tracey realised that she was sounding ridiculous, and why the hell she was trying to defend him now, when the very reason she was here, was that she had every suspicion that at this very moment he was probably up to his armpits in the exotic delights of some foreign tart.

"Of course they do sweetheart," he replied patronisingly, "what else could they possibly get up to?"

"I don't know, you tell me, you're a bloke and in your game you probably have a better idea than most. How did you get into it anyway? To be honest you don't look like a porn baron."

Simon leaned forward.

"Now that's a very long story. Why don't we slip away and get a bite to eat somewhere a little quieter and I'll reveal all. I know a great little Italian place, two minute walk from here."

Tracey shook her head.

"No thanks. Look I might be pissed off with my husband,

but I have no intention of having a fling with anyone, let alone some king of porn who I've just met in a bar. Give me some credit."

Simon didn't smile but took her hand.

"Look, I don't have you down as a quick shag, I'm offering to take you for a bite to eat because I'm hungry and I think you, like me, have had enough of this place. I'd also enjoy your company. We can eat, then I'll order you a taxi home and you'll never have to see me again, promise."

Tracey looked around the bar. He was right, she'd had enough and the thought of something to eat was appealing, although it was just past midnight.

"Will the restaurant still be open, isn't it a bit late?"

"This place is always open. Come on you'll love it."

"Just food, nothing else."

"Nothing else. I told you, I promise and as a Queen's Scout I don't break my promises."

Tracey laughed.

"How the hell did a Queen's Scout get into the porn business?"

"Say yes and I'll tell you over dinner."

With the help of a hefty tip, Cavendish and two of the hotel waiters had managed to get all of the boys back to their rooms. It had been a great night, one of the best as far as he was concerned. He had purposefully not organised anything for tomorrow, he didn't expect to see many of them at breakfast. Golf was available for anyone fit enough, but most of the guys would probably opt for a day by the pool. Whatever, his job was done, they could organise themselves. Remembering he had promised to speak to Maggie in the morning, he made a note in his diary and turned off the light. He hoped the conversation wouldn't get too heavy. Compassion wasn't his middle name.

The ladies' toilet at Randolph's was alive with champagne fuelled excitement and Tracey was the centre of attention. Virginia couldn't contain herself.

"Oh my God Tracey, he is *so* gorgeous, I couldn't care less if he's a porn star, he's just so shaggable. Did you look at his lips, and I just love that floppy messed up hair look. I am so absolutely bloody jealous."

In between rearranging her cleavage and retouching her lipstick, Sarah joined in.

"I couldn't take my eyes off his arse actually, although I have to say, that naughty little Irishman has rather taken my fancy. Rick isn't it? You're right Virginia, it's the accent, does it for me every time. What did he say he did again? Gambling wasn't it? So dangerous, but hey, what the hell."

Sarah pursed her lips and replacing the lipstick in her handbag, turned to Tracey.

"So where's he taking you, you sly little devil. Must say I would never have had you down as a player, but I knew you'd pull, you're so annoyingly gorgeous, and I bet you haven't even had any work done. It's really not fair. These bad boys cost Tommo a fortune, but he says it was worth every penny."

Trying to avoid staring at Sarah's ample breasts, Tracey looked away embarrassed.

"Honestly I'm not a player," she sighed, trying not to sound too pious, "I've never done anything like this at all since I've been married and I'm not about to, I'm just going for dinner that's all, mainly because I'm hungry, and then he's getting me a taxi home, he's promised."

"And you believe that?" giggled Virginia. "Believe me sweetie he has absolutely no intention of getting you a taxi home. God I would be so disappointed if he got me a taxi, seriously if you don't want him I'll have him."

Tracey laughed and headed towards the door.

"Well I think I'm doing you all a favour and saving you from yourselves, and as I'm now absolutely starving, I'm off to get some food. Sorry to be a lightweight, but I can promise you all, that I will definitely be going home in a taxi and sleeping in my own bed."

As Tracey and the rest of the girls headed back into the bar, Susie Jamieson grabbed Jules' arm. Jules groaned and held her head in her hands.

"Look," whispered Susie excitedly, "she's going back to him, she's picking up her coat and he definitely looks as though he's going with her."

Jules was exasperated. "They're probably just old friends, for God's sake Susie, will you please get a grip, you're starting to sound completely deranged. Look there's a whole group of them, just stop it will you. Simon's married and you can't have him, just find someone else, preferably someone who's single."

Susie wasn't listening. She was fascinated by Tracey and fired up with the realisation that finally, there was a glimmer of hope. Draining her drink, she reached to the back of her chair for her coat.

"Come on, get your jacket on, we're going."

"Going where?" Jules answered, despite already realising just what Susie had in mind.

"Where do you think, they're definitely up to something and I owe it to Simon to tell him the truth. Come on hurry up, before we lose them."

Simon caught Tracey's eye as she picked up her coat, and

standing up, he smoothed back his hair and smiled.

"Ok then, shall we get some food? It's not raining and the restaurant's only five minutes away, so if you don't mind we could walk?"

Tracey felt suddenly more confident.

"I think my shoes will manage a five minute walk, and remember sunshine, dinner only, please don't think you'll win me over, because believe me you won't. You promised me a taxi home don't forget."

Simon looked at her and sighed, she really was very attractive.

"Unfortunately, I do remember, and as I told you before, I do actually keep my promises. Come on let's go."

As Tracey said her goodbyes, Sarah winked and tapped her nose.

"Have fun Trace, and remember, what goes on tour, stays on tour, your secret's safe with me."

Tracey shook her head. "I told you, it's just dinner, which is probably more than can be said for my husband this evening. Thanks for letting me join in Sarah, it's been fun, and stay away from that Irishman for God's sake, he's definitely trouble."

"Oh I bloody hope so," giggled Sarah, "I'll let you know tomorrow."

Having tried again to sleep, Maggie lay awake in the darkness listening to Callum's slow breathing. She'd given him a couple of sleeping tablets which she'd found in her handbag and finally they appeared to have taken effect. The darkness, however, felt claustrophobic and flinging back the covers she once again got out of bed. She desperately needed to talk to Callum, to try to make sense of everything. She needed to know how bad things were so that she could make a start on sorting things out. If they could be sorted out. She thought of the girls. How was she going to tell them that their whole world could be about to fall apart. Maggie Dunbar was not used to uncertainty. Not being in control was an alien world.

Out on the balcony, the air was warm but fresh and in the streets below, the restaurants and bars were still very much alive. The apartment, in contrast, was heavy and oppressive. Agitated, and with a sudden realisation that she needed to get out, she threw on some clothes, picked up her bag and headed for the elevator.

Maggie wasn't the only one who couldn't sleep. Simon was desperate. Sober and alone in his room, he stared at the images on his mobile. Who on earth, he wondered, had sent them. His stomach churned. When was the last time he had seen her in red lipstick. No wonder she hadn't wanted to see Sophie. He was stunned. Never, ever, in their life together had he had any cause not to trust her? But it was definitely her in the photo, and who the hell was he? He looked at the time. It would be one-fifteen in the morning back home. With shaking hands he called her mobile. No answer. He called home, maybe she was asleep. The answer phone clicked in. If she was home she would have answered, in case it was the kids. He called her mobile again and waited for voicemail.

"Hello, it's your husband here although it appears that you've forgotten that you have one. Just wondering why you've never worn that lipstick for me. You're obviously still out as I've tried the house but it looks like we need to talk. Can't believe you've done this Trace, I really thought everything was great. Call me please, whatever time it is I need to speak to you."

Simon hung up and staring again at the image of his wife walking arm in arm with another man, he began to cry.

Stepping out of the hotel foyer into the street, Maggie felt a surge of relief. She felt uneasy walking alone in a strange town late at night, but the anonymity was liberating. The restaurants were still busy and the steady stream of ambling pedestrians quickly distracted her from her troubled thoughts. She wondered whether anyone noticed her and whether they thought her strange. Catching her reflection in a shop window, she smoothed down her hair and looked at herself critically. She hoped she didn't look like a hooker. She kept walking. She wasn't ready to face the silence of the hotel room and the unknown shadow of the man that had become her husband. She felt more comfortable out here within the lights and buzz of the street. She stopped outside a lively cafe bar. Most of the clientele looked young. They would only be interested in themselves. They wouldn't notice her.

"Excuse me, are you still serving?" she asked a waiter busily clearing away glasses from the tables outside.

"Of course Madam, you would like to sit inside or outside?" he replied graciously.

"Oh outside I think, it's a little quieter. Can I take this one?"

The waiter smiled. "No problem, you would like just a drink or coffee?"

Maggie realised she was hungry."Can I get a little something to eat or is it too late?"

"No problem, I will bring you the menu, please sit I will be two minutes."

Maggie sank down into one of the cushioned chairs, she was

tired now. The waiter was quick and placing some nuts on the table in front of her, he handed her the menu.

"You are very hungry or you just want small snack?" he asked.

Maggie smiled. "To be honest I don't really know, I don't even know what time it is? I am actually quite hungry. What do you suggest?"

The waiter pointed to the menu.

"Maybe you like this one, a selection of small dishes, you can try different things. They not too big, good for night time. Not give you big tummy," he said patting his stomach.

Maggie laughed and handed back the menu.

"Well that sounds just perfect and a large glass of white wine please. Thank you."

As the waiter disappeared, Maggie sank back into her chair and closed her eyes. At this moment, her old life seemed a million miles away, how quickly things could change. Nothing, she suddenly realised, was guaranteed. Was anyone or anything ever what it seemed?

"Maggie, is that you?"

Startled, Maggie opened her eyes and took a few seconds to focus.

"Oh my God Myles, what the bloody hell are you doing here?"

As Tracey and Simon walked into the restaurant, the elderly, moustached waiter bustled over.

"Good evening sir, nice to see you again," he smiled at Tracey. "A nice quiet table for two sir or will there be more of you?"

"Just the two of us Carlos, thank you. Do you have a table in one of the alcoves?"

"Of course sir. Madam may I take your coat?"

Tracey was suddenly extremely self conscious. She wondered

whether he had noticed her wedding ring, she felt guilty and slightly angry with herself. The waiter smiled at her as he took her coat and ushered them to their table.

"Thank you Carlos. Could you get us a bottle of champagne please."

Tracey stopped him.

"No please not for me, I think I've had enough champagne, I really just need to eat."

"Are you sure? The champagne here is excellent; please let me treat you before I send you out of my life forever. It's the least you can do."

Tracey shook her head. She had to hand it to him;he was smooth, too smooth. She needed to be careful.

"Ok, if you want to waste your money, because I'll only have one more glass. It's up to you."

"Thank you Carlos, champagne please."

Tracey looked around the restaurant. It was elegant and obviously expensive.

"I hope the waiter doesn't think I'm one of your porn stars?"

Simon looked indignant.

"I don't date porn stars, why would I want to do that?"

"You men are such hypocrites. It's all right to use them to make money but you wouldn't take them out. Do you actually view them as human at all?"

"They don't have to do what they do; they do it out of choice. Believe me, there isn't a shortage."

Tracey shook her head; she had seen some of the porn on offer these days.

"I just don't believe that, some of these women must be desperate to do what they do. Why would any self respecting woman want to spend her life having some revolting guys dick shoved down their throat, because that's all porn is these days, I've seen it and most of it is vile. Why would you want to be part of that?"

Simon leant back in his chair as Carlos brought the champagne and poured two glasses.

"Well my very nice bank balance tells me that I am supplying a demand in our very screwed up society. There's a demand for fantasy. You're right, most self respecting women like yourself wouldn't go there but there are plenty that will, for whatever reason. It pays better than Tesco's and it's usually all over in half an hour. I can introduce you to a couple of girls if you like and let them speak for themselves."

Tracey took a sip of the champagne. It was good but she was determined to stick to one glass.

"No thanks, but I still don't believe they enjoy it, how could they?"

"I didn't say they enjoyed it, I said they had a choice. I'm sure stacking shelves in Tesco isn't enjoyable but people do it. Come on, get off your soap box and relax. I don't want to talk about work. What do you fancy to eat?"

Tracey took the menu but the choice was too much at this time of night.

"Any suggestions? Nothing too heavy or I'll not sleep."

Simon was tempted to say something but resisted. She was beautiful and intelligent, and unlike the majority of women he had taken out lately, it was obvious that she was still in love with her husband. He could see that he would be sticking to his promise.

"The sea bass is good, you may like that or the mushroom risotto, I've never had it but I'm told it's delicious. I'm having the duck."

Tracey ordered the sea bass and drained her champagne. Simon poured another. Before she could protest, he interrupted.

"You don't have to drink it, there's water here, it just makes me feel better and saves me having to drink anymore. Blimey this isn't the easiest date I've ever been on."

Tracey laughed.

"That's because it's not a date but you obviously don't give up that easily. It's that old macho thing, the chase. You just can't help yourself can you? Have you ever been married?"

Simon looked at her. She looked so serious. She had a beautiful mouth. He wanted to kiss her.

"Nope", he sighed, "not even close. Now what about you? I think it's your turn. How long have you been happily married and why the hell are you sitting in a restaurant in the early hours of the morning driving a complete stranger insane with desire?"

Tracey lowered her head.

"I don't know," she whispered guiltily, "I honestly don't know."

Chapter 33

Cavendish stared at Maggie and sat himself down in the chair opposite.

"I came out for some painkillers, bloody hotel wouldn't give me any. What are you doing out here by yourself, where's Callum?"

Maggie was embarrassed. Maybe she shouldn't have left him. She was also aware that she wasn't looking her best.

"He's asleep, finally. I gave him some of my sleeping tablets. It's awful, he just won't speak, hasn't said a word, I couldn't bear the silence, so as soon as I knew he was asleep, I came out here. I've just ordered some food; do you want to join me?"

Aware that she was starting to sound a little desperate, she continued.

"Sorry Myles, of course you don't want to join me, not with a raging headache and in the middle of a boy's trip. We can catch up in the morning, it's not a problem."

Cavendish looked at her. He admired her; admired the fact that she was trying to be brave and hold her head up, despite the fact that her dickhead husband had caused such chaos.

"You know what Maggs, I'm a bit peckish myself. Let me get these painkillers down my neck. Can I use that glass?"

Maggie handed him the water glass.

"Are the rest of the boys out cold or are any of them still up? How did you manage to stay relatively sober?"

Cavendish grinned. "Well I'm in charge, need to try and keep some semblance of control. I think they're all tucked up safely in their beds though Maggs. Everyone's safe and sound."

Maggie stared at him. He was a complete rogue, but she couldn't help but like him.

"I wouldn't count on it. We women aren't stupid you know, we know what you're like."

"Honestly Maggs, they are all in bed, I know because I helped put most of them in it."

The waiter arrived and Cavendish ordered a small beer.

"Hair of the dog," he grinned mischievously.

"I'm so sorry about all this Myles, ruining the trip. I had no idea he was so miserable. I can't believe he's done it."

Cavendish swallowed the painkillers, and draining the water, placed the glass back on the table.

"I'm sorry too Maggs, and I'll be the first to admit that I gave him a hard time for being miserable. I never thought he would do anything like this, honestly, I would have laid off him if I'd known."

Maggie leant forward and took Cavendish's hand.

"It's not your fault Myles, please believe that. There was obviously something going on of which none of us knew anything about. I thought he was having an affair for Christ's sake but was too scared to ask. Doesn't say much for me does it? I couldn't ask and he couldn't tell. Makes me wonder what my marriage has been about all these years. I must be so selfish that I didn't want to see the cracks."

Cavendish held onto her hand and gripped it tight.

"My father killed himself," he said suddenly, not quite knowing where it had come from, "killed himself while I was still at school. At least Callum didn't succeed and the kids still have a father."

Maggie stared at him. He looked miserable.

"Oh sweetheart," she whispered, "I'm so sorry, I had no idea."

Cavendish was staring at the floor desperately trying not to crack. He wasn't used to sympathy.

180

"Well it wasn't something I wanted to brag about really. In fact, you are the first person I've told. I hated him for leaving me with my bitch of a mother; she was the cause of it all. There wasn't one of my father's friends she hadn't shagged. She was insane and beautiful, but a complete whore. She humiliated him and me. It was his only chance to redeem himself. But it was still bloody selfish. Callum has everything to live for Maggs, a beautiful wife, gorgeous kids; he just needs a bloody good kick up the arse."

They both smiled, and as the waiter arrived, Maggie withdrew her hand. Cavendish picked up one of the forks and passed it to her.

"Come on, let's eat, then I'll walk you back to your hotel."

As Simon went to fill her glass for the third time, Tracey placed her hand over the top.

"Seriously," she said, "I really don't want anymore. I've had a lovely evening and I really just want to go home."

Simon placed his hand on top of hers. She didn't move.

"I know you do, and with great regret I am about to order you a cab."

"Thank you and I'm so sorry that you've wasted good champagne."

Simon took her hand in his.

"No regrets, you haven't led me on, I took a gamble and lost. But hey, that's life and despite what you think, the champagne wasn't wasted."

Simon reached in his pocket and handed her a card.

"As I'm absolutely positive that you aren't about to give me your number, on the off chance that you ever fancy another bottle of champagne when you've been left to your own devices, here's my card."

Tracey took the card.

"Simon Montgomery. That's very grand. Is that you're real name?"

181

"Of course," he said laughing, "you don't trust me do you?"

This time Tracey took his hand.

"Actually I do Simon Montgomery, and I like you very much. Now let's get that cab ordered and say goodbye."

Cavendish and Maggie walked back to the hotel in silence. Enough had been said and they were both lost in their own thoughts.

"Well here we are Maggs, do you still want to see me in the morning or will it be difficult?"

Maggie didn't answer. Back at the hotel, the reality of what was waiting for her in the darkness made her shiver.

"Please come in with me Myles, I don't want to go in by myself."

Cavendish stiffened.

"What if he's awake, believe me I'm the last person on earth he'll want to see."

Maggie took his hand.

"Please Myles, I'll go in first I just need a bit of support."

Reluctantly Cavendish took her by the arm.

"Come on then, lead the way."

Carlos indicated that the cab had arrived, and helping Tracey on with her coat, accepted his tip graciously from Simon. The air outside was fresher and Tracey realised that she had consumed far too much champagne. As they neared the cab, Simon turned her to look at him and wrapping her in his arms, kissed her fully on the lips. Tracey didn't struggle and as he released her she kissed him again.

"Thank you Simon Montgomery, thank you for keeping your promise and letting me go home."

Simon held onto her hand. "Aren't you even going to tell me your surname?"

Tracey shook her head.

"Best not. I'm sure it would lead to trouble don't you? Take care and thank you again."

And as the taxi pulled away, Tracey wondered what on earth she had started.

Chapter 34

Cautiously Maggie opened the door to the apartment and they both walked inside. It was quiet, with no sign of life.

"Wait here," Maggie whispered. "Let me check the room and see if he's still asleep."

Cavendish did as he was asked and waited by the door; leaving it ajar in case a hasty exit was required. How he had managed to get himself into this one, he had no idea, but the fact that he could be of some help, made him feel a little better about his part in Callum's downfall.

"It's ok," Maggie said quietly as she closed the bedroom door behind her, "he's out cold and thankfully still alive. I think I'll sleep in the double room, might be easier."

Cavendish felt awkward.

"Well if you're ok now I'll be off, better get some sleep myself. You sure you'll be alright?"

Maggie turned to him.

"Yes I think so. Here give me a hug, thank you so much for looking after me, I really needed someone to talk to and you appeared out of thin air like a knight in shining armour."

Cavendish put his arms around her and kissed her on the top of her head. Her hair was soft and perfumed.

"Well I can quite honestly say I've never been called that before, plenty of other things but never that."

Maggie buried herself into Cavendish's chest and breathed him in. She could smell the musky odour of his body, intermingled with the fading perfume of his cologne. Cavendish held her close and feeling her push herself closer into his body, he ran his hand gently down her back and over her buttocks. She flinched, and letting out a gentle moan she lifted her head and opened her mouth. Cavendish ran his tongue gently over her lips and as he pushed his tongue into her mouth, he felt himself stiffen. Maggie ran her hand down his chest and rubbed her hand over his crotch. How badly she wanted him. Panting she opened the double bedroom door and pulled Cavendish inside.

"What are you doing? What if he wakes up?" Cavendish gasped. "We can't do this to him."

Maggie wasn't listening.

"Just lock the door."

Cavendish locked the door and fumbling in the darkness, he pushed her up against the wall. She had already removed her shirt, and pulling her skirt up around her waist his hand found his way into the silkiness of her underwear. He wasn't used to hair these days, but on Maggie it was strangely erotic. God she was wet. Expertly he pushed his fingers inside her and Maggie let out a gasp.

"Oh yes, please, don't stop it feels so good."

Cavendish slid his tongue into her mouth again and gently moved his fingers in and out of the wetness, toying with her erect clitoris, enjoying her ecstasy. Lowering his head, he found her nipple through her bra and played with it between his teeth. Suddenly she pushed his hand away and unzipping him allowed his rampant cock to spring free. Squeezing him hard, she moved her hand expertly over his shaft. He was big, just as she'd imagined.

"Fuck me Myles," she groaned, "I need you to fuck me so badly."

Cavendish lay her down on the floor and removing her knickers he opened her legs wide. Pushing his fingers inside he pressed his thumb back and forth until she started to quiver, then without warning, he thrust himself hard into her, holding his hand over her mouth to stop her crying out. Digging her nails into his buttocks, she pulled him into her, her hips thrusting. Cavendish couldn't hold back and as Maggie arched her back again he exploded into her.

As they lay together in the darkness, Cavendish stroked her hair. Neither of them spoke, there was no need.

Back in the house, Tracey threw her bag onto the hall table and threw her coat over the banisters. Her feet were killing her; her shoes were definitely not made for walking. Turning on the kitchen light, she walked over to the fridge and took out the jug of filtered water. It was late, too late, and she knew she would have a headache in the morning, not ideal for a Monday. Thank God the boys were away. As she took out a glass from the cupboard, she looked at the answer phone. No messages, but three missed calls. She checked the number, Simon. How did he like it when he couldn't get hold of her, wasn't much fun then was it? It wasn't like him to call so often though. Maybe something was up. Tracey walked back out to the hall and opened her bag, and taking out her phone, opened the text. She went cold. What did he mean? With shaking hands she phoned voicemail. He sounded distraught. "Oh my God," she said to herself, as she sank down onto the stairs. "What have I done?"

"I think I'd better go," Cavendish whispered, "before we get caught and make things even worse. Are you ok?"

Maggie took his hand. "Yes I think so. Oh Myles, what must you think of me? I'm so sorry, I just couldn't help myself. It's been such a long time since…"

Cavendish stopped her. "We needed each other Maggs, that's all it was and don't worry, it'll be fine. Callum will never have to know. I'm certainly not going to tell him."

Maggie couldn't believe that she felt no guilt.

"Do you want a shower? There's one through that door."

Cavendish grabbed his trousers. "No, I think I had better get away while I've got my chance and before it gets light. Do you still want to meet for coffee?"

Maggie wasn't sure. "I'll see how things are in the morning, I'll call you."

As he stepped out onto the now quiet street, Cavendish was stunned by what had just happened.

Simon had dozed into a half sleep when his phone rang. He cleared his throat and picked up the phone.

"Hello," he answered huskily.

"Simon it's me, are you ok?"

Simon leant back against the pillow. With too many emotions churning he didn't know what to say. Where did he start?

"What's going on Trace, I don't understand, I thought we were good. How long has this been going on for?"

Tracey was shaking. How the hell had he found out. Surely one of the girls hadn't dropped her in it. Why would they? They were all just as bad as each other.

"What are you talking about Simon, are you drunk?"

Simon felt angry now.

"No I am stone cold bloody sober, and at this moment I am sitting alone in my hotel room, staring at some photos of you which somebody, somewhere, thought I ought to see. I'll send them to you. You'll like them. Who is he Trace?"

Tracey was horrified.

"It's not what you think Simon, I don't know him. I met him in a bar this evening, he took me to dinner and then I came home. Nothing happened, I swear. Honestly, it's not as bad as it looks, I promise."

"You met him in a bar and then went out to dinner and nothing else. That's all he wanted, to take someone out to dinner just for the hell of it. I doubt that. Do you do this every time I'm away?"

Tracey was angry now.

"So it's all right for you to go away and get drunk and shag Cavendish's hookers while I sit at home and watch the telly, but not alright for me to go out with some friends, get chatted up, taken to dinner and then sent home in a taxi. I didn't have sex with anyone Simon, I had dinner. He was very kind and he sent me home in a taxi because he knew he didn't have a chance because I was happily married to my husband, or at least I thought I was."

Simon was quiet for a moment.

"Do you really think that I come away on boys trips to shag hookers?"

Tracey was crying now.

"Well according to Sarah that's the norm. The sleazy golf trip she called it. All the other women seemed to know apart from me, I felt such an idiot."

Simon sighed. If he had told her before he left would it have made any difference? Probably not.

"Look Trace, it's not the norm. This year Cavendish was in charge and he organised dancers, ok hookers, for after the dinner. It's never been done before and most of the other guys weren't happy about it. That's why I'm sober Trace, I've spent most of the evening trying to save some of my best mates from being led astray, because they were all so legless they had no idea what was going on."

"But why didn't someone say something, if no one wanted it. Why couldn't someone say something?"

"Because some of the guys weren't bothered and some of them probably did want it, and Cavendish is in charge so we all have to go along with it. That's the way it is. I was going to tell you before I left because I was worried about it, but I just thought you'd worry and tell the other wives."

"There are so many things in that last statement which are making me angry Simon, I really don't want to talk anymore about it tonight. Please can you send me those photos? I want to work out who took them."

"Is that all you're worried about, who took the frigging photos?"

"I didn't do anything Simon."

"Yes you did. Because you didn't trust me, you tarted yourself up, hung around in an expensive bar until some poor unsuspecting sod tried to chat you up. You let him take you out to dinner, which I have no doubt wouldn't have been cheap, and then just say goodbye. You were trying to hurt me by acting like a hooker yourself."

"I was not acting like a hooker; I told him from the start I wasn't interested. He had a choice; he didn't have to take me to dinner."

"And so did you. You could have said no to dinner but you didn't. You were tempted weren't you? If you really weren't interested you wouldn't have gone. I've never taken another woman out for an intimate dinner Tracey, never. I haven't even thought about it."

"Well I've never done it before either, and yes, I was bloody angry sitting at home thinking you were up to your armpits in tarts."

"I can't believe you didn't trust me."

"Well not all men can be trusted can they if Sarah's stories about Tommo are to be believed. I bet he wasn't hanging back."

"Men, despite what you might think, are not all the same and yes some of them are definitely not to be trusted, but Sarah's not exactly the Virgin Mary either is she? Cavendish has a few stories about that lot I can tell you. What made you go out with them anyway?"

"Probably the same reason you go on your trip, for a laugh, to get away from the norm and I was so bloody angry I wanted to be like them and give you a taste of your own medicine."

Simon sighed.

"Well you did a bloody good job. I still can't believe you didn't trust me. What have I ever done to make you not trust me?"

"You didn't tell me about the hookers."

"So if I'd told you what would you have done then? Not let me go. What would you have done?"

"I don't know."

"The bottom line is, you didn't trust me and it didn't take you long to go flinging yourself around in a bar to try and get me back. You didn't even give me chance to explain. Think about it. I love you Tracey, I'd never do anything to hurt you."

Neither of them spoke. Eventually Simon broke the silence.

"Did you like him? Are you planning on seeing him again?"

Tracey was horrified. He was right, she did like him. She didn't want to, but she did. She'd taken his card when she should have said no.

"Of course I'm not going to see him again; I didn't even tell him my name." Simon wasn't convinced.

"I love you Trace."

"I love you too," she whispered.

Tour Ch 35

Steve was woken by the sound of his mobile. He felt terrible. Trying not to move, and without opening his eyes, he reached for his phone. His throat was dry.

"Hello," he croaked.

"Hi, it's me. You sound terrible. Good night was it?"

"Don't know, can't remember. What time is it?"

Lucy looked at the clock; she'd just got back from the school run.

"Nine-thirty here; some of us have been up for a while. I just wondered how Callum was and whether you'd seen Maggie yet. I didn't want to phone her just in case it was difficult to talk."

Steve was still half asleep. He had no idea how Callum was and he hadn't even seen Maggie. All he knew was that he had a splitting headache and the last thing he wanted was idle chat.

"Sorry love, I have no idea. Simon dealt with it all yesterday, I haven't seen her yet. I'm sure everything's fine."

Lucy was annoyed.

"You don't sound very concerned, it obviously didn't stop you having a good time. What time did you actually make it into bed?"

At this line of questioning, a sudden flashback brought Steve to his senses. Sitting up, he realised that his kilt was up over his chest. One of the girls had carried him back. She'd put him to bed, he remembered now. Shit, had anything happened? He couldn't remember. Replacing his kilt, he sat on the side of the bed. His head was spinning. A pair of lacy black knickers lay accusingly on the floor.

"Fuck," he whispered aloud.

"Steve are you ok? Are you listening to me?"

"Sorry love," he croaked, "I'll ring you back; think I'm going to be sick".

Maggie was woken by the sounds of activity from the kitchen. She had showered before going to bed, but guiltily looked around for any evidence of what had taken place last night. Walking into the bathroom, she looked at herself in the mirror. Last night she had had spontaneous wild sex with Cavendish. She could still smell him, feel him inside her. She shivered. It had been so good. Staring into her own eyes, she realised that she felt different now; stronger, more powerful. Pulling back her hair into a knot, she cleansed and carefully moisturised. Maggie Dunbar; who would have thought it? She smiled as she tried to picture the look on Lucy and Christie's face if ever she told them, which she knew she wouldn't. She knew her choice of partner would be too shocking and she really couldn't trust them not to tell. Cavendish didn't deserve that.

Maggie Dunbar put on her robe and went to the kitchen. She didn't need her makeup today.

Steve banged on Mike's door. Mike was annoyed.

"Who is it?" he barked.

"It's Steve mate, can you let me in?"

Mike opened the door and let him in. Steve looked awful. He still had his kilt on, his shirt was unbuttoned and his socks were rolled down to his ankles. He was white as a sheet.

"Where the hell have you been? Did you actually make it back to your room last night?"

"Yeh and that's the problem, I think I had company." Steve looked terrified.

"What do you mean? Oh shit, you didn't shag one of those tarts did you? How did that happen?"

192

Steve was now pacing up and down. He wished he could remember.

"That's the problem, I don't know whether I did or not, although I'd be surprised if I could have managed anything, the amount I'd had to drink. I remember there was a girl in my room, I definitely let her in and then I can't remember. When I woke up, my kilt was over my chest and her knickers were on the floor. Doesn't look good does it?"

Mike didn't know what to say.

"Well I bet you're not the only one, Christ knows what happened to everyone else last night. Simon put me to bed, thank God."

Steve had another flashback.

"Oh Jesus," he moaned, banging his hand against the wall. "I remember Simon, he tried to take me away from her but I told him I was alright. I fucking said it was ok." He banged his hand against his forehead. "Shit, shit, shit. Why am I such an idiot?"

Not knowing what else to do, Mike put the kettle on as Steve continued to pace the floor.

"Look mate, there's nothing we can do about it now. No one knows apart from me and possibly Simon, so there is absolutely no way that Lucy is going to find out. You were completely pissed for Christ's sake. Just forget about it."

Steve couldn't forget it.

"Lucy was right; she said this would happen if we had Cavendish in charge. She knew exactly what would happen and she's bloody well right. She sounded good on the phone too, looked like we had a chance to patch things up. I was actually looking forward to going home and making mad passionate love to my wife and now I won't be able to risk it in case I've picked up some horrible festering disease from some cheap tart. Sorry dear, I'll have to use a condom because I slept with a hooker when I was supposed to be playing golf. That'll go down well won't it. God I am in so much trouble. You wait till I see Cavendish; I'm gonna fucking kill him."

Mike tried desperately to calm him down. If his own performance was anything to go by, he was useless after a night on the skite, and he was pretty sure that Steve would not have been capable of much either. But Steve was right; the not knowing was the killer.

"I don't suppose there were any condoms in the room, did you look?"

"Course I looked. The only evidence was the knickers."

Mike went to hand him a coffee just as Steve's mobile beeped. Steve picked it up and opened the text. The photo left nothing to the imagination. It was him all right, with his dick very firmly in the mouth of a very attractive and very young whore. The other photos were just as bad. He certainly didn't look too drunk as he held her tits in his hands while she rode him. Steve handed the phone to Mike.

"Like I said, the only evidence is the knickers and these."

Callum was trying to make coffee but Maggie could see that he wasn't focused. He looked so lost. Taking the cafetiere gently from his hand, she placed it on the counter.

"Leave it, I'll phone room service for breakfast."

Callum picked it back up. He was tired of feeling useless.

"I'm ok, I can manage to make some bloody coffee, I don't need you to tell me how to make it. I know you think I'm useless but I think I can make a pot of coffee by myself."

Maggie was taken aback. Where had this come from? He'd never raised his voice to her before.

"Callum I don't think you're useless, why would I think that?"

"Don't patronise me Maggie, don't talk to me in that superior bloody tone. I know you think I'm useless and I'm sure everyone agrees with you now. Useless, fat, Callum Dunbar. Fined for being fat. Fined for being the worst at golf. Bet I'm really popular with the boys now, now I've ruined their trip. Cavendish'll be happy though won't he, the bastard, he's always made my life a misery, fucking bully. He's probably going to fine me for not killing myself properly. I bet he was gutted I never managed to do it. Sums me up though doesn't it? Couldn't even manage to do a good job on that either."

Maggie suddenly felt a pang of guilt.

"Well you're wrong about your friends, they've been fabulous, even Cavendish if you must know, and they've done a great job in keeping it a secret from everyone else. Only Mike, Steve, Simon and Cavendish know and it will stay that way. Cavendish feels terrible about it."

"Yeh I bet he does. The only time Cavendish ever feels terrible is when he can't get a shag."

Maggie froze. It hadn't been like that with Cavendish. She had wanted him, he hadn't pushed her.

"Look, let's try and talk this through. I don't think you're useless and I want us to work this out. If we lose everything, we lose it, we can always start again. The girls need you and love you and so do I. Please Callum, if you talk to me we may have a chance but I can't help if I don't know where to start."

"Well you can start by letting me make the bloody coffee!"

"Bloody hell," gasped Mike, "these don't leave much to the imagination do they? She looks about seventeen. Nice tits."

"That's not bloody funny. Why would she send me a photo though and someone must have taken it."

Steve's phone beeped again. Mike opened the text.

"Oh shit, I think you owe the young lady a bit of cash. She says you didn't pay her."

Steve was exasperated.

"Course I didn't pay her. How much does she want?"

"£5000, God she's not cheap is she?"

"Have you read that right, £5000, she must be joking, why

195

would I hand over £5000?"

Mike looked at Steve.

"Because she knows where you work?"

"Bollocks!"

"And she also thinks Lucy might like to see them."

Steve held his head in his hands.

"I think I've been framed pal. What the hell am I gonna to do?"

Tour Ch 36

Andy couldn't move. His head felt as though someone had put an axe through it. Why did they do this to themselves? He tried to swallow but his tongue seemed to have glued itself to the roof of his mouth. Moving his left leg slowly, he winced as a sharp pain flashed through his buttocks. God, he ached all over. Sitting up, he looked down at himself. His shirt was ripped and his tie was strapped around his right wrist. From the waist down he was naked. Bloody hell, what a state. He looked at his phone. Ten twenty-five am. Getting up from the bed, he winced again and catching sight of himself in the mirror he looked at the bright red wheals across his arse. Shit! As if he wasn't in enough trouble as it was. Limping into the bathroom, he ran the shower and filled himself a glass of water from the tap. He had bruises on his chest too, but he remembered falling off a chair when it was up on the dining table. The night had been wild and he had gone too far. He couldn't remember getting to bed, but he could remember having his face in one of the girl's crotch. He reached for his toothbrush and stared at himself in the bathroom mirror. You complete arsehole, he hissed to himself.

Cavendish hadn't slept well and sitting in the restaurant by himself he checked his phone. Maggie hadn't called, so he presumed she didn't want to speak to him now. Or maybe she couldn't. He hoped she was ok. He poured himself a coffee. Where was everyone? Surely someone wanted a game of golf. He picked up his phone. He wondered how Sinclair was feeling this morning. Steve didn't answer. He phoned Mike.

"Morning," Mike replied curtly, "where are you?"

"I'm down in the restaurant, by myself. Is anyone getting up this morning? This is supposed to be a golf trip. Where's Sinclair, is he still in bed?"

"In the shower and you're not flavour of the month mate, so I'd keep your mouth shut if I were you."

Cavendish laughed.

"If he couldn't keep his dick under his kilt that's not my fault, feeling a bit guilty is he?"

Mike was irritated now.

"Well it's a little bit more serious than that mate and if we don't get it sorted asap, this may be the last bloody trip any of us will be on. You'd better get yourself up here. We've got something to show you."

Cavendish suddenly felt nervous.

"What is it?"

"Just get yourself up here. Don't worry I won't let him at you, not yet."

Simon had showered. He was hungry, but the thought of the chat over breakfast wasn't appealing. He was still reeling from the revelations of last night and he just wanted to go home. Picking up his phone, he stared again at the photos. He had sent them to Tracey but she hadn't replied. The guy was good looking, definitely younger than him. Tracey was beautiful though, any man would find her attractive. He wondered who'd taken the photo. Highlighting the number he pressed call.

"Hello," answered a woman's voice.

"Hello, this is Simon Lewis, who am I speaking to?"

After a few seconds silence, she hung up.

Sophie had called in sick and surprisingly had managed to get herself a doctor's appointment for four-fifteen. If Andy phoned now, she wondered whether she would be able to stop herself from telling him. She hadn't slept well, her mind a whirlpool of emotions.

She still had a couple of credit card companies to phone and the bailiffs had given her a stay of execution, but she was worried about the house. It wouldn't matter so much if it was just the two of them, but now they had a baby to think about and no money. Vic had promised her that he would keep a roof over her head and Andy's parents, she knew, would do the same. But it wasn't fair on them. They'd worked hard and been sensible all their lives, why should they carry the can? Her other worry was the baby. She was an older woman, that's what the doctors would say, which meant endless possibilities for things to go wrong. Could she bear it if things didn't work out? She picked up her mobile but then changed her mind. He wouldn't answer; they never did when they were on a boys trip. She'd have to wait until he got home.

Cavendish knocked on Mike's door. Thankfully he was alone. As he closed the door behind him, Mike handed him Steve's mobile. Cavendish took it and stared at the photos. He recognised Catalina at once.

"He's been set up poor bastard," Mike sighed. "She wants £5000."

Cavendish scrolled through the photos.

"And what's she going to do if she doesn't get it?"

"Send them to Lucy, as well as work. The whole fucking world can see them if she feels like sticking it on You Tube. She's got the photos, she's in charge. If Lucy gets them, then it's curtains for all of us, well all except you of course."

Mike was interrupted by a knock on the door. Cavendish jumped. Steve still looked furious but Cavendish was relieved that Sinclair didn't look as though he was about to deck him.

"Well I hope you're fucking pleased with yourself," he growled, as he snatched the phone from Cavendish's hand. "Where did you get these bitches from because you can get over there and get it sorted. I'm not bloody handing over any money, especially not five grand."

Mike was trying to stay calm.

"But if she's got the photos she can easily send them to Lucy and they don't look good do they? Even if you say you were pissed, which you were, the fact is, we had hookers on our trip and I'm sure Lucy's not going to keep that quiet."

"She might," Steve answered unconvincingly.

"Not," replied Mike. "Cavendish, who did you book them through? Surely they wouldn't let the girls get away with this, they wouldn't last long otherwise. You told me they were reliable. Can't you call them and ask them to sort it out?"

Mike and Steve waited for an answer. Cavendish was saved by a knock on the door.

"Who is it?" bellowed Mike.

"Simon, can I come in?"

Cavendish sighed, that was all he needed. Mother Theresa. Mike opened the door and immediately Simon realised that something was up. Steve didn't waste any time. Handing the phone to Simon he glared at Cavendish.

"I'll let him explain, seeing as it's all his fucking fault that I've been set up. £5000 she wants or she's sending them to Lucy and we're all done for."

Simon looked at the photos as Steve carried on.

"So, you haven't answered his question. Why can't you phone the company and get it sorted?"

Cavendish sighed.

"Because it would probably get her into serious trouble."

Steve was incredulous.

"Get *her* into trouble, what about me? What about us? It's all right for you, you don't have a wife and kids to worry about. So fucking what if it gets her into trouble, I don't give a shit."

Mike looked at Cavendish. He couldn't believe that Cavendish would give a toss about the welfare of some tart. Cavendish continued.

"She'll be working alone, trying to get some extra cash. If we drop her in it you can be sure as hell that these guys aren't going to smack her backside and send her to bed. These guys don't follow the same rules as us, they don't give a shit either. She's trying to find a way out because she's got a five year old kid."

Steve and Mike stared at him.

"How do you know?" Steve asked.

"Because he shagged her the first night we were here," said Simon quietly. "I saw her coming out of his room, didn't look like she'd had a great time either." He looked at Cavendish accusingly. "No wonder she's looking for a way out."

Nobody spoke. The silence was interrupted by a beep from Mike's phone. Taking it out of his pocket, he opened the text message.

"Oh shit," he said, putting the phone back in his pocket. "It's Christie asking how Dunbar is. How can I say I haven't got the faintest idea after the poor sods just tried to drown himself. Doesn't say much for me does it?"

Cavendish stood up.

"Dunbar is ok, I've seen Maggie. He's still not speaking and she can't get a flight back until tomorrow. She's going to call us later when she's tried to get him to talk."

Mike was put out.

"When the hell did you see Maggie?"

Cavendish hesitated. He couldn't look any of them in the eye.

"This morning. I met her in one of the shops; we were both after painkillers. She seemed ok. She said she'd call if she needed anything."

Mike looked relieved.

"Well that's a relief. I'll text Christie back and then give Maggie a call and see if she wants us to go over. Meanwhile, I think we'd better get the boys together for a team meeting and decide what we're all doing about these bloody photos."

Sitting alone in her kitchen, Tracey scrolled through the photos. From the angle they had been taken from she was sure it hadn't been any of the girls she was with. They had obviously been followed out of the bar, but she hadn't noticed anyone. Who would want to do this? She looked again at the photos, they looked like a couple, arm in arm, him leaning over to talk in her ear. It looked as though he was kissing her. He was handsome and she had kissed him. She had let him kiss her and she had kissed him back. She tried to blame the champagne but she knew she had wanted to. Opening her bag she took out the business card he had given her. She should throw it away. Poor Simon. If she'd received photos of him doing the same, she'd have been devastated. They were happy. She loved him. Why the hell had she kissed another man? Guiltily, she replaced the card in a compartment in her purse and opened her laptop.

Andy had showered and was now sitting gingerly on his bed, searching the net for information on sexually transmitted diseases. He could vividly remember what he'd done and he was horrified by the list of possibilities unfolding on the screen in front of him. Unconsciously he wiped his hand over his mouth. How did you know if you'd caught something? If he kissed Sophie now, could he pass it on? He'd never been with a prostitute. He'd slept with other women before Sophie, but apart from the occasional drunken snog in a bar on a boys' night, he'd been completely faithful. Wincing as he got himself up from the bed, he opened the door of the mini bar. Maybe whisky would do it. It was antiseptic wasn't it? Opening the bottle, he swilled some around his mouth and gargled before swallowing it down. He hated whisky. Shaking his head, and with his eyes smarting from the sensation at the back of his throat, he picked up his phone and called Simon.

Jules thrust her phone into Susie Jamieson's hand. She had managed to slip out of work for an early lunch in order to catch Susie before she started her shift.

"I told you this would get awkward. You are such a bloody idiot and I am really pissed off with you for using my phone. He phoned me this morning and he's sent a text saying he'll keep on phoning until I tell him who I am. He says he'll find out. You are so stupid. I knew it was a bad idea."

Susie looked concerned. Maybe she'd made a mistake; drink had obviously affected her judgement.

"What did he say? Did you speak to him?" she asked hesitantly.

Jules was furious. She was annoyed that Susie had compromised her phone and got her mixed up in what was now becoming a more serious situation. She was obsessed with Simon Lewis and was becoming completely unbalanced.

"Course I didn't speak to him, what the hell was I supposed to say? He asked who I was and I hung up. He kept phoning for about ten minutes, but I didn't answer. I don't think he'll give up too easily. I bet he's furious. It's getting out of hand Susie, I think you'd better own up before he finds out."

Susie had absolutely no intention of owning up. She'd dealt the cards and she'd be there to pick up the pieces when his marriage fell apart. She could wait a little longer to make her next move.

"Don't worry, I'll get you a new phone, it's easy to change your number. There's no way I'm owning up now, it'll ruin everything."

Jules shook her head as she stormed off.

"Well good luck you stupid cow, I am seriously not having any more to do with it."

Mike decided to call Maggie. He wanted to make sure everything was ok before he called Christie back. It took several rings for her to pick up.

"Hello, Maggie Dunbar."

"Hi Maggie. It's Mike. How's Callum? Is everything ok?"

Maggie walked out of the bedroom onto the balcony. Callum was in the shower. She could talk for five minutes.

"Oh thanks for calling Mike, I was going to phone you but haven't found the right moment. Callum's in the shower. I can talk for a few minutes."

After the chill of the air conditioning, it was hot out in the sun on the balcony and removing her cardigan, Maggie sat down on one of the chairs.

"Cavendish said he had spoken to you and thought you were bearing up. He said you had a flight booked for tomorrow."

Maggie hesitated. Did Mike know anything she wondered briefly?

"Yes I bumped into Cavendish last night. He was very helpful and he's right, I've got a flight tomorrow morning, ahead of you guys so we shouldn't bump into you at the airport."

Mike listened. He thought Cavendish had seen Maggie this morning. He didn't interrupt.

"He's speaking now Mike but I'm not getting very far. He obviously feels completely humiliated and more than anything he feels he's let us down, what with the job and everything. I don't really know what else I can do at the moment until I get him home and get him to see a doctor. I've phoned his partners and tried to explain, but I've no idea what else to do. I've just got to get through today and hopefully, when we get home we can get some help. I'm so sorry about ruining the trip Mike, I really am."

Mike felt terrible. He didn't know what to do either. And as for ruining the trip, Cavendish had managed to do that by all by himself. The wanker.

"Do you want us to come over Maggs? Do you think he would see us or would it make things worse? It might take the pressure off you for a few minutes and let you take a break."

Maggie desperately wanted to get out of the apartment. It felt good in the sun and Callum was becoming a little aggressive.

"That would be wonderful Mike, but you boys have paid good money to come on this trip, don't worry about us, we'll be fine. Go and enjoy yourselves. I'll call if I need anything."

Mike wasn't convinced.

"Look Maggs, we've got a few little issues to sort out here but one of us will be over in an hour or two. I'll phone before we come round though, just in case."

Maggie tried not to cry.

"Thanks Mike, I'm really grateful."

Mike hung up. Simon was still in Mike's room, Cavendish and Steve having left to round up the rest of the boys. Despite redialling the number, no one was picking up.

"How is she?" he asked not looking up. "Does she need one of us to go round?"

"Yeh I think so, she says not but I could tell she didn't mean it. Probably best if Steve or I go. I'll see what Steve says but he's probably got enough on his plate. So much for playing golf, it was hardly worth bringing my clubs. Cavendish has a lot to answer for. Wish I'd listen to you now, sorry mate."

Simon stood up and put his phone away. He felt miserable, but trying to put a brave face on it, he put his hand on Mike's shoulder.

"Don't worry about it. If it's any consolation it's the first time I've ever seen Cavendish show the slightest bit of remorse.

I don't think he bargained on this much carnage. Don't think any of us will forget this trip though will we? Come on mate, let's go and find out who else is up shit creek. Andy's been trying to get me for the past hour; the poor bugger's probably after a cure for his red arse."

Tour Ch 38

Cavendish and Steve had managed to round up the boys, and one by one they had filed into Cavendish's suite. Most had managed to get themselves together, but sore heads and some remorse was keeping the banter to a minimum. Andy continued to torture himself with photos of the latter stages of sexual diseases. Passing the phone to Tommo, he looked anxious.

"Look at that. That's what I could have now. What's Sophie gonna say when my gob turns into mass of puss filled boils?"

Tommo laughed. He'd taken plenty of chances and not been caught yet.

"It's your dicky diamond you need to worry about mate, I saw where that went last night, could be the blobby knob clinic for you sunshine."

Andy stared at him. He didn't remember doing anything else. He remembered the redhead sitting on his face while one of the other girls held him down, but he didn't remember his dick getting any attention. He didn't have his trousers on when he woke up though. Tommo grinned. Andy was so easy to wind up. He hadn't a clue what Andy had got up to, he'd been too busy getting his own share of the action. Alex joined them.

"I feel like shit," he croaked. "I'm bruised all over and I was covered in some sort of gunge, no idea what it was, don't want to know either. What the hell were we drinking?"

Andy couldn't tear himself away from his phone.

"It says here that catching a disease from oral sex with a prostitute is quite common and that I should see a doctor if I'm worried." Alex grimaced. What on earth was he talking about?

"Were you up to no good last night?" he asked. "I don't remember much to be honest. I don't remember seeing you at the end."

Tommo laughed.

"That's because he had tart on his face and you were having your wee willy winky massaged by some ample young filly. She was gorgeous mate; don't tell me you don't remember. What a bloody waste. Davie took her on later though; he's a real man, bet he remembers."

Alex and Andy looked at each other, both trying desperately to remember the night's events, and with both now fearing the worst, they remained silent.

As Mike and Simon walked into the room, Steve stood up and called for quiet. Cavendish didn't move. The boys immediately realised that something was up. Steve cleared his throat.

"Right boys, I'll cut to the chase, as probably, like me, you're all feeling like shit. The reason we're here and not on the golf course, is that we have a bit of an issue to sort out which although I am the main target, ultimately affects us all."

"You're pregnant!" shouted Rex. "Congratulations."

Despite the laughter, Steve didn't smile.

"Last night, I was set up by a couple of the girls and they have photographs of me which they intend to send to Lucy and to work. They don't leave anything to the imagination and if Lucy sees them I'm dead."

The implication of Lucy getting the photos was not lost on any of them, and an unnerving silence fell upon the room. Steve continued.

"Basically, if Lucy gets those photos, believe me, its curtains for another trip. The girl wants £5000 but I'm not sure how we stop her from using them again. If we give her the cash she might want more. What does everyone think, do we pay her or what?"

Alex was the first to speak. He felt sorry for Steve. It could have been any of them.

"What do you think Lucy would do if she got the photos? What if you told her you'd been set up and blackmailed, surely she'd believe you?"

Steve shook his head; it was more complicated than that.

"That's the problem though isn't it? Even if she didn't divorce me, she wouldn't be letting me away on any more trips and you know what women are like, it'd be round the wives like a dose of measles."

"Or herpes," laughed Tommo, slapping Andy on the back. Andy looked grim, the new revelation only adding to his misery. Mike stood up.

"I think Steve's right; we don't want Lucy getting the photos. I think we have to take a chance and hand over the cash and hope she keeps to her word. Hopefully, she'll take the cash and run."

"But what if when that runs out she wants more and we have to pay up again?" asked Rex, "we could have this hanging over our heads for years. If we pay up once, she'll know we're scared and she'll see us as an easy target. I think we should just come clean and own up. The women'll soon get over it; you know what they're like. It'll cost us an expensive holiday or some new clothes or whatever, but they won't divorce us over some lap dancers."

At this statement, the room was divided, with half the room unconvinced that their marriages and bank balances would survive. And as the possible outcomes were thrashed out, the volume in the room increased. Up until this point, Cavendish had remained silent, but with the noise in the room becoming intolerable, he called for quiet. The room fell silent.

"It's my fault," he said simply, "and I'll sort it. Go and play golf and let me sort it."

Steve didn't trust him.

"I think you should let us know what you intend to do, after all, it's not as if we've just got to pay for a broken table, we're dealing with blackmail and marriages here. I think we all need to know how you think you're going to sort it"

Cavendish looked at him. There was no arrogance.

"Please Sinclair, just trust me, I know what I'm doing. I got us into this mess, just let me sort it out."

Steve hadn't phoned Lucy back, and still wondering what was going on, she tried Christie. Christie, on her way to meet a client, was happy to chat.

"Have you heard what's happening? I texted Mike this morning but he hasn't replied. Have you spoken to Steve?"

"For about a minute. He told me he hadn't seen Maggie yet but he thought everything was ok, then he hung up as he said he was going to be sick. He said he'd call me back but he hasn't, but nothing new in that is there? I suppose if anything was wrong we would have heard."

Christie felt slightly annoyed. Mike usually found time to give her a quick call, and under the circumstances, she thought he would have let her know what was going on. If Steve had thrown up though, it obviously hadn't stopped them having a good time.

"Maybe I should try Maggie, what you think?" asked Lucy. "I'm off to have my hair done, maybe I'll text her from there. Might cheer her up a bit to think I've taken her advice."

"Good idea," replied Christie, "I'm going to be tied up for a while so probably won't get chance to phone until this afternoon. If you find out anything, let me know, and if you speak to Steve you can get him to tell Mike that he's an arse. I can't believe he hasn't let me know what's going on. Bloody thoughtless; it's only a bloody golf trip for Christ's sake."

With the promise of golf and responsibility handed over to the tour leader, the boys dutifully filed out of Cavendish's room. Simon, however, held back. Cavendish looked annoyed.

"Don't say a fucking word," he growled, "I know what you're about to say and I don't need it. I said I'll sort it out and I will, ok. I don't need one of your self- righteous bloody lectures thank you."

Cavendish walked over to the small kitchen and poured himself an orange juice.

"Do you want one?" he mumbled.

"No thanks," replied Simon not moving. Cavendish was irritated.

"Well what do you want then?"

Simon handed Cavendish his phone and showed him the photos.

"I just wondered whether you knew who he was?"

Maggie sent a text to Cavendish. "*Mike coming over later to see Callum and give me a break. Not good idea for you to come. Sorry about last night but no regrets. Thanks for everything. Maggie x*"

Deleting the sent text from her phone, she poured herself a drink and took a magazine out onto the balcony.

Cavendish looked at the photos on Simon's phone. He was as shocked as his friend. He'd never have put money on Tracey having an affair. He scrolled through the rest of the photos. Poor Simon. Here he was playing Archangel Michael, while his wife was out on the town with a slut like Montgomery. He needed to play this carefully.

"Does Tracey know you've seen them?"

Simon sighed.

"Yep, she denied it, well sort of. Said she was out with Sarah, Tommo's Mrs and the rest of her bloody coven. Sarah had spread the word that we had lap dancers on the trip so Tracey went out with them on the pull. She said he took her to dinner and that was it, he got her a taxi home."

Cavendish had his doubts but this wasn't like Tracey. He had known her as long as he'd known Simon and she'd always been a good friend to him despite his behaviour. She'd even managed to forgive him for Simon's stag do which was pretty admirable. She adored Simon. Montgomery wasn't one to mess about though. Would he have given up after dinner? He doubted it. Not when he had a beautiful married woman like Tracey in his sights.

"Tommo's in for a massive bloody fine for leaking tour details, fucking big mouth. Do you believe her? It's not like her is it? Sarah I can believe, she hangs around in that bar all the time, Tommo and her are made for each other, but not Tracey. She's probably telling the truth mate, she probably got herself wound up at the thought of you having a good time and thought she'd give you a taste of your own medicine. I doubt she's having an affair."

Simon looked at Cavendish. He wanted to believe him.

"I can't believe she didn't trust me."

Cavendish smiled, he was so pious.

"You obviously don't trust her either or you wouldn't be taking this any further by discussing it with me."

"Well she doesn't have photos of me escorting another woman to dinner and God knows what else does she?"

Cavendish didn't reply.

"So you don't know who it is then? Maybe I should call Sarah."

Cavendish handed back the phone. Simon wasn't going to drop it that easily.

"Oh come on, that's not fair on Sarah, is it. It's not really her fault. Leave it mate. Look if you want, I'll have a phone around and see if any of the guys know anything. Another interesting question is who took the photos? It's either someone who hates Tracey or someone that's got the hots for you. Do you know who sent them?"

Simon shrugged his shoulders.

"Nope. It's a woman though, I called the number back, a woman's voice answered but when I spoke she hung up. She obviously won't pick up now. How would she have my personal number?"

Cavendish had no idea. Whoever it was must be a devious bitch. He looked at his watch. What he did know was that the day was fast disappearing and he wanted a game of golf.

"Must be someone who knows you then, I've no idea. Look mate, we've got one day left, go and play golf and try and enjoy yourself for once. I know I've fucked up but I'm trying to redeem myself here. I'm sure Tracey's telling the truth but I don't think you can do anything about it till you get home."

As Simon closed the door behind him, Cavendish called Montgomery.

Back in his room, Andy took another bottle of whisky from the mini bar and taking some cotton wool from the container in the bathroom, carefully wiped it over his nether regions. He would get himself checked out when he got home, just in case. He thought about phoning Sophie but changed his mind. He was feeling too guilty to talk at the moment and women had that sixth sense, it was in their DNA. They knew instinctively if something was up. A game of golf with the lads was what he needed. Hopefully the sunshine and banter would clear his head and he could call her when they got back.

As Steve and Mike walked back to their rooms, the discussion had turned to Maggie.

"Look you don't need to go mate," said Mike resolutely. "I'll go and see them, it's only round the corner and I'll catch up. I can probably play with Cavendish as he'll be last going out."

Steve for once, wasn't in the mood for golf.

"No mate, I'll go. You did your share yesterday and you're team captain. You go and play and I'll go and see Dunbar. Lucy'll kill me if I say I didn't go and see him and spent the whole trip getting pissed and playing golf. I can catch up with Cavendish and he can explain how he thinks he's going to get us out of this bloody mess."

Mike didn't put up a fuss. He hated drama and he was desperate to get one decent game of golf in before he went home.

"Thanks mate, appreciated. Do you know where you're going?"

"Just round the corner isn't it? Can't be far if Maggie bumped into Cavendish this morning. I think I've still got the address in my phone."

"Yes, strange that," said Mike quietly. "Maggie said she saw Cavendish last night not this morning, wonder what the bloody hell he was up to? Probably feeling guilty and trying to squirm his way out of any responsibility. Don't say anything to Maggie though; she's got enough on her plate."

Simon tried the number again. He didn't expect an answer but it gave him something to do.

"Look," Jules answered angrily, "you don't know me and those photos are not my fault, someone used my phone to send them. I'm really sorry but it's nothing to do with me, so please will you stop calling."

Simon was taken aback. He hadn't expected an answer and the woman sounded genuinely upset.

"Well as you can imagine," he said quietly, "quite a lot of damage has been done. So if you didn't send them, who did?"

Jules went quiet.

"Look you must understand I can't tell you, she's my best friend, you wouldn't drop your best friend in it. I told her not to do it but she wouldn't listen. She's in love with you, well she thinks she is and when she saw your wife with that guy she thought it was her chance to well, I don't know, ruin your marriage I suppose. I tried to tell her it was wrong but she wouldn't listen. I'm really sorry but I can't tell you anymore."

Simon was flabbergasted.

"Well how did you get my number? She must have had my number in her phone to send the photos from the bar. Do I know this woman? She obviously knows me but do I know her well? I must do. Come on you have to tell me."

"I'm sorry," whispered Jules, "I can't tell you anymore. Please just leave it."

Simon didn't push her. It obviously wasn't the poor girl's fault and at least she'd had the balls to give him some sort of explanation.

215

"Well thanks, whoever you are, but you can tell your friend that despite her best intentions, I have absolutely no intention of leaving my wife and if I ever find out who she is she'll be bloody sorry she ever met me."

As Montgomery hung up he smiled to himself. Cavendish, the biggest tart on the planet, had actually warned him off, the arrogant bastard. The hilarious thing was he'd had no intention of pursuing her, despite the fact that she was gorgeous and intelligent and he'd thought about her all morning. He'd had every intention of keeping to his word. He could easily track her down if he wanted to but he'd promised to let her go. That was, until she'd called him and arranged to meet him for lunch.

Tour Ch 40

"Right, what are we playing?" Mike asked cheerfully, as the guys gathered in the hotel foyer to wait for the minibus. He couldn't wait to get on the golf course. He loved the competition and the banter and he lived for his trips away with the boys.

"Cavendish and Steve are catching up, which means we are down to thirteen which isn't ideal. Simon what do you think? Texas Scramble, two fours, a three and a two, even if we have teams of three we're still stuck with a two. Mind you by the time we've got ourselves sorted and had lunch, Cavendish and Steve shouldn't be far behind."

He looked around the group. No one offered an alternative. Everyone looked awful and he was convinced that the ferocious heat wasn't going to help the situation. The sooner they got going and took their minds off their hangovers, the better.

"Right, we'll go with the Texas Scramble. Let's try and mix the teams up a bit. I'll go out first with Alex, Simon and Tommo. Second group we'll have Andy, Davie, Rex and Fats. Third group will have to be Smithie, Murphy and Charlie and then Sinclair and Cavendish can join you two. Is everyone happy with that? Hope so because I'm not changing it. Usual tour rules apply. Right looks like the buses are here, lets rock and roll."

As the boys picked up their clubs and shuffled towards the exit, Mike was relieved that the trip appeared to have returned to some semblance of order. It had been carnage so far, absolute bloody carnage, and he could tell that some of the boys were suffering. Hopefully, they could have a bit of a laugh on the course, a trouble free dinner this evening and head home a little happier than some of them were today. If they'd known the truth about Dunbar it would have been even worse but hey, he said to himself, life had to go on, moping didn't get you anywhere.

As Steve headed towards Dunbar's hotel, he was nervous. He had no idea what he was going to say. None of them were good at this sort of thing, which is why Mike hadn't put up much of a fight when he had offered to go in his place. Steve couldn't blame him; all he'd done on this trip so far was sort out hassle. He deserved a game of golf. He wondered what Cavendish was going to do and how the hell he was going to sort the blackmail out. Although that was the thing with Cavendish, you never really knew what he was up to. He always seemed to know someone somewhere, who knew someone else who could sort it out, and Steve had to admit that it was never a dull moment when he was around. What a wanker though, organising those bloody women when he knew it would cause trouble. Steve liked to think it would teach him a lesson, but he knew it wouldn't. Steve was cross with himself. Why did he let her into the room in the first place? What if he told Lucy? Wasn't it best just to come clean than try to keep it all a secret? The rest of the boys were the problem though. If Lucy did tell the other wives, that would be the end of it, and he didn't want that responsibility. Stepping into the hotel foyer, he checked the room details on his phone and headed for the escalator.

Cavendish dialled the number from Steve's phone. After a few rings he got voicemail.

"Catalina, its Myles Cavendish here regarding your text to Mr Sinclair. If you would like to call me back on this number I may have a proposal for you."

Within twenty seconds she had returned his call.

Steve knocked on the door of the apartment and did not have to wait long before Maggie opened the door. Steve was both surprised and relieved to see that she looked remarkably good under the circumstances, which was probably more than could be said for him. He hoped that his aftershave masked the smell of the alcohol that still seemed to be emanating from every pore in his body.

"Steve darling," smiled Maggie, "oh come on in and thank you so much for coming round, I am so pleased to see you. My God sweetheart, you look worse than Callum, come on I'll get some coffee ordered. Good night was it or was it very bad, don't worry you don't have to answer that, I know tour rules and all that."

If only she knew, Steve thought to himself. He followed her through to the kitchen. There was no sign of Callum.

"Coffee would be great Maggs," he answered, looking around for any sign of him, "I feel as shit as I probably look. How is he feeling now, does he want to see me?"

Maggie suddenly lost her sparkle. He probably didn't want to see Steve, but she wasn't going to give him the opportunity to say no. He needed one of the boys right now even though he didn't realise it. She knew it would help.

"He's out on the balcony. You go on out and I'll bring the coffee through when it arrives. Do you want anything to eat? Silly question of course you do, I'll order something."

"Maggs," said Steve, "what do I say? I really don't know what to talk about."

Maggie smiled at him; he looked like a little boy.

"Oh I'm sure you'll think of something, what do you boys usually talk about?"

Steve looked bewildered.

"Well nothing, that's the problem Maggs, we don't really talk about anything. Men aren't good at small talk; you should know that by now."

Taking him by the arm and leading him towards the balcony, Maggie laughed.

"Rubbish, just go and see him and I'll get the coffee."

Cavendish hung up the phone and put the piece of paper on which he'd written Catalina's details into his wallet. That was that sorted, it hadn't been too difficult. He looked at Maggie's text. Should he call her? Steve would probably be there now; maybe he could meet her in the cafe around the corner. He opted for a text.

"If you can escape could meet for coffee. Have to wait for Steve anyway as golfing together. Probably not good for me to come there x"

The reply was prompt.

"Thanks so much for the offer but best not. You've done more than enough. Enjoy your day x"

Disappointed, Cavendish realised that a reply was not required and throwing the phone on the bed, turned his attention to the golf.

Steve walked out onto the balcony and replaced his sunglasses. He felt more comfortable behind the dark lenses. Callum was sitting, eyes closed with his back to the open door. He seemed unaware of Steve's arrival. Steve pulled up a chair and sat down, and as he did so Callum opened one eye. Closing it again, he readjusted himself in the chair.

"Shouldn't you be on the golf course," he mumbled.

"So should you," replied Steve. "You've really buggered up the numbers you know."

Attempting a smile, Callum opened his eyes and picked up his sunglasses from the table.

"Maggie's getting coffee," Steve said, looking for conversation. "She said I looked as though I needed it."

"Good old Maggie," said Callum sarcastically, "coffee's her answer to everything. She's ordered so much coffee since she's been here she must be wired to the moon."

Steve hesitated.

"How are you feeling mate?" he asked cautiously.

Callum sighed.

"Like a complete fucking idiot. What do you think?"

Steve smiled.

"Well if it makes you feel any better, after what happened last night, you're not the only one."

Maggie ordered coffee and croissants and turning on the TV flicked absent mindedly through the channels. She was relieved to see that the conversation out on the balcony wasn't too strained. If Steve could get him talking it might improve the atmosphere a little. She felt guilty about Cavendish, but if she didn't knock it on the head now, things could get even messier, and right now she had enough of a mess on her plate to keep her going till Christmas. A knock on the door signalled the arrival of the coffee, and taking the tray, Maggie walked silently out onto the balcony just in time to catch the end of Steve's sentence. Placing the tray on the table, she raised her sunglasses, and with a look that would terrify any man, she glared at Steve.

"If Lucy found out what exactly?" she asked menacingly. "Steve Sinclair, I hope you haven't been a naughty boy?"

Steve and Callum looked at each other as Maggie waited for an answer from Steve. Maggie repeated the question.

"I'm obviously hoping that I didn't hear right, but unfortunately I think I did Steve. Have you got yourself in trouble? Is it serious?"

Steve, still leaning forward, eyes to the ground, ran his hands through his hair. What was he going to say now? Catching Dunbar's eye, he silently pleaded for help, but Callum remained quiet. Maggie poured the coffee, then looked at him again, waiting once more for a reply.

"Oh come on Steve, I'm not stupid, something's up I can tell, so if it's serious and you need advice maybe Callum can help. He is a lawyer after all."

"Not a very good one though," Callum mumbled. Maggie looked at him.

"You know that's not true darling," she added abruptly, "tell him it's not true Steve, he might listen to you."

As soon as the words had left her mouth she realised how ridiculous she sounded. Callum was right; she was treating them like children. Maggie Dunbar; bossy, arrogant and now increasingly desperate. Before Steve could answer, Callum interrupted.

"That's enough Maggie," he replied almost forcefully. "Leave Steve out of this. This is our problem not his and whatever you think you may have heard from Steve, it is absolutely none of your business. Whatever happened on this trip is for the boys to sort out amongst themselves, not you, so just back off and leave him alone."

Maggie was taken aback. Steve was impressed. Maybe he had a bit of fight in him after all. Maggie, however, wasn't to be deterred that easily.

"Well I think it is my business; especially if it's serious and it affects one of my best friends don't you?" she said, glaring at Steve. Steve wasn't convinced that Maggie and Lucy were bosom buddies but he could see her point. His continued silence was only enflaming the situation and fuelling Maggie's imagination. He needed to calm things down a bit.

"Look Maggs," he said gently, "I do appreciate your concern, but there really is nothing to be worried about. Cavendish has been a bit of an arse as usual and caused a few upsets, and I didn't want Lucy to find out because she dislikes him so much and she'd be gloating for weeks that she was right about him all along if she knew what a nightmare he'd been. Obviously the trip hasn't been one of the best, for various reasons, but Cavendish has learnt a few lessons and hopefully we can all move on. Lucy doesn't need to know about anything because there is nothing to be worried about."

At the mention of Cavendish, Maggie felt her stomach lurch. How could she so easily have forgotten what had taken place last night. While her husband was asleep, she had seduced the pantomime villain in the next room. If anyone had anything to hide, she did and with this much animosity towards him, could Cavendish be trusted to keep it to himself. She wasn't so sure now. She took a sip of her coffee.

"So it would appear that Myles has a lot to answer for this year. If you all dislike him so much why on earth do you let him on the trip at all? If he causes so much trouble shouldn't you just ask him not to come next time? From the things you've said about him you obviously think he should take some blame for what happened to Callum and that's pretty serious don't you think?"

Callum looked at Steve. It was Steve who spoke first.

"It's not as simple as that Maggie. Cavendish stood in for someone else on the trip and he gets to keep his place. It's tour rules, we can't just drop him."

"Why not?" replied Maggie, infuriated. "If he behaves as badly as you say he does and everyone hates him, why don't you just do something about it?"

"Because we can't Maggie, it's tour rules and that's that," said Callum.

"Pathetic," hissed Maggie.

"And we don't all hate him," added Steve, "he can be a complete arsehole but he has his good points."

Callum looked at Steve.

"Does he? And what would they be? I can't think of any can you?"

"Well he paid for this hotel for starters," said Maggie, "so that we could have some time together."

Callum looked furious.

"Cavendish is paying for this hotel? The arrogant bastard, who does he think he is? I don't need his money or his sympathy."

Sensing the direction this was heading, Steve tried to calm things.

"To be fair Callum, he was trying to help, to give you some privacy so that we could keep what had happened from everyone else, and that when Maggie came out, she would have somewhere to stay. We were trying to think on our feet to be honest and if we got it wrong then I'm sorry. Seriously, Cavendish just wanted to help."

"Probably because he felt guilty for being such a complete shit," hissed Callum.

"Or more likely," interrupted Maggie, "that he was horrified because his own father had killed himself when he was a kid and left him alone with an insane mother."

Callum and Steve stared at Maggie. She was triumphant

now in her superior knowledge of their tour leader.

"How do you know?" asked Steve. "How come we didn't know?"

It made sense now, Cavendish's reaction when he heard the news about Callum. Maggie's triumph, however, was short lived. Should she have broken his confidence when he had so very obviously trusted her? Suddenly she wondered whether she was skating on very thin ice.

"Well it's not something you want to go bragging about is it, and to be honest, you lot have absolutely no interest in anything too complicated or emotional so would it have made any difference if he had told you, I doubt it."

Maggie took another sip of coffee and tried to calm herself. There were too many issues to deal with here and she was at risk of losing the plot all together.

"I need a drink," she said standing up suddenly, "does anyone else want one? There's a very good whisky in the bar."

Callum looked at her. She was unbelievable. Every time he thought he had the upper hand, she out played him.

"So when exactly did you see Cavendish?" he shouted to her as she walked back into the apartment. "When did he tell you all this?"

Steve was fascinated by the unfolding drama. This was going to be very interesting. Maggie walked back out onto the balcony with a bottle of whisky and three glasses.

"Please don't shout at me Callum, I can hear you perfectly well. Did anyone want a whisky?"

Callum shook his head.

"No thanks and you haven't answered my question. When did you see Cavendish?"

Maggie calmly poured herself what looked to Steve like a very large whisky.

"Last night," she replied.

"Last night? When last night?" continued Callum.

"But Cavendish was with us last night," said Steve. "At least I think he was."

Maggie took a deep breath and inhaled the aroma of the whisky deep into her lungs.

"For God's sake, both of you, I went out last night when you were asleep Callum, because quite frankly, I needed some fresh air and a walk. I stopped at a cafe for a glass of wine and something to eat and I happened to bump into Myles who was out to try and find painkillers. He stopped and asked how you were, I asked him to join me, which he couldn't really refuse, and we had a drink and a chat. He told me about his father because he thought it was a blessing for the girls that you hadn't actually managed to kill yourself. Then he walked me back to the hotel and that was it."

Callum stared at her.

"Great," he mumbled, "I'm lying fast asleep in bed and you're out in a bar with Cavendish. Unbelievable."

Maggie stood up, the emotion of the weekend bubbling just below the surface.

"No Callum Dunbar, I'll tell you what's unbelievable," she erupted. "What is really unbelievable is that you chose to try and kill yourself rather than talk to me, your wife. Ok, so you are about to lose your job, which is a bloody disaster, but it's not the end of the world. The world will carry on and so will we. I came out here to try and help and take you home, because despite what you may think you stupid bastard, I actually do love you and all you've done is ignore me. I know you're struggling Callum, but believe me I'm am too, and you know what, I am so glad that I met Cavendish last night because he appears to be the only one who can understand that, probably because just like the rest of us he's hurting too."

As Steve closed the door of the apartment behind him, he was relieved to see Callum get up from his chair and take Maggie in his arms. Looking at his watch, he was also relieved to see, that despite all the drama, he was still ok for time and reaching for his mobile he texted Cavendish to say that he was on his way.

Chapter 42

As Callum took Maggie in his arms she began to cry with relief at his offer of intimacy. She actually couldn't remember the last time he had hugged her or shown any hint of interest. They hadn't had a proper conversation for so long, in fact, they had hardly had a conversation at all. She had done the talking while he listened, if in fact he had listened. Why had it taken her so long to notice that he was quietly slipping away?

"I am so sorry Callum," she whispered, trying to hold it together. "Why couldn't you talk to me?"

Callum stroked her hair. Where did he start? How could he possibly describe the feeling of utter hopelessness that had been facing him every day for the past year? He didn't even know when it had started or why. Yes, the pressure had been on at work, but he'd always coped before. How could he tell anyone that for the past few months it had taken every ounce of will power he had to get out of bed in the morning, and that sometimes the darkness was so overwhelming he could hardly breathe? How could he tell her that no doubt about it, he had wanted to die in that swimming pool, to check out of his responsibilities and fade quietly away?

"I don't know," he answered hanging his head, "I just couldn't. I just felt such a bloody failure. My brain doesn't seem to function properly anymore, I keep wanting to hide myself away in a corner and cry and I don't know what to do about it. I feel so ashamed, I've let you and the kids down and all my mates, I just want to be normal again Maggs but I don't know how."

Maggie looked at him, his haunted expression was disturbing.

"Why didn't you say anything at work? Surely they would have tried to help or your friends, why couldn't you talk to them? They had no idea anything was wrong until you arrived on the trip."

"Because I was ashamed, don't you see, no man wants to admit that he can't bloody cope, that he's a pathetic wimp who needs some time off because life's getting a bit stressful. If I'd been paralysed from the neck down that would have been more acceptable, but no, paralysed from the neck up and that's a different story, that's not worthy of time off, that's worthy of a good talking to, a slap on the back from the boys, a few pints and a bit of well meaning advice on pulling myself together. It wasn't worth saying anything Maggs, it just wasn't worth it."

Maggie kissed him gently on the cheek and held him in her arms.

"We'll get this sorted sweetheart, I promise. When we get home we'll see the doctor and get some help. Please don't ever think about leaving me or the children again Callum Dunbar, do you hear me? I love you. It doesn't matter about work or the house, all that matters is that we get this sorted out and we work through it together. Do you hear me? We'll work it out, I promise."

Callum forced a smile and squeezed her hand. How he wished he could believe her.

As Tracey stepped off the tube she felt self conscious, as if everyone in London knew that she was about to meet a man who wasn't her husband for lunch. Two days ago the scenario wouldn't have entered her head. She knew she could have discussed the issue of the photos with him over the phone but she'd wanted to meet him, just one more time. Why? She didn't know, other than the fact that when she thought about him she felt an excitement that she hadn't felt for a very long time, the excitement that comes from the not knowing, the challenge, the first touch or kiss. She knew it was madness but she couldn't help it. As she reached the restaurant she prayed that no one would recognise her, but she'd prepared a number of plausible stock answers to any inquisition should the need arise. As she neared the restaurant she wondered whether he'd arrived, she hated being first and she was nervous now, without her champagne courage.

"That's what I like to see, a woman on time, a sign of good manners."

Turning round she saw Montgomery striding towards her and blushing, she smiled at him in acknowledgement.

"Well that's good timing," she said nervously. "We must both be very hungry."

Grinning like a Cheshire cat, Montgomery took her arm.

"Ravenous," he replied mischievously, "absolutely ravenous."

As Steve walked into the foyer of the hotel, Cavendish looked up from his newspaper and taking a mouthful of his bottled beer, he signalled to Steve to join him. Steve, eager to get on the golf course, didn't want to be sidetracked by a beer and rather than sit down he hovered beside Cavendish's table.

"Well how was he?" Cavendish asked. "Was he ok?"

Steve hesitated. Was Callum ok? He had no idea. To his disgust he realised that he hadn't really asked and that he'd spent most of the time talking about himself and his own problems. Callum had looked ok but he hadn't said much, probably because he and Maggie hadn't really given him much of a chance.

"I think so," he mumbled guiltily, "oh shit I don't know, he didn't say much and Maggie was there and ..."

"In other words you wimped out," Cavendish interrupted, "and before you fly off handle I'm not blaming you, we're all as bad as each other, none of us knows what to say. Mike hasn't even been to see him and he'd probably cut my throat if I went round. But one of us has to get him to talk mate, he has to know that no one's laughing at him. Imagine how you'd be feeling if one of us had fished you out of the swimming pool. If you want my opinion, I think you and Mike should go back round after the golf and just sit and bloody listen. Let him know that you want to help. I'll take Maggie for a coffee or something, you won't be able to talk properly if she's hovering around, you know what she's like. There'll be time before dinner tonight."

Steve, for once, didn't argue. Cavendish was right, possibly because as Steve now knew, he had felt firsthand the devastating consequences of suicide; poor bastard.

"Right ok, I'll drag Mike round later," he sighed. "Can you text Maggie then and let her know what's happening? I need to go and get my stuff. I'll be fifteen minutes."

Cavendish stood up.

"Make it twenty mate, I've got a couple of calls to make. See you at the entrance, and by the way, your wee problem has been taken care of."

Steve looked at him, not sure whether to believe that he could have taken care of it so easily.

"How did you manage that?"

Cavendish tapped his nose. He didn't need to give all the details. Catalina was more than happy to accept a plane fare home and a monthly transfer to her bank account, large enough to keep her off the streets and to bring up her son. He could afford it. After all, where she came from, the equivalent cost of a few executive lunches went a very long way.

"Don't worry, all above board and legit and no one will get hurt. She didn't take too much persuading. See you back here in twenty."

Tracey looked at the menu but couldn't take it in, aware that he was staring at her and waiting for her to speak.

"Any suggestions?" she asked him without looking up but

taking in his tanned, perfectly manicured hand as he toyed with his empty wine glass.

"Don't tempt me," he answered. "Shall I order wine or are you planning on being sensible in case I lead you astray?"

Tracey looked at him; he looked younger than Simon. She hadn't really noticed that in the bar last night.

"I think it'll take more than wine to lead me astray," she said smiling at him. "I'm sorry but I haven't asked you here to seduce you and before you say anything I am planning to buy the lunch to pay you back for all the champagne and dinner you bought last night. I shouldn't have let you, I'm sorry."

Montgomery sighed and leaning forward he took her hand.

"For God's sake, you really are very complicated and you know what, I don't believe you for a second. If you just wanted to pay me back you could have sent me a cheque."

He was right, she could have sent him a cheque but she hadn't. She had instigated this lunch; she had called him when she should have left well alone. Removing her hand she started to panic.

"Well actually it wasn't just that I wanted to pay you back, things got a little complicated last night, with my husband. Someone sent him photos of us in the bar and walking to the restaurant and he's obviously very upset."

"So I hear," interrupted Montgomery, "I had a phone call this morning from one of his friends warning me off."

Tracey was suddenly confused.

"Someone called you? It wasn't Simon was it, sorry you have the same name which is a bit unfortunate, how did he know who you were? Do you know my husband?"

Montgomery grinned.

"No, thankfully I don't know your husband but unfortunately I do know Myles Cavendish. It seems we share the same unsuitable acquaintances. Small world isn't it?"

Tracey went cold.

"Oh my God," she whispered, covering her face with her hands, "not Cavendish. Did he see the photos?"

"Well he must have done and must have recognised me and decided to give me a courtesy call on behalf of your husband. I told him that I'd taken you for dinner and that was it and that I didn't have your number and had no plans to see you again, which actually was the truth when he called me. You, however, seem to have other ideas."

As Tracey struggled to take in the implications of this revelation, her mobile rang and distractedly she fumbled in her bag.

"Hello," she answered curtly.

"Hi Tracey, its Myles, have you got five minutes for a quick word?"

Chapter 43

Flustered, Tracey stepped outside the restaurant to take his call, leaving Montgomery to watch her through the window as she paced up and down. He could see that she was panicking and it amused him. Maybe he should just leave well alone; he couldn't see this going anywhere. It was far too complicated and she obviously wasn't ready to play the adulteress. Not yet anyway.

"Myles, what on earth do you want?" she asked nervously. "Aren't you on the golf trip?"

"Yes I bloody well am Mrs and I should be on the golf course so I'll make this quick. I've seen the photos Trace and they don't look good do they, and as you can imagine, Simon is completely gutted. I told him I didn't know Montgomery because I didn't want him to think that his wife was hanging about with one of the biggest slags in London. I know him Tracey, he's bad news."

"The words pot and kettle come to mind here Myles. I can't believe you just said that," said Tracey defensively. Cavendish was irritated.

"Look, what I get up to has nothing to do with it; it's you and Simon I'm worried about. Please don't tell me you're shagging *him* Tracey, for God's sake the man's a complete tosser."

Suddenly Tracey realised that the whole situation was getting out of hand. She had no defence. She had asked him out. She found him attractive and hadn't thought twice about the effect that this could have on Simon. It had all happened so quickly and too many people were already involved; and what about the kids? She hadn't thought about them either but then she didn't have a plan, she hadn't planned an affair; she hadn't anticipated any of this. She'd just wanted to see him one more time, but maybe that's how these things started by not being able to say no.

"Look Myles, it's not what you think; I'm not shagging him as you so delicately put it. I met him in a bar, he took me out to dinner and that was it, no shagging, just dinner. I have no idea who took those stupid photos but I'll bloody kill them if I find out."

"Well that's what he said too so I suppose I'll have to believe you both. Trust me, Montgomery is bad news, he doesn't deserve you. Don't blow it Trace you've got too much to lose."

As a mixture of emotions tumbled through her brain, Tracey flew off the handle, infuriated by his condescending tone.

"Oh please don't patronise me. Honestly, I can't believe that neither you nor my darling husband trust me to behave myself when I'm on my own, yet I'm supposed to trust him when you've organised a bunch of hookers to entertain the troops. You're such a hypocrite Myles so you can lay off the lectures because I can look after myself thank you very much, I don't need your advice."

Myles sighed, exasperated.

"Well I'm sorry Tracey," he said firmly, "but where Montgomery's concerned, I really think you do."

Maggie picked up the text from Cavendish, she was relieved that Steve had decided to come back later with Mike. Now she and Callum had managed to talk, it might be easier for him to talk to them. He was going to need their support whether he realised it or not. She was less enthusiastic about meeting Myles for a drink though but she supposed she would have to see him again sooner or later; she might as well get it over and done with. She texted back.

"*That would be good thanks. I'll text you when the boys arrive and I'll meet you at the same place as last night. See you later. Maggs*"

"Callum sweetheart," she called from the balcony, "Mike and Steve are coming round after their golf so I'll pop out when they arrive and get a few bits and pieces and leave you in peace. Does that suit you?"

Stepping out on to the balcony, Callum handed Maggie a cold beer and forced a smile.

"That's fine with me, maybe we should pop out and get a few more beers though, the boys will need a drink by the time they arrive and to be honest I could do with a walk."

Maggie took the beer and answered enthusiastically.

"So could I my darling and there are some really pretty restaurants down beside the harbour where we could get some lunch. Sit down for a while and have a drink and I'll shower and smarten myself up a bit and we'll get out of here for a while."

As Maggie chatted about nothing in particular, Callum sat down beside her and took a swig from his bottled beer. If she only knew how hard it was to maintain this charade she'd be devastated. The problem was he had no idea how much longer he could keep it up, and as the dull ache in his chest increased with the impending departure for home, the more he wished he was dead.

"So shall I order a bottle of wine or are you leaving me again?" asked Montgomery as Tracey returned to the table. She was flushed but her eyes were sparkling.

"Well, according to our mutual friend Cavendish, I should be leaving you because you are extremely bad news, which if someone with the morals of Caligula thinks so, you must be. But as I now need a drink, will you please order a bottle of wine and I'll let you explain yourself over lunch."

Montgomery laughed.

"Well I'll order a bottle of wine but I have no intention of explaining myself. Cavendish is right, I'm very bad news and I make no excuses. But I haven't put a foot wrong with you now have I? I saved you from that God awful bar and your so called friends, I took you out to dinner and bought you champagne and then against my better judgement kept my promise and sent you home in taxi. And I'm not cheating on anyone else. You, however, a married woman, accepted dinner and champagne, kissed me and then invited me out to lunch. Believe me darling, I'm not the one who needs to explain myself."

Tracey stared at him. His arrogance was unbelievably attractive.

"I know," she replied quietly, "I have no idea why I'm here. I shouldn't be but I am."

Montgomery leaned forward and took his face close to hers. The smell of his cologne excited her.

"The reason you're here Madam, is because not only do you find me unbelievably attractive but because unexpectedly, a little bit of excitement has crept back into your life and last night you were not Mrs whatever, someone's wife and mother, you were and still are a beautiful, sexy, woman who another man finds agonisingly gorgeous. You just don't want to let that go, that's all."

He was right. She loved Simon, she loved her children but her relationship had become dull. The thrill of last night and the anticipation of the unknown was like a drug; a sudden high from which she didn't want to come down. She knew, however, that the down would come from crossing the line. She didn't want to cheat on her husband, especially with a man like Montgomery; he would drop her anyway when he'd caught his prey and the thrill of the chase was over. What she was enjoying, was the excitement that disappears after seventeen years of marriage, the same thrill that Montgomery was enjoying, the taste of forbidden fruit.

"I know you're right and obviously you are an expert in these matters but you know and I know, that despite me fantasising about you I'm not going to take this any further. There's too high a price to pay and my husband doesn't deserve it. You could move on but I couldn't, I'm not tough enough for that."

Montgomery leaned forward and kissed her gently.

"It would have been good though," he whispered.

"Oh I know it would," she sighed.

Back in his hotel room, Steve realised that he hadn't phoned Lucy back, and picking up his mobile he dialled her number.

"Hi darling, it's me, sorry about this morning. I must have eaten something that didn't agree with me."

"Fifteen pints probably," replied Lucy, "you sound a bit better now though. What are you up to; I thought you'd be golfing?"

Steve continued to get his golf bag sorted as he spoke.

"I'm just off now. I've just been round to see Callum, and Mike and I are going back round after the golf. He seems ok, quiet but ok. He and Maggie are on the early flight. You should give her a ring, she's fine to talk."

"I will in a while, I've just had my hair done and now I'm waiting to have a couple of treatments. Maggie thought I should treat myself, well and you actually, you might have a few surprises when you get home."

Steve was intrigued; he had no idea what she was talking about although by the tone of her voice it sounded like he could be in for some fun.

"Marvellous, can't wait to come home now. How are the kids? Is everything ok?"

"Yes fine. Oh got to go, sorry, oh and Christie says to tell Mike he's an arse for not phoning her about Callum, so you'd better pass that on. Bye, see you tomorrow."

Well, Steve thought to himself, there's a turn up for the books. For the first time in a long time she actually sounded happy, and for the first time in a long time, he was actually looking forward to going home.

Chapter 44

"That is such a pussy putt," Tommo mocked, as Alex left his putt short. "Dropping your lipstick back there must have put you off."

Alex smiled. "Sod off Tommo, with a short game as shite as yours I wouldn't bloody gloat."

"Not when he hasn't hit the fairway yet," Simon added. "Must be all the guilt he's carrying from last night, must be affecting his swing."

"Don't know what you're talking about," Tommo answered innocently as they walked towards the next tee, "I don't remember a thing."

"Unfortunately I do," grimaced Alex, "you were shameless; it was absolutely gross. Poor Sarah, she doesn't deserve you. How can you live with yourself?"

Tommo placed his ball on the tee and for once managed to hit the middle of the fairway.

"Poor Sarah my bollocks, she can handle it, believe me she gives as good as she gets," he laughed, "and anyway I don't recall you going to bed with your trousers on, do you Simon? In fact my last recollection before I passed out is of those spindly little legs sticking out from beneath a very ample tart with a rather large arse, and if I'm not mistaken you didn't look as though you were putting up much of a fight."

"That's because she was bigger than me," Alex replied, grimacing as he remembered the details. "I actually thought I was dying, I couldn't breathe."

"Thank God you got me out of there early Simon," said

Mike as he watched his ball edge towards a bunker. "I owe you one. It could have been any of us in Steve's position we were all so pissed. Bugger did that ball go in?"

"Andy's shitting himself," laughed Tommo as he watched Alex tee up. "Not only has he got massive whip marks across his arse, he thinks he's got a disease from one of those tarts sitting on his face. He'll be in so much trouble he'd be better off slitting his wrists."

Mike and Simon looked at each other, the implications of that remark lost on the other two. Steve had texted Mike to let him know about the plan to visit Dunbar and he wasn't looking forward to it, but Simon had explained that Callum was obviously suffering from depression and would need as much understanding as he could possibly get. Why hadn't he noticed though? Had he missed something obvious? He would never forget pulling him out of that pool and if he could erase it from his memory he would. All he hoped was that he'd done the right thing and that Callum would forgive him.

"Pured it," whispered Alex triumphantly as his ball flew down the fairway, "absolutely bloody majestic, up yours Tommo."

Tommo laughed. "We'll see chicken legs, we'll see."

In the group behind, Andy was struggling with both the heat and the banter. His head was throbbing and the aroma of the whisky he had plastered over his body was not helping his nausea. The ribbing from the other guys had been relentless.

"Tell you what Bob, you certainly like living on the edge," heckled Davie, "I don't think any of us have ever lied about going on the trip before, it's pretty impressive."

"Fucking dumb," replied Rex, "how the hell did you think you'd get away with it? Your wife must be as stupid as you are? Where did you say you were going anyway?"

"That's fifteen Euros for you already," replied Andy, his sense of humour failing him, "it doesn't matter what I said does it, she found out and if I wasn't in enough shit as it was I now have to go home with a red arse and probably some foul disease. I just hope she's not speaking to me so I can get myself sorted before she finds out. Why aren't you lot as worried as me? Am I the only one concerned about my sexual health?"

Davie laughed. He'd been primed by Tommo.

"Well we didn't go as far as you did we you little tart, didn't think you had it in you. Simon tried to stop you but you weren't having any of it. Beast of a shot Fats, bloody glorious, what a finish."

Andy didn't reply. Simon hadn't tried to stop him had he? He didn't remember speaking to Simon. His head was throbbing now, he felt awful. Andy stared at his ball. He couldn't focus and the ringing in his ears was getting worse. Automatically he swung his golf club and as the ball headed towards the green Andy hit the deck.

As Maggie applied sunscreen in the bathroom, her mobile rang. Walking through to the bedroom and wiping her hands, she picked up her phone. It was Lucy. Maggie was delighted to hear her.

"Maggie, it's Lucy, I hope it's ok to call, we weren't sure whether to or not, we've been worried about you both."

"Oh Lucy, it's good to hear you. We're ok thanks. Simon Lewis says Callum is obviously suffering from depression so we'll have to see a doctor as soon as we get home. He's worried about losing his job and it's all a bit of a nightmare but we'll just have to take one step at a time. He says he's been feeling bad for ages but couldn't tell anyone, he doesn't know how it started or why. It's pretty scary actually Lucy, why didn't I notice or why couldn't he tell me?"

Lucy could identify with some of those comments. She'd had plenty of days lately when she hadn't wanted to get out of bed or face the world. It wasn't easy to explain those feelings and silence was often the result. She hadn't felt like killing herself though, thank God.

"Steve said he'd been round and he's coming back later with Mike, that'll help won't it?" Lucy asked.

"Well I hope so. I'm going to pop out and have a coffee with Cavendish, he's feeling pretty awful about the whole thing, but Callum and him don't exactly see eye to eye so I'm going to see him."

"I don't believe that Maggie, Cavendish will only be feeling awful because his trip's not going to plan. He's a horrible man."

Maggie was defensive.

"Oh he's not as bad as you think Lucy, I know you don't like him but he's paid for our hotel and it turns out his life hasn't been as rosy as we think it has. Did you know his father killed himself when he was a kid; explains a lot don't you think?"

"Maybe," replied Lucy, "but it still doesn't excuse him for some of his behaviour."

Maggie smiled.

"No it doesn't Lucy, you're right, but I'm sure we've all got a few skeletons in our own cupboards if we care to think about it."

"I wish I had," sighed Lucy, "my life might be a little more interesting. Anyway I've done the deed so Steve's in for a bit of a surprise when he gets home. I hope he likes it, I'll kill you if he doesn't do you know that, it was bloody agony."

Maggie laughed, it was good to laugh.

"Oh text me when he gets back, I want to know all the details."

"Yes ok. Look I'll let you go. Look after yourself and please if you need a chat don't be afraid to phone, whatever time, I mean it, and give my love to Callum. Text me when you get back tomorrow so I know you've landed safely. I'll tell Christie I've spoken to you. Bye Maggs take care."

"Thanks Lucy, you too. I'll call you tomorrow."

Maggie hung up and walked out of the bedroom.

"I'm ready love, shall we go?" she called. "Have you got any cash?"

Callum didn't reply; she hoped he hadn't fallen asleep again. She looked in the bedroom but there was no sign of him. Walking out onto the balcony she was horrified to find him slumped in the chair having obviously drained most of the whisky she had so stupidly left on the table.

"Oh Callum," she whispered kneeling down beside him. "What on earth have you done now?"

Chapter 45

"So do you always go for married women?" asked Tracey as she passed Montgomery the butter, "or are you not fussy?"

"I am extremely fussy which is why I'm sitting here with you, and no, I do not go around preying on bored, married women if that's what you're implying."

Tracey buttered her bread.

"Do you think you'll ever settle down? You don't want to end up a sad lonely old man do you?"

Montgomery smiled.

"Why on earth would I want to do that and why is it that women assume that men will end up sad and lonely if they don't get married. I haven't missed it so far?"

"Well that's because you're extremely attractive and probably flash a bit of cash around so women aren't exactly difficult to find. Won't be so easy when you're old and wrinkly though will it? When you're in a home."

He liked it when she teased him. God he wanted to take her to bed.

"Well when I'm old and wrinkly you can look me up and tell me whether I'm still attractive, and there's usually more women than men in the homes anyway, so I'll be alright. Shame we have to wait that long though. Have you been completely faithful to your husband or am I your first?"

"My first what exactly?" Tracey asked, flirting with him over her wine glass.

"Love interest."

Tracey laughed.

"Love interest? Oh for God's sake where did you get that expression from? I've known you less than twenty four hours, you are hardly a love interest."

"Well how about lust interest? Does that sound more appropriate? Isn't that why you're here? You more or less admitted it earlier."

Realising that the conversation was taking a wrong turn again, Tracey tried to change the subject but Montgomery brought it back. He didn't plan on giving up without a fight, especially as there were still a few chinks in her armour.

"So when we leave this restaurant is that it? Will I be deleted from your contact list?"

"Probably," Tracey answered. She didn't really know.

"Probably? Well I suppose that's better than definitely." He paused. "No one would ever have to find out you know."

"Find out what?"

"That you had great sex with a man you find very attractive."

Tracey flushed and looking down at the table, shook her head.

"You make it sound very simple and I've already told you I couldn't go through with it."

"Well isn't it? It seems pretty straightforward to me. You know you want to and I'm certainly not going to tell anyone or beg you to leave your husband. What could be easier?"

Cavendish was right, he was very bad news and she was now in very dangerous territory.

As Andy came round he had no idea what had happened to him and as Fats and Tommo helped him into the golf cart he suppressed the urge to throw up. His mouth was dry, he needed a drink. Simon checked his pulse and handed him a bottle of water.

"I think you're a bit dehydrated mate, have you had much to drink this morning? You're looking a bit sunburnt too, did you put sunscreen on?"

Tommo, despite feeling like throwing up himself after the sprint back, still managed to find the situation amusing.

"And what about your pants, did you put clean pants on?" he asked in a perfect impersonation of Simon, and Andy, despite feeling terrible, finally managed to smile.

"No to all of those. I'm sorry but can someone please get me back to the hotel, I think I'm going to die. I need to lie down in a dark room."

"I'll take you mate," offered Simon. "Tommo, throw the golf bags in the cart and you two carry on. If I see Cavendish I'll let him know what's happened."

And as they drove off, Simon promised himself that he would never agree to come on another bloody trip ever again.

Maggie gently took the empty whisky glass from Callum's hand and placed it quietly on the table. Placing her hand upon his forehead, she brushed back his hair. He was perspiring heavily in the sun.

"Oh my God Callum, why did you do this, can you hear me? Answer me please."

She tapped his cheeks and gently moved his head from side to side, hoping for some sort or response, but apart from a throaty grunt as his head lolled forward, Callum did not reply. Increasingly desperate Maggie stood up, and taking his hand, attempted to pull him up from the chair.

"Come on you stupid, stupid man, get up will you, please Callum, I can't take any more of this, please don't do this to me. Come on!" She pulled, but he was too heavy and releasing his hand, Maggie slumped desperately to the floor and burst into tears.

Back at the hotel, Andy was grateful for the cool, darkness of his room. He felt slightly better after the bucket full of water Simon had forced down him but all he wanted now was to sleep off his headache.

"Can I get you anything else mate?" Simon asked as he stood in the doorway. "Are you sure you're feeling ok? Maybe you should order something to eat?"

Andy shook his head. He wasn't hungry; he was just hungover and emotional. Gratefully he sat down on the bed and pulled off his shoes.

"No, I'm fine now thanks, I think I just need to sleep. I'll tell you what though, I don't think I could go through another trip like this; it's been a fucking nightmare. What am I going to do when Sophie sees my arse and what if I have got something from that bloody woman, what the hell am I going to do then?"

Simon smiled; the poor guy was worried sick.

"Well you blame your arse on Cavendish and tell Sophie it was some weird perverted public school boy punishment that he dished out, Sophie would believe anything of Cavendish, and as for any horrible disease its highly unlikely as the boys were just winding you up, well apart from her sitting on your face, but if you'd had any sense you would have had your gob shut. Seriously, the chances of you having caught something is about the same as Cavendish getting the Nobel Prize for Peace."

Andy smiled. "It's not been much fun for you either has it, sorting out all the bloody devastation."

If only you knew the half of it, Simon thought to himself, it had been a bloody disaster from start to finish.

"But at least you don't have to go home and face Tracey with a guilty conscience, that's got to be a bonus."

At the mention of Tracey, Simon's stomach tightened. Andy was right, he didn't have a guilty conscience but he bloody well hoped that she had.

As Steve and Cavendish headed towards the golf club, Cavendish's mobile rang. Cavendish looked at the screen, it was Maggie.

"Hi Maggie, what's up?" he answered casually. He could tell

by the look on Steve's face that he was put out that Maggie had called him. Steve watched him. What was this new found friendship with Maggie all about? Cavendish listened for a few moments before replying.

"All right sweetheart," he said gently, "Steve and I are on our way, we'll be with you as soon as we can. Don't worry, it'll be all right, just stay with him, we'll be there in ten."

Cavendish hung up and leaning forward asked the taxi driver to take them to Maggie's hotel.

"What the fuck's happened now?" sighed Steve exasperated. "He hasn't tried to kill himself again has he?"

Cavendish looked concerned.

"The stupid, selfish prick downed a bottle of whisky and is out cold on the balcony. Maggie can't move him. She doesn't think he's taken anything else; she very sensibly kept hold of her sleeping tablets and painkillers. The poor woman's at her wits' end. He is being such an arsehole."

Steve put his head in his hands. He couldn't believe his friend could have been so desperately unhappy and not one of them had noticed.

"So, shall I order coffee or shall we have coffee back at my place?" Montgomery asked with a wink. "It's five minutes in a cab or a ten minute walk, what do you think?"

Tracey had had more wine than she intended, it would be madness to go through with it but she was shocked by how badly she wanted to. This wasn't the sort of thing women like her did, but then she'd never put herself in the way of temptation before. Up until now she'd never had to think about whether she did or didn't. Her Simon didn't deserve it, she knew that he would have wanted nothing to do with Cavendish's stupid antics but here she was having lunch with a guy who was, by his own admission, bad news and enjoying it. But would it be such a bad thing to have just one afternoon of madness? Montgomery moved his leg and let it rest gently against hers under the table. His touch made her shiver. She jumped as her phone rang. Distracted she answered without looking at the screen.

"Hello," she answered guiltily.

"Hi, it's me," said Simon cautiously, "just wondered what you were up to. Andy wasn't feeling too well so I had to bring him back to the hotel. I'm back in my room on my own and thought we could chat. Where are you? I tried the house."

Tracey was flustered. Moving her leg away she began to panic and raising her eyes to Montgomery, she signalled to him to be quiet.

"Oh hi," she replied, trying to sound casual, "I'm in the cafe bar at the gym, thought I'd try out the new salsa class that everyone's talking about."

Montgomery grinned at her and moving his leg back against hers he blew her a kiss. She looked away. How could she do this?

"Oh well, probably not a good time for a chat then. What time will you be home?"

"I don't know, not too late. I said I might meet up with Sally after the class and the boys said they would be back by sixish, so will definitely be back then. Look sorry love, I have to go or I'll miss the class. Speak to you later. What time are you back tomorrow?"

Simon could tell by the tone of her voice that things were not right. "Don't worry, I'll be out later, I'll see you tomorrow probably back by late afternoon. Do you want me to bring anything back?"

Tracey felt awful.

"No thanks, you could maybe pick up something for the boys though. I'll see you tomorrow."

As she put the phone back in her bag she was shaking.

"Well," whispered Montgomery leaning forward, "seeing as you have already woven such a beautiful alibi I think it would be a travesty to waste it. Waiter, could I get the bill please?"

Chapter 46

As Sophie left the surgery her mobile rang. It was Andy. He never phoned from a trip. It seemed uncanny that he should phone now. Getting into her car she closed the door and answered his call.

"Soph, its me," he said gently. He sounded awful.

"You sound terrible," she replied, "are you all right?"

Andy's head was still thumping and more than anything right now he wanted to be at home.

"Not really, I can't keep up these days and to be honest I'm not sure if I want to anymore."

Sophie was amazed, he really did sound miserable.

"Are you ok Andy?" she asked gently, "has something happened?"

Guilt ridden, Andy desperately wanted to confess but with the rest of the boys having generously funded his trip, there was no way that he could break their confidence.

"Yeh I'm ok," he sighed, inwardly cursing himself for his weakness. "I'm just hung-over, tired and very emotional and I feel really bad about being out here when I know we can't afford it. I don't know what I was thinking Soph, you don't deserve all this and I just wanted to say sorry that I've been such a prick."

Sophie swallowed hard; she couldn't let him take the blame any more.

"I'm sorry too Andy," she whispered almost choking on the words, "and it's not all your fault, I've let you down as well." Looking herself in the eye in the rear view mirror, willing herself on, she knew it was time to confess. Andy was confused.

"What do you mean sweetheart, how could you have let me down? I'm the tosser who can't get any work, you're the only one bringing any money in."

Sophie went silent, desperately trying to stop herself from crying. It would be so easy to go along with him and keep it to herself. She couldn't speak. Andy was worried now, the silence was deafening.

"What is it Soph, what's wrong, please tell me, what is it?"

Sophie tried to pull herself together enough to answer. If she didn't tell him now she knew she never would.

"It's not just your fault," she stammered, her voice breaking. "I've been so stupid and I know you're going to go mental. I'm really sorry but not being able to have a baby, I just couldn't help it."

"Couldn't help what?" Andy interrupted, a knot of fear creeping into his stomach. "What is it Sophie, what have you done?"

Sophie was physically shaking now.

"I've spent too much," she sobbed. "I owe a lot of money, it's not your fault Andy, you've been working so hard to get work and I've been throwing it all away, it's my fault we're broke, not yours, I'm so sorry."

Andy was stunned. He was finding it very difficult to digest. Here he was, guilt ridden and desperate to confess and Sophie had beaten him to it. Maybe he could get away with his red arse after all.

"Oh Sophie, why didn't you just tell me? I wouldn't have come on this stupid trip, it's been pretty crap anyway, I think it's definitely my last. You should have told me love instead of getting yourself into such a state." Suddenly empowered, he felt a surge of relief that their problems were not entirely of his making.

"Look love, don't worry about it now, we'll sort it, it's only money. Between the two of us we'll survive, we'll just have to tighten our belts for a while."

Sophie suppressed the urge to cry again.

"Well that's another problem," she said quietly.

"What is?"

"Tightening my belt, I'm not going to be able to do that very easily either."

Andy was confused. "Why not, what are you talking about, you're not making much sense love, are you sure you're alright?"

"Because I'm pregnant, Andy, I've just left the doctors' and I'm bloody pregnant. Can you believe it?"

Andy sat bolt upright, was she telling the truth?

"Fucking hell, are you sure? How can that be after all these years?"

"Yes," sobbed Sophie, "I'm sure. I've just been to the doctors, I can't believe it either but it's such bad timing."

Andy was ecstatic. Jumping up from the bed and pacing round the room he could hardly contain himself.

"It's not bad timing, it's fucking brilliant, I'm going to be a dad. Sod the money, I don't care if we have to live in a bloody tent, it's fucking brilliant."

As the taxi turned around and headed towards Maggie's hotel, Steve sent a text to Mike updating him on the latest turn of events.

"Do you not think it would be sensible for one of you to fly back with Dunbar and Maggie?" Cavendish interrupted, removing his sunglasses and placing them on top of his head, "because it looks like he can't be trusted not to do anything daft as soon as he gets the opportunity. We can't let Maggie try and deal with him by herself can we?"

Steve looked out of the window, Cavendish was right. In fact, Cavendish appeared to be the only one with any common sense in this whole sorry situation and if he was really honest with himself, he and Mike had been pretty bloody useless. Dunbar's two best mates were in reality both floundering and completely out of their depth. Steve tried to think back to any tell tale signs that things were bad for Callum but he couldn't recall anything. The first time he'd had any concern was at the airport. Up until that point, nothing in Callum's demeanour had given him any cause for alarm. The poor bastard had been desperate and none of them had noticed. Cavendish was right though, Maggie would need their help; they couldn't let her deal with this by herself.

"Yeah, you're right," he sighed, continuing to stare out of the window, "he's obviously in a bad way, we'll have to help Maggie get him home somehow. How are we going to keep this from the rest of the boys now, it's starting to get bloody complicated."

Cavendish shrugged his shoulders.

"It doesn't really matter now the golf's over. The most important thing is getting this sorted and giving Maggie a hand, sod the rest of them." Cavendish looked at his watch. "Bloody hell, how much longer is this taxi going to take? Maggie'll be beside herself."

Steve looked away. He agreed with everything he said but Cavendish's new found compassion, especially with regard to Maggie was starting to intrigue him. He couldn't believe a leopard could change its spots that easily.

As the waiter brought the bill, Tracey grabbed it before Montgomery had chance to take control yet again.

"I said I was paying," she said confidently, "that makes us even and gives me a clear conscience."

Montgomery smirked.

"Oh I'm sure it doesn't. A married woman takes another man out for lunch, the same man that she snogged the night before. I'm sure your husband would be delighted with your expenditure, oh silly me, I forgot you're having lunch with Sally. Paying for lunch won't clear your conscience now will it, especially when I take you back to my place and let me finish what you started?"

Tracey couldn't look at him. His left hand was now under the table, his fingers feeling for her thigh under her dress. With the other he stroked the inside of her wrist.

"Look at me," he whispered, "come on; don't look away, look at me."

Tracey looked at him and closed her eyes as his fingers found the lace of her underwear.

"Open your eyes," he whispered again, "come on look at me, I want you to look at me while I touch you. Open your legs a little." Stroking her through the black lace he smiled. "Aah I can feel how much you want me. Shall I make you come here or shall we go somewhere more private?"

Tracey was speechless. What was she doing? She was happily married, she had two children and here she was being exquisitely fingered by a man she hardly knew in the middle of a restaurant. She couldn't believe how badly she wanted his fingers inside her. His fingers teased her expertly through the fabric; he knew exactly what he was doing. She didn't want him to stop. She opened her eyes and as she looked at him he pushed his finger inside her. He didn't speak as she shuddered and moved herself against his probing hand. Suddenly he removed his hand and she gasped as gently stroking he teased her once again. The longing was unbearable.

"Come on, we're leaving," he whispered, as removing his hand from under her dress he touched her lips gently, enticing her to open her mouth and taste herself on his fingers. Glancing at the bill he tossed some cash onto the table, and taking her hand he led her from the restaurant. Stepping out onto the pavement, her phone rang.

"Leave it," growled Montgomery arrogantly, tightening his grip on her hand. "It can wait."

Tracey wasn't so sure.

"I can't leave it, it might be one of the kids; they're on a rugby trip," she said breathlessly.

"Well they can wait, won't do them any harm."

Struggling to free her hand she hissed at Montgomery.

"Let me go, I need to check my phone, something might have happened."

"Oh for God's sake," Montgomery groaned, releasing her hand. "Bloody well answer it then, Jesus Christ this is hard work."

Tracey rummaged in her bag and looked at her phone. It was Sophie. Declining to answer it, she replaced the phone and looked at Montgomery.

"Well?' he questioned her, raising his eyebrows sarcastically, 'it wasn't the kids was it? Now turn the bloody thing off and let's get back to my place."

Tracey didn't like his tone and suddenly she didn't like this situation.

"No it wasn't the kids, but it could have been and I am actually responsible for my children. I'm sorry, I've made a big mistake, I have to go, I can't do this, I'm sorry for leading you on but this really isn't me."

Montgomery took her hand again and realising that his attitude wasn't helping the situation, tried a different tack.

"Oh come on Tracey please, you can't leave it like this, you want me as much as I want you, come on what's the harm," he said gently, pulling her towards him. She loved the smell of him.

"No, I said I can't, I should never have called you, I'm sorry. Please just let me go." And releasing herself from his arms, she turned and fled.

Chapter 47

Cavendish and Steve found the hotel room door ajar and knocking gently they entered the hallway. The room was silent. Closing the door quietly behind them, Cavendish let Steve go first, still wary of any reaction his presence might evoke from Dunbar. Walking through to the sitting room, Steve could see Maggie on the balcony through the net curtains which were moving gently in the warm breeze. She was kneeling on the floor beside Callum who still appeared to be out cold in the chair.

"Maggie?" Steve called apprehensively. "We're here love, are you ok?"

As Steve and Cavendish stepped out onto the balcony, Maggie stood up and bursting into tears threw herself into the arms of Cavendish. Steve looked at Dunbar, he was snoring, dead to the world but thankfully for them still alive. He looked ridiculous, his head covered with a towel to keep him from the sun. The last time Steve had seen him in a similar position he'd been wearing a blonde wig and a red dress, it seemed like an age ago. God if only they'd known just how fragile he was. Maggie was sobbing now.

"I didn't think, I left him to go and have a shower, we were supposed to be going for something to eat and get a few drinks in for you boys coming round tonight, I wasn't very long but then Lucy phoned and I forgot I left the whisky but he seemed ok when I left him."

Cavendish held her while she sobbed into his chest.

"He must really hate me, he must do. Why else would he do this?"

Steve looked at Cavendish. He was stroking Maggie's hair, holding her protectively.

"Sssh," Cavendish replied soothingly, "it's not your fault, he obviously needs medical help, he doesn't know what he's doing at the moment. Come on, go and get yourself a tissue or something and dry your eyes and Steve and I will get the old boy through to the bedroom."

Maggie left the balcony to sort herself out and Cavendish turned to look at Dunbar.

"Come on then," he sighed looking at Steve, "I'll get his arms, you take the legs. It's not going to be easy." Steve grasped Dunbar around his ankles and waited for Cavendish to get a grip on the other end.

"Right lift," grimaced Cavendish, straining, "bloody hell he weighs a fucking ton, if I do my back in I'll kill him my bloody self."

Steve tried not to laugh. If it wasn't so pathetic it would be hilarious but somehow they managed to lift Dunbar off the chair and get him to the cool of the sitting room.

"Just leave him here for a minute," groaned Cavendish, "it's miles to the bloody bedroom."

Maggie walked in blowing her nose.

"We could always try that thing where you use a blanket or sheet and try dragging him to the bedroom, it might be easier. He's quite heavy isn't he?"

Restraining himself from insulting Dunbar any more, Cavendish said nothing and acknowledging Maggie, agreed that the sheet idea might in fact work. Fifteen minutes later, Dunbar was placed in the recovery position on one of the single beds and leaving the door open Maggie and the boys slumped down on the white leather sofas in the sitting room. Maggie felt emotionally drained.

"Can I get you a coffee sweetheart?" asked Cavendish softly. "I can order something to eat too if you want, I'm a bit peckish myself now. Steve do you want something, we could be here for a while?"

Maggie protested.

"Oh boys, seriously you don't have to hang around, you've already missed your golf. I just couldn't lift him by myself and I was worried about him being out in the sun. I can manage now, honestly."

Steve got up and sitting down beside her, took her hand.

"Maggs, we have absolutely no intention of leaving you by yourself again, it's just too dangerous. Mike and I will take it in turns to stay with you and one of us or both of us will fly back with you. Seriously, it's not a problem; we just want to get your old man back in one piece."

Cavendish leaned forward running his hand through his tousled hair. Maggie couldn't help but think how attractive he was.

"If you give me your passport details I'll try and sort some flights out and see if I can change Steve and Mikes. Between the three of us we'll get you both home. Now let's order something to eat, I'm hungry. What do you both fancy?"

Tracey closed her eyes as she sat in the back of a black cab. Even though every cell in her body had screamed out to go with him, she knew she'd made the right decision. Opening her eyes and pulling her hair back from her face she breathed in deeply as she caught the scent of him on her wrists. Instantly she could feel his fingers again and the exquisite ecstasy that he had invoked. How could she face Simon and pretend nothing had happened? She hadn't slept with him but she had definitely crossed the line. She jumped as her phone signalled a text. She didn't recognise the number.

"I can still taste you on my fingers. Delicious! See you soon x"

"Oh my God," she said aloud as she deleted the text and called Sophie.

Andy was beside himself. Utter despair had turned to elation in the space of fifteen minutes. How the hell could she be pregnant? They hadn't had sex that often lately, what with the pressures of everything else. Maybe that was it, stop trying and start worrying about something else and bingo, there you go. Desperate to share his news, he called Simon, who was happy to be distracted from the crap that the TV was offering.

"How are you mate," he answered, "you feeling any better?"

Andy was almost shouting down the phone.

"You'll never guess what, I've just phoned Sophie and guess what, go on have a guess, guess what's happened?"

Simon had absolutely no idea what Andy was talking about but whatever it was it was obviously good news.

"I've no idea, it could be anything."

"Just have a guess," continued Andy, "I've just had the best news ever, go on have a guess."

"You've got a new contract?" Simon offered.

"Nope, better than that."

"Bloody hell, I don't know, your arse has miraculously healed, how the hell am I supposed to guess, it could be anything."

"Sophie's pregnant mate, I've just spoken to her and she said she's pregnant, can you believe it? After all that hassle, we give up and boom, just like that. We're still broke but hey, money's not everything, we'll be ok. I'm going to be a dad."

Simon couldn't help but smile, Andy was such a nice bloke he deserved to be happy.

"Congratulations mate, that's fantastic news," laughed Simon. "There's only one problem though. She'll be so happy to see you that she'll want a shag. Better make sure you keep the lights off."

As Sophie drove back to Vic's house, the relief she felt from confessing to Andy was enormous and she realised now just how much it had been affecting her both mentally and physically.

She felt as though a huge weight had been lifted off her shoulders. Andy had been ecstatic when she had told him about the baby, she had never realised just how much it had meant to him too. She'd been so wrapped up in her own misery that she'd paid no attention to his. He was right, the money thing would sort itself out, and they would still have a roof over their heads and a family that loved them. If only her mum had been here to see her grandchild, she would have been over the moon. As she pulled up outside the house her phone rang. It was Tracey.

"Oh hi Tracey," she answered chirpily, desperate to share her news, "I tried to phone you earlier."

"Yes, I know," replied Tracey, "I couldn't answer at the time. Look Sophie, are you free right now, I really need to talk to someone?"

Sophie could tell that she was upset. What on earth had happened?

"Well yes I suppose I am; I've just pulled up at my dad's. Do you want to come here or shall I meet you somewhere?"

"I'm in a cab right now, how far are you from Danielli's coffee shop, could we meet there?"

Sophie looked at her watch; she had promised Vic that she would give him a hand. Danielli's was probably ten minutes away if the traffic was ok. She was tired but Tracey had been good to her this weekend.

"Yes ok, I'll meet you there. I'll just have to let dad know. Are you ok Tracey, you sound really upset?"

"That's because I'm a stupid, selfish fucking idiot. Oh Sophie, Simon is never going to forgive me if he finds out."

Chapter 48

Finishing the last of the cheese from lunch, Cavendish sat back on the sofa and glanced over at Maggie. He couldn't believe how fond he'd become of her in the space of a few turbulent hours. Catching his eye she smiled at him before looking away and starting a conversation with Steve.

"Did you say Mike was going to come over this evening?"

"Well that's the plan," he replied, replacing his beer on the table. "He's golfing at the moment so we haven't finalised a time but he'll definitely be here later. It's probably best that we're both here when Callum wakes up. He'll have a hell of a hangover, as if he wasn't miserable enough already."

For a fleeting moment Maggie almost wished he wouldn't wake up, not that she wanted him dead. It was just that while he was asleep she didn't have to face the reality of the situation, and to be honest, his unpredictability was frightening her. Standing up, Cavendish brushed the remnants of lunch from his lap and picked up his phone.

"Right, I'm off to try and sort out these flights, have you got your passport numbers Maggs? I'm not sure whether I need them or not. I suppose I'll need Callums' flight details too so that I can change it. Steve can you text me yours and Mike's?"

Steve took out his phone and texted Mike. Mike would have to get them from their rooms when he got back. As Scottish team captain he had all the details.

"I've sent a text to Mike but you'll probably see him back at the hotel before he comes over here."

"Fine. Let me know as soon as you can so I can get this

sorted. Right Maggs, I'll see you later."

Maggie stood up; she was reluctant to see him go.

"Thank you so much Myles, you've been so kind, I really can't thank you enough. Let me see you out and I'll get the passports. Steve would you pop the kettle on in the kitchen please? I would actually like a cup of tea, even if it is a crappy foreign teabag."

As she escorted Cavendish to the door, she took his hand and squeezed it gently.

"I mean it," she whispered, "thank you so much, you have been more help than you could possibly imagine. I am just so sorry that we've caused so much trouble and ruined your trip."

Cavendish kissed her on the cheek.

"Believe me Maggs, you haven't ruined this trip, I've managed to do that all by myself. Hopefully they'll all forgive me one day. Bye sweetheart, I'll call you later when I've got everything sorted."

Maggie closed the door behind him and went to check on Callum. He was still snoring which she assumed was a good sign. She wondered what Cavendish had meant about ruining the trip himself, he didn't seem too upset about it but then with men you never could tell what they were really thinking. Walking into the tiny kitchen she hovered behind Steve who was obediently making tea.

"So it sounds like this trip has been a bit traumatic," she enquired, opening the tiny fridge for the milk. "Poor Cavendish looked a bit despondent, he said he'd ruined the trip for everyone. What on earth was he talking about? It doesn't have anything to do with what you were talking about earlier with Callum, does it?"

Steve handed her the mug of tea, desperately trying to avoid her gaze. It reminded him of being back at school and knowing that if you tried to lie they would see straight though you. He knew he looked guilty.

"Come on, let's go out on the balcony," she said soothingly. "I've checked Callum, he's sleeping like a baby, let's get a bit more sun before we head back to sunny Scotland."

And as Steve meekly followed her outside, he braced himself for the inevitable inquisition.

In Danielli's, Sophie poured herself a cup of Earl Grey as Tracey cupped her hands around an extra large cappuccino. The cafe was busy and she was grateful that their conversation was unlikely to be overheard over the background chatter. As Sophie cut a very generous slice of carrot cake in two, she could see that Tracey was agitated.

"So what's wrong?" she asked, placing the cake on a separate plate and passing it to Tracey. "You look really upset, has something happened?"

Tracey rested her forehead on her hand and toyed with her spoon. She didn't know where to start. She didn't want to tell Sophie about the lap dancers as poor Andy was in enough trouble as it was, but how else could she explain her behaviour. She would have to tell Sophie the truth. After all, didn't all the wives deserve to know what their husbands were up to? Calmly Sophie listened as Tracey talked through the extraordinary events of the past twenty-four hours and by the time she was finished, a mixture of emotions were flooding through Sophie's mind. How could Tracey do such a thing to poor Simon and with someone that she'd picked up in a bar? She hadn't slept with him but she'd come pretty close and in a restaurant of all places. And the photos? Who on earth had taken the photos? Then there was the issue of the lap dancers, had Andy been involved? Sophie didn't want to know all this. An hour ago she'd been ecstatic and so had Andy; she didn't want anything to spoil their happiness now. Andy, she knew wouldn't have slept with one of those dancers, he wasn't brave enough. That's probably why he sounded so miserable when he had phoned. How could Tracey not have trusted Simon, the most reliable, most honourable man on the planet?

"Did you really think that Simon would have had anything to do with organising those dancers, you of all people should know what Cavendish is like? Simon's not in the same league. To be honest it's always amazed me how they've managed to stay such good friends. What possessed you to ask this guy out to lunch?"

"I don't know," she replied shaking her head, "I couldn't help myself. I found him so attractive, I know I shouldn't have, but I did." Tracey felt awful. Sophie was right in so many ways. Simon did not deserve it, she should have trusted him. She had everything she could possibly need in life, but the bottom line was that more than anything she had wanted to have sex with Montgomery.

"Simon must be devastated. Are you going to tell him about the lunch?" Sophie continued, still trying to get her head around the situation. "It must have been awful him getting those photos. Do you think it was one of Sarah's friends who took them?"

Tracey sighed.

"No, someone followed us from the bar and I certainly didn't see anyone I recognised and who would have Simon's mobile? It must have been someone who either doesn't like me or likes him. Anyway it doesn't matter now does it? I'll probably never find out and the damage is already done. I'm dreading facing him when he gets back."

Well you should have thought about that, thought Sophie to herself.

"Well at least you did the right thing and didn't go through with it; he can't be very suitable if Cavendish thinks he's dangerous enough to warn you about. To be honest I think you've had a lucky escape. I'm so glad I phoned now, but what if I hadn't phoned Tracey, do you think you would have gone with him?"

Tracey didn't have to think about the answer, she knew she would have and what was worse was that she knew that if he called her again, she'd probably not be able to resist.

"Of course I wouldn't," she lied, realising that Sophie probably wouldn't be agreeable to this confession. "Give me a bit of credit."

As Simon opened a bottle of champagne in the hotel bar, Mike and the rest of the boys arrived back from golf. Flushed from the sun and high on the banter, they wasted no time in heading for the bar.

"Bloody champagne?" roared Tommo looking at Andy, "bit bloody extravagant or is this a cosy little get together for two? You're obviously feeling better now you bloody lightweight."

Simon turned to the barman and ordered another couple of bottles.

"Boys, boys," he yelled above the din, "quiet please. I'd like to propose a toast."

The boys filled their glasses and waited expectantly. Simon raised his glass and turned to Andy.

"To Andy, a bloody good bloke who's just found out he's finally going to be a dad. Good luck mate and congratulations."

As a huge cheer erupted from the group, Cavendish appeared. "Bloody typical," he bellowed to Mike, "disappear for five minutes and you crack open the champagne, did someone lose at spoof or are we actually celebrating something?"

Mike handed him a glass of champagne. "Bob's going to be a dad, poor bugger, doesn't know what he's letting himself in for. Great news though, they'd given up hope."

"And do you think he's the father?" grinned Cavendish.

"Just keep your bloody gob shut for once," glared Mike, "don't give him something else to worry about, you know what he's like and at least he's not fretting about his arse anymore. Anyway what's happening? I've just seen Steve's text."

As they downed the champagne, Cavendish filled Mike in on the situation and took the flight details from his phone.

"Steve's with Maggie at the moment but they're expecting you later. I'm staying out of the way because quite rightly he hates my guts, but I'm sorting out the flights. Are you able to fly back with him and Steve? We can't let Maggie take him by herself in case he tries to jump out of the plane."

Mike didn't think it was a problem and he knew Christie would understand, although if he didn't make the effort to contact her soon, he definitely wouldn't be flavour of the month.

"And did you manage to sort out our other little problem?"

Cavendish nodded. "Course I did, shouldn't hear from her again, well not if she's got any sense. You can all relax, safe in the knowledge that you won't be castrated when you get home. Anyway, cheers, I'd better go and congratulate Bob and I'll speak to you before you head over to Maggie's. What a bloody trip hey, feels like I've been here for fucking months."

Chapter 49

After warmly congratulating Andy, Cavendish managed to get Simon alone. He hadn't forgotten the photos of Tracey or his little chat with her, and her reaction had, in fact, given him cause for concern. He was annoyed with Tommo too but he would have to wait. He didn't want to fine him in front of everyone and embarrass Simon.

"How are things mate, have you managed to speak to Trace? I'll get Tommo back somehow, stupid bastard. Why couldn't he just keep his big mouth shut? He bloody well knows the tour rules."

Simon sighed; it wasn't really Tommo's fault. He obviously had a more solid relationship than he had even if it was a bit unconventional.

"Well we had a right go at each other if that counts; she seemed more worried about who took the photos. She just said she went out because she was annoyed about the dancers and let herself get chatted up by this guy. Why the hell she let him take her to dinner God only knows. I'm just not sure I believe her that it was just dinner. You wouldn't take a woman for dinner and not try for desert would you?"

Cavendish had to agree with him. He definitely wouldn't and he knew Montgomery would have tried every trick in the whole dam book. Could Tracey have fallen for it? For Simon's sake he really hoped she hadn't.

"The thing is," continued Simon, "I just don't know what to think anymore, I really trusted her. It's madness. One minute I'm happily married to one woman and the next it's like she's turned into a complete stranger. She looks so different in those photos. I mean I've never seen her wearing red lipstick. I want to believe her but to be honest I just don't think I do."

Cavendish tried to reassure him that things probably weren't as bad as they seemed but inwardly neither of them were convinced. Fortunately, as Cavendish emptied his glass, Mike came over.

"Do you want to grab a quick bite to eat before I head over to see Dunbar? I suppose I'll have to take my stuff. Has Steve got his?" Mike paused for breath. "To be honest I have absolutely no idea what I'm doing so if you can point me in the right direction I'll do as I'm told. Cavendish, I'll hand it to you, there's no way we're going to forget this trip in a hurry."

Cavendish put his arm around his shoulder and shook him playfully.

"You and me both mate, you and me both."

Lucy was admiring herself in the bedroom mirror, it had been agony but she had to admit the beautician had done a pretty good job. Gently she stroked her hairless mound. It was the first time she'd been turned on in months. Maybe Christie was right, Steve might appreciate a little taster. Rummaging in her bag she took out her phone and set the camera. The results were impressive. *"Recognise this?????"* she texted suggestively, and selecting a suitably graphic photo, she pressed send.

"So did you pay this woman and let her blackmail you?" asked Maggie. "It was obviously a set up because you guys are absolutely bloody useless after a few drinks however much you may kid yourselves. If you couldn't remember having sex, you can rest assured you didn't. Honestly, you boys are so stupid sometimes."

Steve looked sheepish. He couldn't believe he was telling Maggie all this but she'd promised to stick to tour rules and keep it to herself.

"Yeh well it wasn't just that. If Lucy had seen the photos she would have told the other wives and that would have been it, no more trips and none of the boys wanted to risk that. Anyway Cavendish came to the rescue. I have no idea what he's done but he says it's sorted. It's a worry though, knowing that those photos are out there somewhere."

Maggie closed her eyes and turned her face to the sun.

"You have to hand it to Myles," she said smiling, "he might have caused havoc but at least he's tried to put things right. He's been very good to me and Callum."

Steve looked at her. She was right, Cavendish had been unbelievably helpful and if Steve's instinct was anything to go by there was a little more to this helpfulness than Maggie was letting on.

"Good to you I think," Steve replied suggestively. "Come on Maggs, what is it with you two, is something going on?"

Maggie opened her eyes and sat up. She looked flustered. He'd obviously hit the nail on the head.

"What do you mean by that Steve? Are you suggesting that Cavendish and I are having some sort of affair?" she said defensively.

"Yes probably," replied Steve frankly. "Cavendish has been running around after you, you've called him instead of me when you needed help, you threw yourself into his arms when we arrived and as for sending me to make a cup of frigging tea while you said your goodbyes earlier, I don't have to be bloody Taggart to work it out. How long's it been going on?"

Maggie poured herself a glass of water and composed herself. She wasn't used to being questioned.

"It's not what you think Steve. I hardly knew Myles before this weekend, only from the few get togethers we've all had over the years. He's hardly even spoken to me before. We bumped into each other that first night I arrived when Callum was sleeping and I went out to get some fresh air. I asked him to join

270

me and that's when he told me about his father committing suicide. He'd never told anyone before and I think he was genuinely upset that he could have been partly responsible for Callum's behaviour. It was actually really good to talk to him because Callum hadn't said a word to me all evening. Anyway I asked him to walk me back to the hotel and when we got inside I kissed him and one thing led to another. It was all over very quickly. To be honest I don't think poor Myles knew what hit him, the poor love."

Steve stared at her. He was speechless. She really was quite incredible.

"I know what you're thinking, how could she do that with one of her husband's friends when he is asleep in the next room, but it wasn't like that, I just needed a bit of affection. Callum hasn't been near me for months. I'm sorry Steve, but it was just harmless sex and it's all over now. I'm not going to leave Callum and run off with Myles and please don't say anything to Myles or blame him, because it was all my fault. I think we women refer to it as a comfort shag if you're interested, which I actually think is very appropriate in this case. There, confession over. I'm going to put the kettle on."

Maggie stood up and walked through to the kitchen. Well I wouldn't have put money on that one, thought Steve as he stared out over the busy promenade. A comfort shag? Women were bloody unbelievable sometimes. Suddenly his phone beeped. Opening the text he was horrified. "Fucking hell, I knew this would happen," he said loudly, jumping up and sending the chair flying. "I knew it couldn't be that straightforward."

Finding Cavendish's and Mike's number he frantically forwarded the photo along with a desperate text.

"Thought you'd sorted this but that bitch has sent this photo to Lucy. Trust me we're all dead!!!!"

Chapter 50

Mike and Cavendish's phones beeped simultaneously.

"Bloody hell," gasped Mike, "that doesn't leave much to the imagination does it, Lucy will have gone ballistic and she's probably phoned Christie by now. Steve's right we're dead."

Cavendish was confused. He was convinced that Catalina had been happy with his offer, why would she do this? It didn't make any sense at all. As they both stared at the photo Tommo looked over Mikes shoulder.

"Oh very nice," he drooled, "I love silky smooth fannies. I keep trying to get Sarah to go the whole hog but she says I'll have to have my arse waxed first. Who sent you that then, can you forward it to me?"

Mike wasn't really listening, he was still panicking. Christie was going to kill him, especially as he hadn't called her. Her mind would be working overtime. If he phoned now she'd know it was because of the photos. He was surprised she hadn't called him already. What the hell were they all going to do?

"Steve forwarded it. Looks like the bitch that set up Steve has decided to show Lucy what her hubby's been up to."

Tommo whistled. "Well looks like we need another team meeting Captain, the boys'll need to prepare themselves for inevitable hostilities. Boys," he bellowed, "team meeting. You're all gonna love this one."

"What on earth's the matter?" asked Maggie picking up the chair. "What was all that noise about?"

Shaking, Steve handed the phone to Maggie.

"This. Look at the bloody photo. Lucy's just sent it. I knew Cavendish couldn't have sorted it that easily. Lucy's going to kill me. What the hell am I going to do now? I bet she's phoned Christie. I've just told Cavendish he's a complete wanker. Leave it to me he said, I'll sort it, I know what I'm doing. All complete bollocks."

Maggie took the phone from Steve and looked at the photo, and as the realisation dawned, she put her hand over her mouth in disbelief.

"Have you just sent this to Cavendish?" she asked cautiously.

"Yes and Mike, the boys will have to know, as once Lucy gets going she'll make sure everyone suffers, and if all the wives find out then that's it, curtains. Even if we don't get divorced, it'll definitely mean no more trips. God I can't believe all this, just when you think it can't get any worse something else happens."

"Oh my God, poor Lucy," said Maggie stifling the urge to laugh. "I don't believe this either. Steve this is entirely my fault."

Steve looked at her; he couldn't believe she was finding it funny.

"It's not bloody funny Maggie, she'll definitely divorce me now, she's been looking for an excuse for ages, and what do you mean it's your fault? How the hell is that photo your fault?"

Maggie was giggling hysterically now, she couldn't help herself.

"Because I told her to do it."

"Do what? What are you talking about? What's so funny Maggie? I don't think you realise how serious this is."

Maggie handed the phone back to Steve; believe me she knew how serious it was.

"Oh my God Steve, I'm sorry I shouldn't be laughing, and you're right, it is serious because that photo's not of that prostitute. That beautiful vagina that you've just forwarded to all your friends is Lucy's."

Steve was speechless.

"What?" he croaked taking the phone and looking again at the photo, "how the bloody hell can that be Lucy?"

"Oh I am so sorry Steve but you have to see the funny side or should I say fanny side, oh Lucy will be mortified. When we had lunch on Saturday, God knows how, but we got onto the subject of our sex lives, which for Lucy and I we had to admit were nonexistent, don't worry Lucy said it was her fault not yours, and we were discussing ways to spice things up a bit and Christie and I said that she should go for a Brazilian or Hollywood or whatever they're bloody called, and surprise you when you got home and you have to admit, you are definitely surprised."

Steve couldn't believe it. Not only had his wife gone completely, fantastically bonkers and sent him a pornographic picture of herself, but he had gone and forwarded it to Mike and Cavendish and no doubt the whole bloody tour.

"Oh for fuck's sake," he groaned as he called Mike, "how much shit can a man take in one weekend?"

As the photo was passed around, the mood was sombre with the realisation that this had been sent to one of the wives. With the exception of Davie and Cavendish, all of them were silently picturing the fallout and frantically planning their response to the inevitable phone calls, which no doubt would follow shortly. What a way to end the tour. As if on cue, Mike's phone broke the silence and a collective hush descended upon the group. Relieved that it wasn't Christie, Mike answered.

"Mike, has anyone else seen that photo other than you and Cavendish?" asked Steve anxiously.

"Yeh, they've all seen it, we're having a team meeting at the moment, everyone's shitting themselves."

"Oh for fuck's sake," groaned Steve picturing the scene, "I don't believe this."

Mike was confused. Steve wasn't making sense.

"Why, what's happened now?" he asked. "Has Lucy told Christie do you think?"

"I doubt it," replied Steve.

"Well you sound pretty convinced, why wouldn't she?"

"Because that bloody photo is not of that bloody tart, it's my bloody wife."

And as Mike watched Lucy's fanny being passed around the room he didn't know whether to laugh or cry.

Maggie handed Steve a whisky and sat down beside him. Callum had woken but had opted to stay in bed with his raging hangover. Thankfully he had been quite civilised and with the knowledge that she would have the help of Steve and Mike for the rest of the trip, she began to relax. She was tempted to phone Lucy but knew it was too complicated, it was better that she remained in blissful ignorance, despite the tours obvious appreciation of both her efforts and her assets. Steve felt awful, despite Cavendish's assurances that the boys had sworn to keep the whole incident a secret; he knew he'd never live it down and if Lucy ever found out she would never go out with any of his friends ever, ever again.

"I'm sorry," said Maggie, whispering in case Callum could hear, "but you have to admit it's certainly been a tour to remember. You couldn't write it really. When I thought Callum was having an affair it seemed like the end of the world, and then he tries to kill himself and I think an affair would have been preferable. You know Steve, my life has been so in control and now I realise that actually I never had any control at all, I just thought I did. Nothing's ever certain is it?"

Steve sat back in the chair. Maggie was right. How could three days deliver up so much carnage? Even his golf had been crap and the trophy had finally gone back to England and with Cavendish of all people. Things with Lucy were obviously looking up though, despite the fact that most of the boys would never be able to look her in the eye again. He couldn't wait to get home now. Finally managing to see the funny side, Steve smiled and patted Maggie playfully on the knee.

"Yep, we all have a few more skeletons after this trip hey sweetheart, but luckily we're all in this one together. Even you and Cavendish will have to keep quiet thanks to your little *comfort shag* as you so delicately described it. Good one Maggs, might try using that myself, do you think Lucy would buy it?"

"Now now Steve," glared Maggie, "let's just forget all about it now, remember the rules, *what goes on tour stays on tour*, isn't that the mantra?"

"Yep Maggs and for Lucy's sake I bloody hope it does."